EASTER DAY, 1941

EASTER DAY, 1941

1941

G. F. BORDEN

BTB
BEECH TREE BOOKS
WILLIAM MORROW
New York

Library of Congress Cataloging-in-Publication Data

Borden, G. F.
Easter Day, 1941.

1. World War, 1939–1945—Fiction.   I. Title.
PS3552.B658.069E27   1987   813'.54   86-10726
ISBN 0-688-06538-4

Printed in the United States of America

First Edition

1 2 3 4 5 6 7 8 9 10

BOOK DESIGN BY RICHARD ORIOLO

BIB

The word "book" is said to derive from *boka,* or beech.
The beech tree has been the patron tree of writers since ancient times and
represents the flowering of literature and knowledge.

This book is dedicated to the memory of Harry C. Frey, Corporal, Battery C, 304th Field Artillery, 77th Division, American Expeditionary Force.
Killed in action on August 20, 1918, he is buried in one of the 6,012 graves in the Oise-Aisne American Cemetery, Fère-en-Tardenois, France.

ACKNOWLEDGMENTS

My thanks to Hildegard for her calm encouragement and all else; Paul Tempest, friend and first reader, for his kind enthusiasm; Al Hart of The Fox Chase Agency, for his agreement to represent this book and his thoughtful comments about this novel and another; and Jim Landis, publisher and editor-in-chief of Beech Tree Books, for his many editorial suggestions, each of which improved this book.

"But think—this wilderness, this fury of war which I have described, it covered barely twenty-four hours of a conflict which lasted years; and of the millions who took part, how many really wanted it?"

—Commander, 8th Company, 12th SS Panzer Regiment
Quoted in *Caen: Anvil of Victory*
by Alexander McKee (Pan Books Ltd., London, 1972)

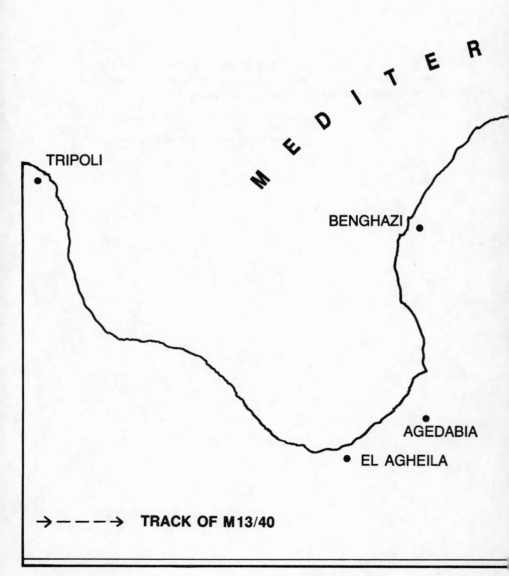

TRIPOLI

MEDITER

BENGHAZI

AGEDABIA

EL AGHEILA

→ ― ― ― → **TRACK OF M 13/40**

M13/40

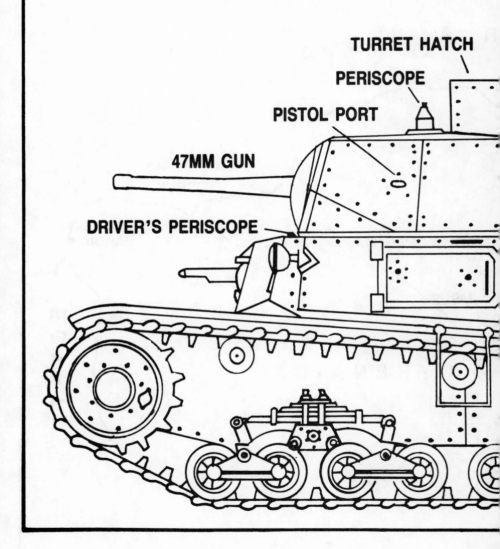

TURRET HATCH

PERISCOPE

PISTOL PORT

47MM GUN

DRIVER'S PERISCOPE

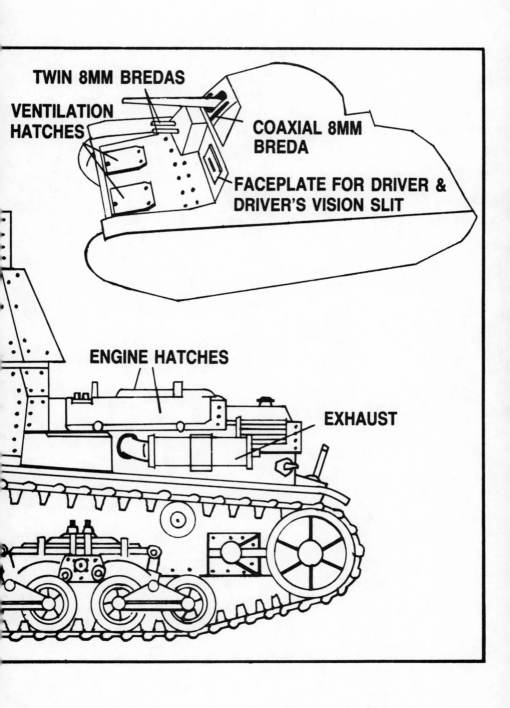

TWIN 8MM BREDAS

VENTILATION HATCHES

COAXIAL 8MM BREDA

FACEPLATE FOR DRIVER & DRIVER'S VISION SLIT

ENGINE HATCHES

EXHAUST

EASTER DAY, 1941

† † †

Up on the hull of the M13/40, his back to the barrel of the 47mm gun, Mackeson sees the rising trail of dust first. He pounds his fist against the slabbed armor of the turret, points southwest across the desert and shouts, "Something's coming."

We stop considering morning tea and start thinking of danger; for in the desert any unidentified movement is potent, and during this retreat, movement to the west is hostile. We are in our second confused week of the great withdrawal to the east. The 2nd Armoured Division is dead, shot down in the afternoon at El Agheila and at dawn nine days later at Agedabia. We are a cast-off remnant, a single armored fighting vehicle far out in the sand, equally distant from the Gulf of Sirte to the west, the Mediterranean to the north, and the Egyptian border to the east.

I am standing on the tank commander's seat, my body thrust from the waist up out of the commander's turret hatch. I have been scanning the desert to the northeast of the shallow wadi in which we have hidden through the night. I turn, raising the fieldglasses to my eyes, and tell Mackeson to get inside and run the engine up.

Mackeson ducks under the barrel of the gun, swings around the sloped side of the turret and wriggles into the fighting compartment through the rectangular hatch in the port side of the hull.

From his seat to the right of Mackeson's, Smythe shouts above the grind and cough of the engine starting, "What the fuckin hell's going on?" Smythe likes to be, as the Brits say, in the picture. Smythe is the machinegunner and radio operator. He sits behind two 8mm Breda machineguns in the right-hand front of the hull. The guns are fixed in a ball mounting. Through the periscope in front of his

15

face he can see nothing but a narrow arc of the wadi in which the tank lies. Smythe becomes nervous when he cannot see, and when he is nervous he sounds exasperated. I understand his exasperation. Death, after all, can come at us from any direction, and it is easier to cope with the thought of its approach if one can *see*. For a moment I listen to Smythe checking his guns and rattling clips of 8mm ammunition to calm himself. He does not have to worry about the radio: something esoteric has broken inside it and we can neither send nor receive. Thus our knowledge of what has happened around us in the desert during the last week is all guess and extrapolation, though none of the four of us would suggest that our side is winning.

Smythe shouts to Mackeson over the roar of the engine, "I'm fuckin telling you, Alan, it better not be the fuckin Germans."

I tell him to shut up. I sympathize with his fear but I can do nothing for him. In a fight only I get to see everything in all directions, for in the M13/40 only the tank commander's hatch can be open when we are at risk: that is the rule in this crew. The rectangular hatch in the port side of the hull, the two ventilation hatches, one in front of Mackeson and the other in front of Smythe, and the driver's and gunner's faceplates must be closed.

I would keep my hatch dogged down if I could; but the view through the gunslits, the pistol ports, the 47mm gun's optical sights and the periscope is imperfect—and to be unable to see when one must is the epitome of danger.

I imagine Mackeson and Smythe sitting in the gloom inside the tank staring through the viewing slits close in front of their eyes. I glance forward along the length of the 47mm gun's barrel. The jut of the gun menaces the empty wadi. In the east dawn is coming, but the sky on the western horizon is still full of night. Early as it is, it is already hot and we sweat in the cramped interior of the tank, which is crammed with the machinery with which we fight. Once men used swords and fought from horseback. Now we ride inside the horse and our 47mm cannon and 8mm Breda machineguns reach much farther than the length of a cavalryman's blade. Modern warfare is impersonal and may be without honor. But then, in the Middle Ages traditionalists may have thought the same of battle between armored knights. Whatever. The purpose—to kill the enemy, or to escape him if he is more powerful—has not changed.

In the growing light I watch the approaching plume of dust and listen to the light rising wind that moves in the desert each day at dawn. My crew waits in silence behind the steel walls of the M13/40. They wait for me to decide. At last Allison, the loader, asks, "Do you see them, Sergeant?"

Allison is a new boy, just come out from England. His seat is to the left of mine, on the port side of the breech of the 47mm gun. Like mine, his seat is fixed to the turret, so that when I rotate the turret, our seats, and we, rotate with it. It is Allison's job to feed the 47mm gun with shells and the coaxial 8mm Breda machinegun with clips. In all the enormous desert his world is the breech of the gun, the sloped steel interior of the M13/40's fighting compartment, the rack of 47mm ammunition behind our backs in the rear of the turret and the coaxial Breda's clips. We carry a lot of ammunition for a medium tank, 104 rounds of 47mm for the gun and 3,048 rounds of 8mm, packed in clips of 24 rounds each, for the machineguns. Now, ten days and more into the retreat, we have 86 rounds of 47mm left, along with almost 2,400 rounds of 8mm.

"Not yet," I tell Allison. Elbows on the starboard half of the raised commander's hatch, I peer through the fieldglasses at the rising dust. The fieldglasses are Zeiss. Five months ago I lifted them from the corpse of an Italian major. The corpse lay on the stony desert just west of the frontier. Bent and dessicated but still pungent, the body

17

was partly hidden by a mantle of sand. It was not until I nudged the torso with my boot that I saw the fearsome wound where the right leg had been taken away at the thigh. The glasses lay beneath the corpse in a leather case that fell to pieces when I picked it up. Leather, like flesh without water, does not last long in the desert. The binoculars were in excellent condition. More than once I have been grateful for German optics and the Italian major's death.

When I have identified the vehicles coming toward us I tell the crew: "Two AB 40s."

"Thank Christ for the little things," Smythe says. The AB 40 is an Italian armored car. It is fast, but as Smythe says, thank Christ—for it is not well armed and its armor is thin. We are in luck.

I let the glasses swing from their strap around my neck and slip on a headset. I speak into the Bakelite microphone. "Intercom check." I know that Mackeson, Smythe, and Allison already have their headsets on and are switched into the M13/40's internal communications system. But running through the procedures calms a crew. And besides, we are in no hurry: the AB 40s are still quite far away.

"Loader," Allison says. After two weeks of fighting and running and hiding and fighting again, the sound of his voice is tinny and uncertain, tinged with fear and exhaustion.

"Ready to roll, Peter," Mackeson says.

"Machinegunner, aye," Smythe tells me.

"Is it good, Sergeant?" Allison asks. He is eight weeks off the boat, fresh from Salisbury Plain. "ABs, I mean."

"Didn't you study your recognition charts, Timothy?" I have the binoculars back up and I watch the ABs coming on as I speak. "Autoblinda 40: six and a half tons, three 8mm Bredas, lightly armored. But fast: it'll go almost fifty."

"Yeah," Smythe says. "And I'll bet they're beating up the fuckin dust like they're in some fuckin wop auto race."

18

"You can't see that, John, from down in this wadi," Mackeson says. Mackeson likes to point out Smythe's exaggerations. "And *you're* in a fuckin wop M13/40. This isn't any fuckin Panzer Three you're in."

"Don't I bloody well know it," Smythe says. He is aggrieved and deflated by the mention of the Panzer III, a German armored fighting vehicle of efficient design employed with dash and cunning by the Germans. But then the Panzer III aggrieves and deflates us all, for we ride and fight in an M13/40. The M13/40 is an Italian armored fighting vehicle dragooned into the 2nd Armoured Division after the great desert victories against the Italians. So many M13/40s were captured, the powers that be thought they might as well be put to use. It wouldn't have been a bad thought except that the M13/40 isn't worth much. For although it has lines reminiscent of the Russian T34/76, that faint similarity, and diesel engines, are all the two AFVs have in common. The M13/40 has a poor power to weight ratio and is slow off the road. It is also poorly gunned and mechanically unsound. It has a high silhouette, which in armored warfare means death. Its plates are held together with rivets. Rivets are unnerving: any solid shot striking the M13/40, even if it does not penetrate, may pound a rivet into the fighting compartment; and any such rivet will be moving almost as fast as the shot that struck the tank's carapace. We are told we are to get tanks with welded plates, but that possibility is meaningless now. We are in the desert, alone, in an M13/40 and we must rely on Italian design and Italian workmanship to see us through. We aren't required to be happy about it, but the M13/40 is all we have.

"All right," I tell them. They've pattered enough to expend their tension. "Driver, reverse."

Mackeson backs the tank down the wadi. Mackeson is our savior. He is the reason we are not dead and not prisoners; for he is a mechanical genius. He ought to be teaching tank maintenance back in England. He has kept our tank operating for two weeks without normal resupply of all those angled metal bits and liquids and maintenance pull-throughs that a tank requires if it is to go on functioning. Tanks are complicated, and although they are large and menacing, they are delicate and require constant maternal handling. Mackeson is the best of mothers; and if we live and are not taken prisoner he will be given most of the credit by the rest of us.

As Mackeson backs the tank, the turret rises inch by inch above the level of the desert.

"Driver, halt," I say when the turret is above the lip of the wadi and I can lay the gun. Mackeson stops the tank and I slip down inside the fighting compartment to the right of the gun's breech. I touch the turret controls. Hydraulics flow, the turret revolves, the gun traverses. I lay the gunmuzzle ahead of the Italian armored cars angling toward us. Our position is textbook: we are hidden in the wadi like a lizard with its head up.

When I have the gun laid I stand back up on my seat, torso stuck out of the turret hatch. A few stars lie low in the last of the night to the west. The sun is behind us. These Italians are insane to drive out of the dark into the sunrise. I tell Mackeson to keep switched on and to be ready. I do not need to tell him this: he has been in tanks since 1937 and he knows more about the tactics of armored warfare than most colonels commanding armored regiments. He certainly knows more about it than the colonels who commanded us at El Agheila.

"Oh, aye," he tells me.

"Loader," I say, "load AP." Sweat seeps down my neck and along my arms. My palms and fingers are gritty with dust and sand. The first flies of the day buzz inside the narrow fighting compartment.

"AP," Allison says. He holds up one of the 47mm shells, the muscles in his forearms tensed. He seems not to know what to do with it.

I put the fieldglasses up to my eyes: the Blindas are whipping up dirt and sand, coming straight for the wadi in which we lie in wait. "Armor-piercing's got a green stripe," I say. "High-explosive red." I do not take the glasses down while I speak. We must try for calm. "Forget the Italian markings."

"Right," Allison says. I hear the oily complicated metal mechanism of the breech shutting on itself.

"Be ready to load as I order, Timothy," I say. "As I call for it. We're not fucking around now."

"Listen at the colonial's language," Smythe says.

"Shut up, John. We don't know what else is out there."

"*I* know what else is out there," Smythe says. "The fuckin eighty-eight-millimeter gun we've heard so fuckin much about. That's what's out there."

I watch the AB 40s coming on. They seem to be moving as fast as they can, whizzing down the desert. It is odd. Anything could get them. A Swordfish lost off an aircraft carrier charging ahead at ninety-three miles an hour armed with a marine torpedo could get them. On the other hand, they have had two weeks of victory, their blood is up, and out here they must feel they can be incautious. After all, they *know* the defeated British are far to the east.

I take a last look at them before I slide down into my seat to the right rear of the gun's breech. I close the halves of the turret hatch so that the sun low in the east behind us will not reflect from the gunsight. I hunch forward toward the gun—it is a comfortable feeling, almost like embracing a dancing partner—and place my forehead against the rubber bumper above the sight. The two magnified armored cars, their turrets trained fore and aft, fixed like the still faces of dead men, are bustling toward me. I can almost identify the regimental markings on the fenders. They are almost into gun range. It will be a clean, no-deflection shot. I lay the gunsight's range marks across the boxy shape of the second AB and traverse the turret to track its passage. If I destroy the farther AB, the nearer one may veer toward me.

Something puffs beneath the target. White light flashes.

Mackeson says, "Jesus," as the heavy thump of the explosion reaches us.

"What happened?" Smythe asks. "Are there more of them then?"

"Mine," I tell them. "The far one ran over a mine."

Through the sight I watch smoke pour from the Blinda as it jerks and slews to a halt, the tires throwing up sand. The flowing smoke flares orange and gold with fire, reaches out a lapping red tongue at the stony desert. Then the fire is sucked back and up into the armored car, the tongue of flame swallowed. The Blinda jerks on its suspension as its fuel explodes. The explosion blows out the AB's port door. The armored car's turret slips askew on the turret race like a hat angled on a drunkard's head. It is a magnificent show.

The nearer Blinda curves away from its exploding twin, passes across the gunsight, obscuring my view of the exploding armored car for an instant. Then it is past and I watch the first AB destroying itself: bounding on its suspension, it begins to glow, white and yellow light flashing inside it as its ammunition explodes. A single man, sleeves rolled up past his elbows, hands held to his eyes, blood spattered down his shirt, runs from the Blinda. He falls to his knees, gets up, and begins to stagger away from the ragged explosions that ravage the vehicle behind him.

"What the fuck's going on?" Smythe asks.

"Yeah," Mackeson says. "Send us a bulletin, Peter."

"The farther AB is burning. The crew's killed—except one. He's in the desert. I think he's blinded." I traverse the turret across the man stumbling with his hands up to his eyes. Blood has stained his shirt, his hands, his arms. I traverse away from him, find the second Blinda. "Second one's thought better of hustling about. I guess he figures there's usually more than one mine put down."

"Whose was it then? The mine that went up?" Smythe asks.

"How should I know?"

"Christ," Smythe says. "We're lucky we stopped right here last night. I mean we could have. . . . It's not on the map, is it? That field. And there was no wire."

"We came from the west. We're going northeast today. We'd never have run through that field."

"What's going on, Sergeant?" Allison asks. They want information.

"The second Blinda's stopped. Range: six hundred yards. Meters," I amend. The gunsight is Italian and is calibrated in meters. "They're traversing the turret, looking around. Coming our way. Past. Went right past us. Hatch opening up now. Big bastard with blond hair and a khaki uniform up in the turret, scanning the ground with field-glasses. Very cool. Going over the desert sector by sector. You'd think he was surveying the place. He's looking this way. Driver, ready. Allison, Smythe, get ready for it. Past us now. He's saying something down the hatch. Door's opening. Three of them getting out. Brown uniforms. Italians."

"Who's the type in khaki?"

"German?" I ask the intercom. "Who knows?"

"German," Smythe says, as though he can see. "I *knew* it."

"The Italians are looking over the ground. Worried about mines. They're yelling at the blinded one. He's stopped. Gone down on his knees. Got the word. The one in khaki's still going over the desert with his glasses."

"Thank Christ the sun's behind us," Allison says.

"Smart lad," Mackeson said.

"He's looking this way again." I see him through the sight, a big blond man in a khaki uniform standing in the turret hatch of the Blinda examining the desert through his fieldglasses. "He's finished looking now. Didn't see us. He's getting down out of the hatch. Hold it. An Eyetie is taking his place. He's taking the glasses. The guy in the khaki uniform . . ."

"Call him a German, for Christ's sake," Smythe says.

"I know them. Saw enough fuckin Germans in fuckin France."

"The old campaigner," Mackeson says. Mackeson was in France, too. In a Matilda thrown into battle in support of infantry. Once he mentioned almost dying inside the Matilda, but he has never detailed this close acquaintance with death and we have not asked. We live too close to one another inside the M13/40 to pry.

"Get stuffed," Smythe says. "I remember, that's all."

". . . the German is getting out of the AB. He's going across. Very methodical. He's talking to them. They're spreading out."

"Too bad," Mackeson says. "I was hoping the next mine would get them all at one go."

"They're heading for the wounded man. Driver, reverse out of the wadi. Fast as you can, Alan. And then at them. Let's try to get in before they can get back to the Blinda."

"We could get them from here," Allison offers.

"We're a long way from the sea, Timothy. And farther from the Frontier. There may be something in that AB we need."

Allison apologizes.

"No need for that," Smythe says. "I was thinking the same fuckin thing, I was."

Mackeson backs us out of the wadi. I brace myself against the sway of the M13/40. As we move backward I traverse the turret, following the four men edging away from the AB with the muzzle of the gun, tracking them as they step toward the blinded man down on his knees in the sand. I consider reloading with HE, discard the thought. An AB is a greater threat than four men on foot. Besides, Smythe is ready with his twin 8mm machineguns, as am I with the one in the turret coaxial with the 47mm gun.

We are right out of the wadi before one of the Italians looks over his shoulder at us. Perhaps they will think we're Italian. As Mackeson turns the tank, grinding the tracks against the stony ground, I say, "Advance two hundred yards," and he drives straight toward them.

The three Italians and the German watch us coming. As Mackeson accelerates the blinded man raises his head to listen to the roar of the engine and the diminishing whine of the gears as Mackeson shifts up. He holds his head cocked to one side as though it helps him to distinguish one sound from another. I guess this gesture will become a habit now he is blind.

One of the Italians points at us and says something to the others. The German sprints toward the Blinda. The Italian in the Blinda's turret drops down through the hatch and the AB's twin Bredas rotate to face us. I look through the gunsight at the running German and press the trigger of the coaxial Breda. The machinegun begins its cyclical hammering: the noise is terrific. The thread of tracer and shot weaves between the running German and the Blinda. He stops, stands, throws himself down. The Italians are down in the sand, their hands over their heads. Only the blinded man is still up, on his hands and knees. He seems to be concentrating, as though the violent crashing of the machinegun and the clank and rattle of the M13/40 are distant thunder heard on a sunny summer day.

"I'll take the German, gunner," I tell Smythe. "The Italians are yours if they try for the Blinda." Beside me Allison changes the coaxial Breda's clip. It is annoying that the gun in not belt-fed. I watch the German crawling toward the armored car, squirming in the sand, shifting like a snake. As he was taught at Fuhlsbüttel or Paderborn. A heavy khaki snake. I traverse the turret and fire the coaxial machinegun. Gouts of sand and chips of rock leap from the desert. I shift the turret and the tracer falls across the dense small target of the German's back.

"Silly fuck," Smythe says. It is an inelegant but accurate epitaph.

"Tells the bugger off for being a hero, doesn't it?" Mackeson says.

"What about the Eyetie in the AB?"

"We'll see." The muzzles of the two Bredas in the AB's turret shift as Mackeson drives the M13/40 forward. "There might be more than one of them inside," I say. "You never know."

"That's for fuckin sure," Mackeson says. "We're coming to the end of the hard. Driver halt?"

We are running across hardpan and small rocks. Ahead of us, spreading as far as I can see to the west and southwest, sand and low scrub cover the stony floor of the desert. "Yes. Driver halt."

As Mackeson stops the M13/40 the Blinda's guns begin firing disciplined bursts. "Likes a sitting target," Mackeson says. I watch the red tracer from the AB's guns speed toward us. Even though I know machinegun fire cannot penetrate the M13/40's carapace, I cringe from the atonal tapping of the bullets against the hull and turret of the M13/40.

"Give him a burst," I say, as though Smythe should make a charitable contribution. He fires, walking tracer across the AB's angled metal face. Sparks jump up the AB's hull, flash on the face of its turret.

"Good shooting," Mackeson says, as though he has just seen an inconsequential task performed well.

"*Fuckin* good, I call it," Smythe says. He is ebullient now he can see.

The AB fires one more burst and then its guns elevate and the turret rotates until the muzzles of its machineguns are aligned fore and aft.

"Bugger's given up," Smythe says.

"I want at least one of us inside the hull from here on," I say.

"Suspicious type, aren't you, Peter?"

"That's me."

"Alive, too," Mackeson says. "Remember that. The sergeant's alive."

"What do we do now?" Allison asks. Back in England

26

they didn't tell him about after a battle.

"Now we see what they're going to do," I tell him. I look through the gunsight at the Blinda. I traverse the gun and watch the three Italians get up and place their hands on their heads, lacing their fingers together. They seem to have had a lot of practice with the gesture.

"That's a good sign," I say.

"Look at the AB, Sarge," Smythe says. I edge the turret to port. The Blinda's turret hatch is open and a man stands up in it, raising his hands as he exposes himself. I see the yellowy brown uniform and say, "Italian." The man puts his hands down and hoists himself out of the hatch. He steps, skidding a little, down the sloped front of the armored car and stands above the desert looking down at the sand as though he were about to dive into a swimming pool.

"Looks bloody silly, doesn't he?" Smythe says.

"He'd look a lot sillier if he jumped down onto a mine," Mackeson tells him.

I traverse the gun and the gunsight across the dead German lying bunched on the sand. Even at four hundred yards I can see the stain dark as molasses on his khaki shirt. I traverse the gun away from the corpse. "Loader," I say. "Eject AP, load HE." Allison opens the breech of the gun, slips out the shell, places it in the rack. He lifts a red-striped shell out of the next higher rack and slips it into the breech.

"Loaded," Allison says. He taps me on the left knee as he speaks, to give me the same message. His gesture is insurance: if the intercom fails we will not be able to hear one another.

"All right, everybody. I'm going to open the hatch and get them over here. Gunner, if they do anything the least bit peculiar . . ."

"My pleasure," Smythe says. He means it, too. Many professional soldiers fight on both sides in this war, and many crazies and fanatics, too. You can never be too cautious. On the other hand, you can never be too bold. It is one of the problems with war: you never really know what to do.

"Loader. You're on the gun while I'm outside. But remember: they're only Italians."

I open the hatch. Sunlight fills the fighting compartment and a hot breeze blows grit in my face. I lean on the edge of the hatch and look at the Italians through the fieldglasses. The Italian on the front of the AB jumps down, wincing as he hits the ground. He puts his hands on top of his head. The other three stand in a tight group, their hands on their heads, waiting to be told what to do. They are privates. The one who has jumped down from the AB is a sergeant.

I take the glasses down from my eyes and wave an arm. "Keep the gun on them as they come, Tim," I say.

"What about the one out there on his knees?" Mackeson asks.

"I don't know yet," I say. "Fuck him."

"Just asking," Mackeson says, as though I have reprimanded him. Brit soldiers punctuate every sentence with profanity but they are embarrassed when the words are spoken with meaning.

The Italian privates come forward. They watch where they put their feet and wince when they step on something hard buried in the sand. The Italian sergeant shouts at the privates and they get in line and walk one behind the other. The sergeant angles across to them. When he is fifty feet from them he takes the lead. He yells at them over his shoulder and they fall back one after another until they are walking fifty feet apart. I don't like them so far apart but there is little they can do that would not be insane, what with Allison on the 47mm gun and Smythe behind the two 8mm Bredas in the hull. As they come on, Allison moves the turret, keeping the gunmuzzle laid on them. The Italians recognize the menace in the tracking snout of the 47mm gun. Allison is doing well for a loader operator just off the boat.

When the Italians are a hundred yards away I tell Smythe: "Take the AA Breda and cover them as they come up." The M13/40 carries a fourth Breda machinegun, for air defense. When it is not mounted on the turret it is clipped in the angle of the floor and the starboard wall.

"What are we going to do with them?" Mackeson asks.

"We're not taking them with us," I tell him. "No passengers this trip."

"You can fuckin well say that again," Smythe says. He removes his headset, slithers out of his seat, unclips the AA Breda and opens the hatch in the port side of the hull. He climbs down the port fender and covers the approaching Italians with the machinegun. "No passengers," he calls out. "Not in a fuckin retreat."

I watch the sergeant coming on. The privates don't worry me, but the sergeant is a career soldier. He is a hundred paces away but close enough so that I can see his face without fieldglasses. As he steps off the last of the sand onto the hardpan he straightens his shoulders as though it is good to find he will at least not die as impersonally as have his friends in the other Blinda.

"Get rid of the pistol," I shout. The sergeant unholsters his pistol and lobs it onto the desert. It clatters on the rocky ground.

"Don't let's forget to pick it up, Sarge," Smythe says.

"Who wants a worthless Beretta?" Mackeson says. "Let the fuckin thing rust."

The sergeant marches forward until I wave at him. He stops twenty yards away. The others follow, each of them relieved to step off the last of the sand onto the hardstanding. When they are all together, the privates milling around the sergeant standing stiff and still like a thick rock, I motion them apart and gesture for them to sit. Hands on their heads, each of them a ragged ten paces from the next, they settle on the ground.

I hoist myself out of the turret and jump off the starboard fender. Smythe moves away to the left as I shift twenty yards to the right. I take my Webley from my shoulder holster. Up in the turret Allison shifts the gun and the coaxial Breda in narrow arcs. Each time he moves the turret I hear the hum of the hydraulics, a sound almost obscured by the mutter of the tank's engine.

I walk up to the first Italian private: a boy, frightened but a little hopeful and a little resentful, too. I do not smile at him and he tries to hide his resentment. I aim the Webley at the boy's chest so that he will understand. I step behind him and he sits up straighter. He sits up straighter still when I shove the muzzle of the revolver into his back. From the corner of my eye I see the other three Italians glance at me. Through the revolver I feel the boy tremble and I realize that to shoot him in the back would be like shooting your youngest brother. Nonchalant and standing easy, Smythe holds the Breda on the rest of the Italians, shifting the muzzle of the machinegun from one to the next.

I search the boy, feeling for the hard outlines of weapons under his clothes. His ribs and shoulderblades flinch when I touch him. I empty the contents of his pockets onto the sand. A bone-handled clasp knife, a cigarette lighter and his paybook are all he has of value. I put them into the thigh pocket of my overalls and go to the second of them: another lad who might have been eager for anything if it weren't for the muzzle of the Webley pressed against his back. I take a sheath knife, a box of matches and his paybook. When I search the third one, I find a clip of ammunition for a Beretta automatic pistol. The Italian winces when I find the clip. I slip it into my pocket along with his papers and a pocket knife.

At last I go up to the sergeant sitting on the stony desert. I go over him with more care than I gave the others. I make him stand and feel in his crotch and down his legs and under his arms. I keep the revolver shoved against his back just above his belt while I run my left hand over his body. The sergeant grunts when I put my hand in his crotch. I shove the muzzle of the Webley into his back and he shuts up. I take his papers, a dagger with a Fascist crest on the haft, a cigarette lighter, his pistol belt and a ring of keys. I pocket the lighter and shove the knife into my belt, fling the pistol belt and the keys out onto the sand.

I go back to the M13/40. Mackeson peers from his vision slit, Allison still traverses the muzzle of the gun. I make a wide circuit, keeping out of Allison's line of fire, giving him a free look through the gunsight. I climb up on the tank and look at the two armored cars, one intact but abandoned, the other wrecked, smoke rising in thin columns from the viewing slits and pistol ports and from the grillwork over the engine. All the combustibles inside it have been consumed by the fire.

"What now?" Mackeson asks, his voice muffled by the steel plate dogged down over his face.

"Hang on a bit," I tell him. I get back up in the turret and take the glasses and search the desert, taking care with the west and southwest. Nothing. No dust, no motion, no reflection. I look again, quartering the horizon. The last of the night is gone and it is hot and will get hotter. I look at my watch. Six twenty-three. Much bloody work hath this morning seen.

I pick up my headset and say, "Switch off," to Mackeson. Mackeson closes down the tank engine and I hear once again the light morning breeze passing over the metal angles of the tank. I listen, cock my head, hope not to hear anything. I glance at the Italians. They seem to be listening too.

"Anything?" I ask.

"Nothing," Smythe says.

"I don't hear anything," Allison says, sticking his head out of the turret hatch.

"Get inside," I tell him. He jerks his head back into the gloom. I get down from the tank and consider, kicking at the desert with the toe of my boot. "Alan, start up." Mackeson starts the engine. I look across at the three privates and the sergeant. The privates look at the ground The sergeant watches me as I pull their paybooks out of the thigh pocket of my pants and flip through them.

"Come with me, John." We go up to the Italians and I gesture for them to get to their feet. The privates draw close to the sergeant.

"Any of you speak English?" I ask. I am polite: perhaps they will talk. They look at me with curiosity, as though I were speaking Tagalog. "French? Arabic? Spanish?"

"I speak a little English slowly, *Sergente*," one of the privates says.

"Good on you, mate," Smythe says. He holds the Breda on the English speaker, his finger on the trigger, the weapon on autoload.

"What unit?"

"I am not sure I . . ."

The Italian sergeant says something in Italian. I point the Webley at him.

"The *sergente* says we only name, our number and our corporal our private . . ."

"Geneva *convenzione*, hey?" Smythe says.

"*Sì*," the Italian sergeant says.

"I've got your paybooks. I want to know what unit you're with and I want to know where you were going. You going to tell me?" I cock the Webley, the double click of the hammer distinct against the light rush of the wind.

"No," the sergeant says, speaking in English. "We not say."

"Bugger speaks a bit of the King's own tongue," Smythe says.

"I could kill you all right here," I tell them, and listen while the English speaker translates. He moves his hands when he talks: to show this is serious stuff.

"*Sì*," the sergeant says. Stiff and still, he stands almost at attention, as if he were about to be shot. The privates stand around looking awkward, as though their sergeant were already lying dead at their feet, half his head shot away. "But I won't," I tell the staring English-speaking private.

"The private doesn't understand," Smythe says.

"Neither does the sergeant." I point the pistol at the private who speaks a little English slowly. "Translate. Tell him I'm not going to kill him."

The private translates and the sergeant nods and speaks, staring over my left shoulder. The private says, "He say he believe you. He say he believe a *sergente* would not shoot another *sergente* in this way."

The other two privates smile as though they are part of the conversation. The sergeant looks grim. "He's not ingratiating himself *at all*," Smythe says.

"Tell him he's lucky he's not a general."

The translator speaks Italian and the sergeant looks less grim. I wonder how much he despises his officers, who have failed so many times and have, every time, found excuses. The sergeant speaks and the translator says, "The *sergente* he ask coulda we get the wounded *tenente* from out of the desert?"

"Sounds like a bloody rescue at sea," Smythe says.

"Of course," I tell the private. I glance at the Italian lieutenant down on his knees between the two Blindas, his face raised to the light wind, his features concealed by a mask of blood. "Tell the sergeant absolutely. We'll hustle over right now. Smythe, you come with me. Alan," I shout over my shoulder at the M13/40. When Mackeson opens the steel plate in front of his face, I say, "Get out here with these two. And Timothy," I call, "keep inside the hull." I turn back to the Italians and say, "Sergeant, you're coming with me. And you, Private," I say to the one who speaks English. I waggle the Webley at the two of them. "No trouble, now."

"*Sì*," the private says. The sergeant nods.

We go out into the desert, stepping in the Italians' footprints. It is like a walk on the seashore except that there is no ocean anywhere. Smythe marches behind the sergeant and the private, stepping from one footprint to the next, holding the Breda on their backs. I follow Smythe.

We have gone a hundred yards when I stop, feeling cold and stupid, and say, "Wait a minute." Smythe and the Italians stop and I call out, "Anyone else in there? In the Blindas? What about that German? Any more Germans? Truth, now," I say, looking at the English-speaking private. The private looks as though he has never heard English spoken.

The *sergente* says something and the private blurts out, "No. No bodies there."

"He's a nit, Peter," Smythe says. "There's got to be bodies, at least in the one that burned."

"We'll see," I tell him.

We go on. I feel exposed and I am afraid. As we approach the undamaged armored car, I hear the Italian lieutenant moaning. His hands are over his eyes and he squats in the sand, blood all down the front of him. I walk across to the Blinda and climb up the handholds on the side away from the open door, keeping the twin machineguns pointing forward from the turret to my right and the single fixed machinegun in a ball mounting in the aft of the hull to my left. Before I stick my head over the open turret hatch I call out to Smythe: "If there's anyone in here, shoot the lot of them."

"Right," Smythe calls back. He's out in the sunlight and he sounds cheerful: he can see all the way to the horizon. He takes a firmer grip on the Breda, aims it at the two Italians. The private speaks to the sergeant and his hands flash in the sunlight. He is excited and I can tell he is trying to persuade the sergeant. The sergeant hesitates, then calls out in Italian and then, again, in German. As he speaks the sergeant crouches a little as though he thinks Smythe is going to shoot him because he has spoken. I press myself against the steel shell of the Blinda. Inside the armored car metal scrapes against metal.

"Watch it, John," I shout. Smythe throws himself down on the sand, squirming like a snake, covering the Italians with the Breda. I wonder if Smythe is all that happy, now, to be outside the tank.

"Is a German, *sergente*." The Italian private screams as though an insect has bitten him. "A *Tedesco*."

"*Kommen Sie heraus*," I say. I am panting. "*Oder ich werde dieser zwei soldaten schiessen*." Ungrammatical, I know. But out here everyone understands very quickly, no matter how bad the grammar.

"I am coming out," a voice says in good English. We're very multilingual out here in the desert. I drop down the side of the AB, fall to my knees in the sand. I look under the armored car, see feet step down into the sand. I see brown desert boots and khaki trousers the color of those on the dead German lying out in the desert.

I get up and go around the AB. The German has his hands over his head. He is big, his face square and un-shaven, blond hair matted against his skull. His mouth is open and his blue eyes dart from my face to a place above my head. I step behind him and take his pistol, a Walther in a shiny black leather holster. I shove the muzzle of the Webley into his back and he walks away toward the two Italians, hands up in the air, a sulky soldier, the silver flashes of his rank glittering on his uniform shirt.

I climb inside the Blinda and glance around the fighting compartment. Nothing. I step down onto the sand and call out to the German to stop. I catch up with him and shove the muzzle of the Webley into his back. I search him, take his belt and holster, empty his pockets on the sand, take his paybook and, the fury at what might have happened rising in me, shove him hard in the back with the Webley's muzzle. The German trips, catches himself before he falls. Then he marches on, back straight, as though he knows he will not be shot in the back.

I go right up to the Italian sergeant. "I ought to kill

you. You understand?" I am furious and afraid.

"Is war."

"No. Is not war. Is shit, you fucking bastard." I hit him on the side of the head with the barrel and triggerguard of the Webley. He croaks, falls down in the sand and lies still, blood on his face. The blind lieutenant crouched fifty feet away speaks a lot of Italian, asking questions. "Tell him to shut up," I tell the private. The private calls out to the lieutenant and the lieutenant shuts up. I look at the German and the German scowls back. He doesn't like being held prisoner by any *verdammt Englander*. I tell him: "I ought to kill you too, you bastard." The German scowls some more and I imagine him up in the turret of the Blinda behind the two Bredas. I hit him as I hit the Italian, but harder, because the German really might have killed us all. I hit him across the cheekbone, raking the blow down across the mouth and chin. The German grunts and falls to his knees, his cheek laid open to the bone, blood spattering the sand. I kick him in the side and he grunts again and slips down onto his chest, coughing and spitting blood and pieces of tooth.

"Sarge," Smythe says. "He's only a fuckin Nazi. Take it easy."

"To hell with him." I cock the pistol. "To hell with the German in particular. He would have killed us all. All that stopped him," I say as I prod the German with the toe of my boot, "was he was worried about Allison behind the gun."

"Easy, Sarge. King's regs and all. Not to kill these buggers. Best put them behind wire."

"Can't." I feel cold and sick as I think of how we might have died. "There isn't any wire."

"You are not English," the wounded Italian lieutenant calls out.

"Fancy that bugger," Smythe says, glad for the distraction and eying the revolver in my fist. "A fucking Eyetie speaking the King's tongue like that. Fancy that, would you."

"You're not English," the lieutenant calls again. "Are you American? Are the Americans in the war?"

"Not bloody likely," Smythe says.

"Shut up, *Tenente*."

"Are you Canadian?"

"I said shut up," I shout and the lieutenant shuts up. He must have a good grasp of colloquial English.

"What're we going to do with these buggers, then?" Smythe asks.

"Don't know. Can't take them with us. You want me to leave them here, so they'll be found by their *Kamerads*?"

"Can't kill them, Sarge. Wouldn't be the right thing." I stare at him. "Doesn't matter, Sarge," Smythe persists.

"Doesn't it? What about this bastard?" I gesture at the German groaning on the sand. "There's a million more like him. *More* than a million more."

"Let it go though," Smythe says. "Come on, we've got to get out of here. Let's get what we need out of the AB and *go*."

"I am from Munich," the German groans.

"I bet. I just bet."

"Come *on*, Sarge."

"All right. Get 'em up and moving. Except you, bud," I say, pointing the Webley at the translator.

"*Sì*," the private says. His English is exhausted.

I order the lieutenant to get up and come to where we stand. It is cruel: the man is blind and in pain, but none of us are going any farther into the desert. He gets up, hands up to his eyes, and veers one way and then the other across the desert, lifting his feet as though they are tender. When he comes up to us the private takes him by the arm and helps him sit down. "*Tenente*," he says, recoiling at the sight of the lieutenant's face, "ah, *Tenente*." Where the lieutenant's eyes should be a welter of blood and clear liquid is coagulating.

I speak to the lieutenant. "Tell the private he's going to drive this Blinda over to the tank. You can ride or walk.

He drives. Tell him one funny move and we'll put armor-piercing through him. Got it? Now tell him." The lieutenant speaks to the private. The private nods again and again, and whenever the lieutenant questions him the private says, "*Sì*."

I wonder what the lieutenant will do without eyes. At least he won't have to do any more soldiering. But then there are worse things than soldiering. One of them is being blind.

While the Italians chatter, Smythe gets the battered German and the battered Italian up, prodding the German with the toe of his boot, saying, "Up, now, Fritz. Time to go walkies. And you, *Sergente*. Up and start toward the tank. *Comprendo?*"

"Does he understand what he's going to do?" I ask the lieutenant.

"He understands. He is not the driver. But he says he can drive it if he must.

"You riding or walking?"

"I will ride with the private."

"Remember the mines."

"I am unlikely to forget them, Sergeant," the lieutenant says. He turns his blind bloody face toward me. It is a reproach. But I remember the Italians in Spain and in Libya and I am not impressed with the lieutenant's misfortune. "The soldier is very young," the lieutenant says, holding the massive trauma of his face up for me to see. I notice for the first time that the lieutenant's forearms are burned.

"He's old enough for the great adventure, isn't he?" He can't expect me to commiserate. The war has gone too far for that. The lieutenant seems to understand my thought: he rises and holds onto the private's shoulder, but he does not answer.

Shepherding the Italian sergeant and the German *Feldwebel* in front of him, Smythe has started back through the sand toward the M13/40. Both of them stumble and hold on to themselves. They are deflated and I am even less sorry I have injured them than I am about the lieutenant's eyes and burned arms. The minor pomp of their noncommissioned rank is gone for good now: they know we are not playing games. After all, I could have shot them both. In the law of war, I could have executed them both and no questions asked. More to the point, Smythe, Allison and Mackeson would never have said a word to anyone about it: it was my decision and my right to act at my discretion. Watching their backs, I think I perhaps *should* have shot them.

Supported by the private, the lieutenant limps toward the AB. "And tell him again," I call across the space between us, "to wait till I signal him to come on. And tell him if he fucks up there's a forty-seven-millimeter round'll come right through the fucking driver's hatch." I am angry at the lieutenant for wanting sympathy.

"I will tell him," the lieutenant says. "Although I believe we have nothing to fear from the Americans."

"Tell him what you fucking well please, *Tenente*." The *tenente* cocks his head at my violent speech but he does not speak. I watch him and the private shuffle toward the Blinda, both of them swaying, the *tenente* exhausted by his wounds, the private by his fright.

I set off behind Smythe and the two prisoners, who are holding their heads and staggering as though they are drunk. We trudge to the M13/40 squatting on the rock, a weird steel box on tracks with a gun protruding from its turret like a fearsome nose. Mackeson sits on the hull, a Webley revolver in his fist angled at the two Italian privates sitting side by side on the ground twenty paces away. He gets down off the hull as we come up and says, "My, my, a damaged *sergente*. And a damaged *Feldwebel*. One of the *Fascisti* and his Nazi offspring. You should have hit them harder, Peter."

"I considered it."

"Aw, come on, Sarge," Smythe says. He gestures for

the two injured men to sit. "You know you wouldn't do anything like that."

"Wouldn't I?" I am not so sure. "Alan, crank it up. Wait for the AB. Let it in first, and then get down in the wadi again." Mackeson climbs into the M13/40. I hear him working the controls. The engine catches, roars, settles to a low rumble. I wave my Webley at the AB. The lieutenant and private are inside the armored car: they have left the starboard door open and I can see the lieutenant sitting inside the fighting compartment in the commander's seat. His head is stuck up out of the hatch as though he can see.

"Keep the gun on them as they come, Tim," I call to Allison. His hand comes out of the hatch and waves. "The one up in the turret is blind. But fire if they do anything odd." The Blinda's engine cranks over, roars, coughs and dies.

"Handy with machines, in't he?" Smythe says. "A real Scotsman, he is."

"He's not the driver." The private cranks the starter again. The engine fires and he keeps it going this time.

The Blinda rolls across the sand, bucking as the private works the clutch. As it rolls off the sand onto the hardpan, the private, awkward and afraid and therefore more awkward, brakes hard and the Blinda halts with a jerk, rocking on its springs. The lieutenant braces himself with both hands against the edge of the turret hatch. He peers around himself, bloody-faced and blinded.

"Tell him to drive it down into the wadi," I shout at the lieutenant.

"Yes," he says. "All right." He sounds exhausted and in pain, but he speaks to the driver and the AB curves away, Allison rotating the turret to track the armored car with the 47mm gun. Mackeson turns the M13/40 on its axis, the steel tracks grating on the rocks. He drives after the Blinda and disappears down into the wadi in which we hid throughout the night just past. Smythe urges the three Italians and the German forward with the muzzle of the Breda. I follow as he gestures them toward the wadi. At the rim I look down on the armored car and the tank. They are fifty feet apart, their engines switched off. The M13/40's gun is trained on the Blinda's rear.

"Down you go," Smythe tells the prisoners. The four of them slide down the bank, Smythe right behind them. I wait until Smythe has reached the bottom and then follow him down. "Over t'other side," Smythe says and the four of them trudge between the tank and the Blinda across the wadi into the shade under the eastern wall.

"Alan," I tell Mackeson, who has climbed out of the tank. "See if we can use anything from the AB."

"No hope for diesel," he says. The M13/40 runs on diesel. Almost every other vehicle in the desert uses gasoline. This is troublesome because fuel is hard to find. On the other hand, diesel is not as volatile as gasoline and will not ignite instantly, as gasoline will, if we are struck by antitank fire. "Still, we'll have a look," Mackeson says. He steps past the *tenente* and the private approaching from the captured armored car.

"You have an Italian tank, Sergeant," the lieutenant says.

"That's it."

"It is a good machine?"

"The treads are weak. And the armor on the flanks. The gun's not big enough. It's a thirties tank in a forties war."

"What is an American doing here, fighting with the British? It is as though we had a Swiss with us."

"Not quite. Tell the private to come with me and get what he'll need to fix you up. You and the sergeant and your German ally."

"We will be here long?"

"You'll find out. Tell the private to come with me. "John," I call to Smythe, "come get the *tenente*." The lieutenant speaks to the private and the private trudges toward the AB. Smythe leads the lieutenant across the wadi, gets him seated with the other prisoners. Smythe gestures at them and speaks pidgin Italian until he has them seated well apart, ten feet between any two of them, backs to the crumbling dirt and rock wall of the wadi. Then Smythe sits down, the Breda across his knees. He taps the stock of the Breda with a knuckle. "Just so you understand, now. You translate, *Tenente*. I'm right up here at the head of the line of you. One funny bit and you're for the kites. Clear? And *Tenente*. I've an eight-millimeter Breda machinegun here—you *comprendo* Breda?—and it's on autoload. Tell 'em."

The lieutenant speaks rapid Italian spattered with what seems to be grammatical German. The Italians nod. The German grimaces.

Inside the armored car Mackeson is peering into one storage bin after another. The private takes a medical kit out of a locker against the rear wall of the fighting compartment. I watch him out the door and across the wadi. "Coming your way, John," I call to Smythe, and ask Mackeson, "Anything?"

"Bags of fuel. Unfortunately it's gasoline. Useless for us. We could take this AB and be in Cairo tomorrow night, though." When I raise my eyebrows he says, "Well, not quite Cairo. But a good piece toward the Delta down the Tarik Capuzzo. And looka these cans here. Funny, aren't they?" Mackeson shows me a stack of flat well-made cans, two and a half feet high, a foot and a half wide, ten inches deep, with a built-in handle. They are strapped against the sides of the fighting compartment. "Neat, hey? Built-in spout in each of the bloody things, too. German. See the writing?"

"What've they got them in here for?"

"Maybe your common Italian's made of asbestos?"

"They're crazy."

"Perhaps they didn't expect to meet anyone out here in the desert."

"They're crazy," I say. I think of a 47mm round flashing into the Blinda's fighting compartment at eighteen hundred feet a second.

"That's why the other one burned so well." Mackeson is telling me something I don't know.

"Take it. Maybe we'll be able to use it." I am thinking ahead. If the M13/40 breaks down we may have to scrounge some other vehicle, if we can find one. "And stow it behind the turret, for Christ's sake."

Mackeson nods, hefts the first pair of cans.

I turn over the equipment inside the armored car. As Mackeson makes one trip after another with the cans of gas, I lay our booty on the steel floor: seven compact wooden boxes of clips of 8mm ammunition for the Bredas, two Walther pistols, and ten waxed packages of 9mm ammunition. I empty the storage bins of food, packages of Italian military cigarettes, maps, papers, and six ten-liter plastic bottles of water. I pile them on top of the ammunition and put two bottles of water, two first-aid packages, and three days' rations for six men in another pile.

"I figure we've got sixty gallons of gas up behind," Mackeson says from the door.

"Anything else you need in here?"

"Can't think of a thing. This what you're leaving them? Not much, is it?"

"The last I heard before the radio went, the word was they were going to be in Cairo in three days. They'll be picked up."

"We're a bloody long way from everywhere out here, Peter."

"You want to bargain with them?"

"I'd leave them five days' rations. And more water." Mackeson beats at a fly buzzing in the gloom inside the armored car.

"You think they'd leave us five days?"

"I don't know."

"You know fucking well they wouldn't."

"Still."

"All right. Five days." I gesture at the two piles I have sorted. "Sort it out and get what you can of ours over to the M13 and stow it. Then take Smythe's place and have him come over here. He can take over what you leave for them when he's had a look at the guns."

"Righto." Mackeson squats and begins to sort a few things from the larger pile to the smaller.

"When Smythe and Allison have what they want in here, drain the sump and run the engine up."

"A pleasure." Mackeson gathers up an armful of boxes and packages and takes them outside.

"Take a look at the guns in here," I tell Smythe when he comes in. "Take anything we can use. Then destroy the guns."

"With what, Sarge?"

"Use some imagination. There's a sledgehammer in brackets on the other side of this wall. Think about it. And bring the rest of this stuff when you come. Leave the smaller pile."

"A sledgehammer. That's a thought, isn't it?"

I step down from the hot gloom inside the AB into the hot sunlight outside and go across and climb up on the hull of the M13/40. Mackeson has tied twelve cans of gasoline down on the slanted engine hatches behind the turret with a latticework of rope. Allison is standing on my seat inside the turret peering through the fieldglasses at the southwest horizon.

"Anything?"

"Nothing. Maybe they're creeping up on us?"

"Not out here." In the desert beyond the wadi nothing grows more than knee high and the flat line of the horizon is unbroken. I think of the two AB 40s coming on at speed. Perhaps they didn't believe there could be a wadi. Or perhaps they thought it was still dark enough. Novices. They'll learn, though. Particularly the Germans. You can count on the Germans to do their lessons with care.

"See if there's anything you can use from the Blinda. Look at the radios. If they're useless, destroy them." Smythe handles the radio, but Allison has been trained to operate and service it. We're all supposed to know one another's jobs. Just in case.

Allison hands me the glasses and lifts himself out of the tank. I slip the strap of the glasses around my neck and let myself down into the hatch. My head is a little higher than the surface of the desert and I lean against the rim of the hatch, the glasses up to my eyes. I examine the emptiness and whistle "Red River Valley." Snow and cold. But that was Spain and we're a long way from snow and cold now. A long way from the Spanish border and the officious French immigration officials. I stop whistling when Smythe begins pounding with the sledgehammer, smashing the fine tolerances of the AB's machineguns.

"There's nothing we can use," Allison says as he climbs up the side of the tank. "It's a different kind of set. I don't know why."

"Italians."

"It's just the way they do it."

"Good for them."

"I mean it's just a different system," Allison explains. Allison is very interested in radio.

"Fuck 'em." Allison looks as though he has made a mistake. I have said the wrong thing: it is not light enough for this situation. "Forget it," I say. "It's nothing."

"Right, Sergeant."

"Get up here and take the glasses." We change places again and I jump down and go across to the Blinda. Smythe is working like a miner with the sledgehammer. "You're getting them nicely broken up."

Smythe takes one more swing and lowers the sledgehammer. "Never thought these bloody guns would be so bloody recalcitrant."

"Allison did the radio?"

"One swing. He's a strong lad."

45

"He's worked out all right."

"*I* think so."

"I guess that settles it, then. Anything more you need in here?"

"To hell with it."

"Take this pile and give it to the Eyeties and the German. Tell Alan to come over. And tell him to hurry. It's damned near seven."

"Time flies."

"So do Savoias and Stukas. And Macchis and Messerschmidts."

"Oh," Smythe says. "Right." He goes off with the armful of bottles and ration packs. I wonder if the Italians and the German will survive. I consider the question for a moment and then forget it. It is a statistical issue in which I have no interest. The only issues that interest me concern ballistics, muzzle velocities, and the increased protection a sloped glacis of armor provides the flesh hidden behind it. Once the deaths of Italians and Germans concerned me. But I have seen the deaths that tank crews die and I no longer have room enough to worry about the odds these enemies face.

I get out of the Blinda with my arms full of packages of ammunition and cigarettes, the pistols in their holsters hanging from my shoulders, and go to the M13/40. Allison is quartering the desert with the Zeiss glasses, pausing as he looks at each successive view. This, after Mackeson's maintenance of the engine and drive train, is our most important and continuous duty. In the desert the proximity of any enemy is death, for out here enemies travel with antitank weapons. It worries me that the ABs had nothing heavier with them than machineguns, for this might indicate their heavier weapons are farther back. Or lurking out there beyond the range of our sight. I think again of the speed at which the ABs were moving. I do not recall any enemy vehicle as fast as the Autoblinda 40 that carries a dangerous caliber gun. But the Germans are pouring equipment into Tripoli and I seem to remember a German armored car with a two-centimeter antitank weapon in the turret. Dangerous, but not a tank killer. Head to head we would shoot them down.

I stow the booty in the tank and turn to watch Mackeson down under the rear of the Blinda working with a wrench. He squirms aside as the last thread of the bolt at the bottom of the sump spins away. The bolt falls and a thick stream of hot black oil reaches down like a black arm to touch the sand. Mackeson shrugs out from under the AB, gets inside and starts the engine. The Italians look nervous. The German looks sullen. The *tenente* only seems to look.

Mackeson revs the AB's engine, building up the rpms. He holds his foot down and the engine roars. The last of the oil spurts out onto the desert and a wisp of gray smoke seeps from beneath the rear of the armored car. Mackeson keeps the rpms up and the engine begins to labor. He increases the speed, accelerating away as he sits in the motionless steel box. Harsh clangs and racketing noises. Mackeson stamps his boot on the accelerator. The smoke from the rear of the Blinda thickens, the color shifting from gray to black. The racketing noise rises to a squeal and something snaps. The engine bangs, begins to thumpthump. Mackeson switches off, sits through twenty seconds of silence and switches on again. The starter grinds. The engine catches and squeals, the Blinda shudders and bucks. A rattling grating and a snap. The engine stalls. Mackeson gets out and says, "Another job properly done."

"Let's get out of here." I walk across and climb onto the M13/40. Mackeson clambers through the hull hatch and fits himself into the driver's seat. Allison hands me the glasses and slides down through the turret hatch and into his seat to the left of mine. Smythe, sitting with the prisoners, stands up and backs away from them. He keeps the muzzle of the Breda on them as he walks backward toward the M13/40. I can see they are not sure what he intends. They are relieved when he hands the Breda to Allison inside the hull and climbs in after it.

Mackeson starts the M13/40. I let myself down into my seat, glance down at the back of Mackeson's head. He cocks an ear at the smooth muttering of the engine. The motion of his head reminds me of the lieutenant's blinded face. Mackeson backs the tank out of the wadi and swings it around and drives off northeast along the track scored in the stony desert. I look back only to scan the western horizon for other enemies.

We find them again two hours later.

Edging northeast, slipping the M13/40 along a ridge of crumbling shale, Mackeson holds us hull down, balancing stealth against progress, hoping for invisibility. His hope is fulfilled: the M13/40, painted in desert camouflage, raises only a faint plume of dust in its clattering passage, and I gauge that no one on the winding track below, which leads toward tea, bully beef, the Delta and salvation, will notice us.

Sitting up on the turret, legs dangling through the hatch, I brace myself against the rim of the hatch with my right thigh, my left boot jammed against the breech of the gun. A handkerchief over my mouth and nose, I ride high up like a bandit through the dust and heat, looking down the ridge at the track, peering west through the fieldglasses that jerk in my hands with each spring and jounce of the M13/40, my vision obscured by a shimmering haze, flung this way and that as the tank's hull sways and bucks against the motion of the tracks on the uneven ground.

On one pass with the glasses I glimpse movement to the west; a second jerky look reveals angles in motion, a flicker of tracks rushing in a whirl of graygold dust. I look a third time, guilty I have not spotted them sooner. In the desert motion seen soon enough may be succor.

Motion not seen in time is almost always death.

Through the glasses I see that some of the vehicles in the column coming on display the comfortable trundling outlines of British and Italian lorries. The rest are unusual. Strange and angular, camouflaged in dust-brown, gray, and olive paint, their progress is slick and smooth, a compact threatening procession of discrete engineering. Even at this distance, the glasses jerking in my hands, through a haze of whirling dust, I see the elegant menace of their design.

Not Italian. Nothing like these machines parades with the make-work vehicles the Italians believe, as they believe in Christ, will carry their army to victory.

I saw the deft engineering of these weapons two weeks ago when the 2nd Armoured Division was shot down as it woke, torn apart like damp cardboard, the dawn on fire with red and green sighting tracer and the flashing muzzles of tank guns. Angled, boxy, and efficient, German armored fighting vehicles are designed with flair. They are theatrical, the essence of propaganda: they look as threatening as they are. Watching them through the glasses, I remember the burning carcasses of British and Italian transport and tanks at Agedabia, the ground littered with corpses. My lieutenant, a hopeful type without experience or cynicism, stood on his seat to see. A long splinter of steel pierced his spine and he could not struggle to escape the turret of his burning M13/40.

Staring through a seep of sweat that queers my vision in the instant before I blink it away, I know none of these vehicles, not even the Italian and Brit trucks, are Italian or Brit. Not any longer. The Germans are coming. In France at the beginning of the Great War the cry of "Uhlans!" put whole villages to flight. Today the cry of "Panzer!" does the same. Still, they don't know we're here. They are in column, and too close to one another. Perhaps we will be able to get the boot in before they see us. Or perhaps we will hide. Who knows?

Now I see them clearly: armored cars, trucks, halftracks and towed guns on two- and four-wheeled carriages. Concentrating on the vehicles, I do not at once acknowledge the larger guns. Then I realize they are 88s, the Wehrmacht's dual purpose antiaircraft/antitank gun. It is the best they have—the best anyone has. It will hit anything the gunlayer sees. Its muzzle velocity is very high and it fires a slim shot that can penetrate three inches of armor four miles away. It is a killer, a fearsome weapon that will rule any battle in which armor fights.

In Cairo the 88 is discussed with ease and circumspection. In Cairo it seems impossible things may not go on as they have. In Cairo disparaging calm is an iron rule. Disparaging calm is considered a great morale builder. But I have noted the Brits' 3.7-inch antiaircraft guns pointed at the hard blue sky above the Nile. I have also noted no one has suggested the 3.7-inch gun might kill tanks as a wolf kills sheep.

I focus the fieldglasses on the first 88 and review the sad specifications of the armored fighting vehicle in which we ride. But perhaps the specifications of our M13/40 don't matter. All armored fighting vehicles are weaker than the 88. No tank in production in 1941 can withstand it.

"Driver halt." Our Italian tank stops, rocks on its springs and shocks, creaks like a rusty box spring.

"Bloody hell," Smythe says. "What now, for Jesus' sake?"

"Something coming," I tell them.

"Fuckin hell."

I wipe sweat from my forehead. Allison looks up through the hatch as though I might have an answer for him.

"German column," I tell them. "Guns and infantry. No tanks. Two 88s at trail. And two PAK 37s, I think." The PAK 37 is a smaller, 37mm antitank weapon: dangerous, even deadly if the guncrew is good; but nothing like the 88.

"Bloody hell," Smythe says.

"Is it all that serious, do you think?" Mackeson asks.

When he is nervous Mackeson speaks with a certain formality.

"Odds and sods. A light column. Two Matadors and two Autocarros. The Autocarros are loaded with ammunition. The Matadors are hauling infantry. They've got some of their own transport. Three Blitz lorries and three halftracked 251s. Two of the Blitzes are hauling 88s and two of the 251s are pulling the PAKs. The third 251 is bringing up the rear."

"Is that bloody all?"

"There's an armored car, eight wheels, a 231 I think, up front."

"With a two-centimeter gun," Mackeson says.

"Thanks, Alan," Smythe says. "It's a fuckin comfort you being around with information like that on fuckin tap."

"And a machinegun coaxial with the two-centimeter gun," Mackeson tells him.

"That's it," I tell them. I can see the muzzle of the MG 34 protruding from the 231's turret.

"What'n the fuck do we do now?" Smythe asks.

"We can let them pass or we can attack and see what happens. If we let them pass we'll have to hole up here. We don't have time for that."

"Oh, God," Smythe says.

"They'll never get those 88s unlimbered," I tell them. I'm selling them something. "It takes ten minutes to unlimber and stabilize a gun like that."

"You're *sure* about that ten minutes?" Smythe asks. Smythe is skeptical. He is right to be so, for I do not know how long it takes to unlimber an 88.

"I'm worried about radio," I say.

"Just radio?" Mackeson asks.

"We'll be all right unless they got off a message."

"And then we'd be in for it," Smythe says. "They'd send Stukas, wouldn't they?"

"Oh, I don't know," I say. "They might send Macchis.

Or Savoias. Alan, move on a little. Let's see if we can find a good stand."

"Oh, oh," Smythe says. He speaks with the tone of a man who has given sound advice and seen it ignored. "I've that feeling we've just taken the second option."

"What about the gas up behind?" Mackeson asks. He is thinking about our weak points. Cans of gasoline strapped on the engine hatches constitute a definite weak point. One good shot and we will burn.

"No time to get it off," I say. "Keep our front to them, would you?"

Mackeson grunts once and again as he drives the M13/40 farther along the ridge. I stay up on the turret, bracing myself and staring through the glasses. I consider what to do and how to do it. I count again: first the eight-wheeled 231, angular and menacing, followed by a 251 halftrack hauling a PAK 37; then two captured Matadors, booty from the disasters at El Agheila and Agedabia, full of troops in steel helmets sitting under canvas awnings holding their rifles between their knees; then a Blitz towing an 88, followed by a second Blitz full of troops, their feet up on drums of gasoline; then two Autocarros laden with wooden ammunition boxes; and then another Blitz towing another 88. Then two more 251s, the first pulling another PAK 37 and the second, the last vehicle in the column, full of troops. I run the glasses back up the column, note an MG34 on the roof of each German and Italian truck. They must not have had time to fit proper gun mounts to the captured Matadors.

Eleven vehicles and four guns. I look back up the track beyond the last 251. I do so with care. It wouldn't do to go into them and have a *Panzerkampfwagen III* come around the bend. I stare through the glasses at the far distance beyond the column.

Nothing. We are alone, then: their eleven vehicles and four guns in convoy and our one retread Eyetie tank stuck out here about as far as we can get and not be in French Equatorial Africa.

"Heading down," Mackeson says. I lower the glasses. Before us the ridgeline lowers toward the track.

"Loader, load HE. We'll do the ammunition trucks first."

"Jesus," Mackeson says.

"We've got the advantage," I tell him. "They don't know we're here."

"Not yet they don't," Mackeson says.

"I suppose it's only fair to take the Autocarros first," Smythe says. He sounds optimistic. "After all, we're from the same firm." The M13/40, like the Autocarro, is manufactured by some firm of former racing-car specialists close to Milan.

"How far?" Mackeson asks.

"They'll be six to seven hundred yards away when we hit them. Loader, I'll fire two HE and then call for AP. Got it?"

"Yes, Sergeant," Allison says.

"Wait till I give you the line on the AP, Timothy. If I miss I'll need another HE."

"Let's not talk about missing," Mackeson said. Mackeson knows that in armored warfare a miss can be fatal.

"Reverse when the first two rounds are gone, Alan. Then bring us forward lower down."

"Aye," Mackeson says.

"Gunner, keep their heads down when we come out in the open."

"I don't know about the bloody armored cars, but the lorries and tracks should be no problem at all. Us being up here with the view and all."

"Driver, halt."

I drop down into the fighting compartment, close the hatch over my head and feel for the gun's controls. From the sight a bright beam of light pierces the gloom inside the turret. As I put my forehead against the rubber bumper of the sight I see the eight-wheeled 231 at the head of the column jounce as it runs into a dip in the track.

"Ready," I say. I touch the turret's controls, rotate the gun. Allison and I and the 47mm gun and the coaxial

Breda machinegun follow the 231 around. Green, dust-brown and gray, its two-centimeter gun and coaxial machinegun trained forward, it comes on, menacing the track. I know it has doors between the two sets of wheels but the camouflage scheme disguises them. I worry about the two-centimeter gun. I consider changing to AP and hitting the 231 first. But I decide that to get the ammunition is still the better plan: the explosion will shock and terrify. The first Autocarro trundles into view. Too soon, the second one appears, closer to the first than it should be. These Germans have no convoy discipline. This is a good sign: it will be easy to kill many of them. Through the sight the second Autocarro seems very near. I see the driver's face and the wooden ammunition boxes behind him in the bed of the truck. The man beside the driver lifts his cap and wipes his face with his wrist. He has brown hair. I fire the gun.

The truck explodes: jets of flame rush from a cloud of black smoke. The blast scatters metal and wood across the track into the desert. 88mm rounds fly end over end in all directions.

"Very impressive," Mackeson says. Allison taps me on the knee: the gun is loaded again.

"Looka that then," Mackeson says. Fire from the burning truck flares out, sets the second Autocarro alight. The driver flings open his door, jumps down into the desert, falls to his knees. The truck explodes as he begins to crawl across the track. 88mm rounds, shattered ammunition boxes and ragged parts of truck are flung away. Somewhere inside the smoke and flame, the driver who tried to escape has died. The man in the right front seat is killed as he considers what to do: the ammunition behind him blows up and the cab disintegrates before he can move.

"Jesus," Smythe says.

"Loader, eject HE, load AP." The breech of the 47mm opens. I glance across the gun at Allison as he extracts the high-explosive round, racks it, slips an armor-piercing one from another rack and thrusts it into the gun's breech. Allison is calm. But then Brits insist on calm at all times. Even in the worst and most disgusting circumstances they strive for calm, humor, insouciance. I watched them joke as they wrote up their diaries and then went out to fight in Spain. They were poised: even in the snow and bitter cold at the French border, at the bitter end of my other war, the few of them left alive held on to their poise. Not many survived. They did not seem to worry much about survival.

I, on the other hand, am afraid and show it. Unlike the Brits, I don't care about poise. Fear makes me agile. It also makes me ruthless.

Smythe is firing short bursts from his Bredas, swiveling the guns across the thirty degrees of arc the ball mounting in the hull allows him. Tracer and shot weave among the trucks, halftracks and armored cars. Halted, shocked into confusion by the explosion of the two Autocarros, the rest of the column is a stationary target. Meat on the block, the cleaver raised to strike.

Men jump from the lorries and halftracks, holding on to their weapons. They are wearing German uniforms. Smythe's guns lash the second Blitz and it bursts into flame. The men in it jump, rushing from the explosion of the gasoline drums on which they had rested their feet. Smythe fires at them as they flee. I traverse the gun up the track. The 231's turret swings toward me. I fire the coaxial Breda as I traverse the gun. Two men in khaki shorts running side by side fall as I lash tracer across them. The coaxial machinegun strikes green flashes from the hull of the 231. Scars the pale silver hue of steel appear where the 8mm rounds chip at the camouflage paint.

I fire the 47mm gun and the 231 runs off the track, its wheels bouncing in the sand and loose stones on the verge. It shudders and halts. Smoke seeps from its turret race. Flame flows pale yellow across the engine compartment. A man is climbing out of the turret hatch: I kill him with the coaxial Breda. Flames rush from beneath the armored car. Two breaths and its fuel explodes. Smoke swirls gray and black from the hatch, disguising the corpse. The boxy menace of the 231 is lost in a rush of flame: only the last inches of the two-centimeter gun jut from the fire.

"Very nice," Smythe purrs. He machineguns running men as Mackeson backs the M13/40. Allison yells, "AP loaded," and strikes me on the left knee. I traverse the gun toward the rear of the column, halt the turret's rotation, sight on the complicated geometry of the first 88's breech and recoil mechanism. I fire the gun: the 88 puffs smoke and dust, the barrel bends from the breech and the gunshield twists. Men cower beyond the bank on the far side of the road. They are peering, rifles and machinepistols up. It is a low bank, no cover at all.

The M13/40 slides forward over sand and rock. Mackeson keeps just enough of the hull up to give Smythe a good view.

Burning boxes of ammunition litter the track. I traverse the gun, see the last 251 in the column leaving the track. It is starting up the slope, tracks grinding on sand and shale, wheels bouncing, throwing up dust and stones. A man stands in the bed of the halftrack behind the armored shield of the MG34. He fires and red tracer zips toward us.

Mackeson halts the M13/40 and I fire the 47mm gun. I fear I have missed but the shell rips through the driver's vision slit and something explodes. The 251 slews and six men vault from the back. One rises from the stony ground and waves his right arm. He holds a cap. An officer. I fire the machinegun and his corpse skids downhill. I weave tracer among his troops, killing some and forcing others down. No place to hide. I kill the last of them where they lie.

"They're unlimbering a PAK," Mackeson says. I wonder how he can see such detail through the narrow slit in the steel plate in front of his face. I rotate the turret and tell him, "Swing it around, Alan. Give John a go at them coming up from the left." Mackeson turns the M13/40 and the tracks grate against stone. Halfway through the turn Smythe begins to fire economical bursts.

I lay the gun, sight, fire. The antitank gun skids on its rubber tires, flips onto its side. The guncrew is thrown down in a ragged semicircle. Blood spatters and an arm whips through the smoke.

The PAK 37 is not as good as the 88, but it is good enough for us, the last of the 2nd Armoured Division to escape the last two weeks of disaster full of burning transport and shot-down armored vehicles, corpses scattered on the sand and files of prisoners on the horizons.

I know who is responsible for this disaster: Rommel the good soldier, a tricky strict decisive man with flair. He holds the *Pour le Mérite*. He is a natural with a sense of balance and, they say, of humor. I have read Rommel's treatise on infantry warfare. Translated from German into Russian into Spanish, it lost nothing in the process of filtration. I lay abed in overcoat and gloves, the barracks frigid even though the coal stove at the end of the long stone room was cherry red. A bunch of twenties Brits and idealistic Americans sat around the stove talking about this and joking about that. They are all dead now. But I remember Rommel's book. I remember everything from the Spanish winter of 1937.

As I feel the sweat on my face and smell the stink of cordite in my nostrils, I recall his theses. First, exert surprise and force against a narrow front. Second, be bold. Strike the giant in the face. Who knows, he may die of fright.

Down the slope around the PAK, dead men lie among the dying. One of the dying lifts his right arm, looks at the palm of his hand. His right leg is missing below the knee and the sand beneath the shattered stump is black with blood. It is too bad he must die like this. But I read his master's book and he is part of the lesson.

"Loaded," Allison says, tapping me on the knee.

I recall my other—my last—Spanish winter. It was the coldest winter ever. The wounded froze to death, ice clogged the streams, the reporters had all gone home. The Republic was moribund, the cause defeated, the *Fascisti* creeping closer. The novelists had fled, the war was lost, the night outside the barracks full of snow. The Russians and their nominees passed among us doling out political jargon and, believers who would soon be consumed themselves, departed for a Russia far colder than Spain, leaving nothing behind but the echo of their exhortations.

I remember it all. In particular, I remember the instant when, reading Rommel through the linguistic prism of two translations, I understood the sturdy theses expounded by the victor of Longarone. Still, all warfare, and armored warfare in particular, requires equipment. So long as you have the equipment, you can break through and exploit. Without it no breakthrough is possible. In Spain the Russians provided politics, shoddy equipment and bad tactics for the fight against the *Fascisti* and their German patrons' *PzKW IIIs*. Russian advisers, unshaven and grubby, told us doctrine won wars. And besides, they told us, the T26B was a magnificent machine, a weapon without equal.

In fact it was a primitive beast of a tank, a horror with weak mechanics and a dangerously exposed fuel system, a three-man crew and armor little thicker than plywood.

None of us believed anything the Russians said, but we learned to listen to every word they spoke. Alan Carl, a foolish Canadian, criticized the T26B in the hearing of our Russian armored-warfare expert, who was as pompous as his pseudonym, Marschal, was pretentious. Alan Carl said the T26B was a deathtrap. Marschal, who knew as little about mechanics and armor as he knew about economics, ruled Alan Carl a deviationist. Two of the Republic's battle police, pseudonymed like Marschal, as grubby as he and from as far east of Warsaw, appeared. They tied Alan Carl's thumbs together behind his back with dirty twine, marched him out of the barracks and shot him at the edge of the tank park. It was no worse for Alan Carl than being captured and shot by the rebels, though the Russians thought it far more heinous. For them Alan Carl was not just dead. He was politically unreliable, too.

"They're swarming down there," Smythe says. "A bunch of fuckin Germans like fuckin ants."

I ignore Smythe and lay the gun on the 251 dragging at the destroyed PAK it had in trail. It grinds at the earth. Its tracks spew out dust and its front wheels judder as it tries to tear free. I see a spatter of blood like a frond of some prehistoric plant on the dust-brown and gray side of the 251. I fire the gun. The shell strikes the 251 high on the side of the driver's space. The machine goes mad, grinding at the track as though it is trying to dig itself into the earth. Then the engine stalls. No one gets out.

"Good shooting," Mackeson says, as though I have just winged a pheasant.

"Do the other one, then. The one with the other PAK," Smythe says. "The crew's not even trying to get it unlimbered."

"Loaded," Allison whispers down the intercom.

"Yes," I say. I traverse the gun, thinking of the Spanish winter and Alan Carl, his thumbs tied together behind his back. Then I thought I would never be warm again. Now I sweat and stink and my face is powdered with sand and dust. Cold and snow, heat and dust. Snow was easier on the tracks and the mechanics than sand; but shooting is easier in the desert: the ranges are greater, the angles less acute.

The gun swings, shifting up the column of burning vehicles. I see spatters of blood on the stony surface of the track. Discarded bodies lie like bits of twisted wire. None of this is new. I have seen it all before on other roads in another country. Only the customs of burial distinguish North Africa from Spain. In Spain death required ceremony. Even in the Republic, from which all the unmurdered priests had fled, ceremony followed death. A priest was unnecessary: a commissar harangued the fallen hero's comrades. In the desert our customs are informal and apolitical, though the unceremonious insects, mice and kites are no less diligent than the muddy burial squads of the communists.

I fire careful bursts from the coaxial Breda as I traverse the gun. Down in the hull Smythe works his guns, killing Germans trying to hide among the litter of destroyed vehicles.

I lay the gun on the other halftrack. Its PAK 37 is limbered, the muzzle plugged, the sights capped with rubber covers, the breech under canvas, the crew crouched in the ditch beyond. I fire: the shell explodes against the PAK and the gun bounces on its wheels to the edge of the track. The 251 begins to burn. The fire is surprising. The driver and an officer jump down from the cab. I kill the officer with a lash of sighting tracer, kill the driver with the same burst. The pounding bullets tear the officer's chest apart and throw him down. His corpse lies on the narrow track, the sunlight flashing on his uniform badges. I glance at the driver's corpse: askew on the track, the bullets have cut him in half.

I hold my watch near the bright shaft of light pouring from the gunsight: 9:10. The watch is a Gallet, a gift from my father. "What's left?" I ask the intercom.

"The other 88," Mackeson tells me. "They're dancing around. Thinking about trying something. They've no time, though. You were right about the ten minutes they need to unlimber, Peter. They'll never make it."

"The other 88, then. Loader, HE."

The breech closes. "Loaded." Allison's hand touches my knee.

I traverse the gun, firing the Breda as the turret rotates, giving the *Infanterie* short three second two second four second bursts, killing the men I see as I swing the 47mm gun. Smythe, hemmed in by the thirty degrees of traverse of his guns, says, "Swing it around, Alan. For fuck's sake give me *room*." He sounds like a man swinging an ax in a dense forest.

"John, lad," Mackeson reasons, "let the sergeant get at the 88 and I'll swing you around as much as you please." Mackeson has his priorities straight. They are: armor first, antitank guns second, light armor third, infantry fourth, artillery fifth, soft vehicles sixth.

The 88 slides into the gunsight. I check the rotation of the turret, bring it back, fire a burst with the coaxial machinegun. Tracer flickers against the 88's gunshield. I fire the 47mm gun and the 88 jumps on its tires, the breech pounded and bent, the steel beneath the camouflage paint glittering bright.

"Seven rounds, was it?" Mackeson says. "Very economical. Shall we go down and finish the buggers off?"

"Get us back up the ridge, Alan." The M13/40 lurches backward. "Timothy, throw these things out." Empty 47mm casings litter the floor of the fighting compartment. For some unaccountable reason the Italians did not install a hopper to catch the brass. Allison opens the hatch in the port side of the hull, gets down from his seat and throws the casings out one after another. The light from the opened hatch is bright and blinding but the stink of burned powder inside the tank does not diminish. I fling open the hatch above my head and peer out.

"Careful, now," Mackeson says.

I look down from the turret past the gun. The hatch in front of Mackeson's face is open. "What the *fuck* are you doing, Alan?"

"Can't see a thing through the slit," he advises me.

"Goddamnit you don't need to see."

Safe behind the armored face of the M13/40's hull, Smythe enters a plea: "You ought to be grateful, Peter. He saw that PAK they were unlimbering."

"If you ever open that plate till I tell you I'll shoot you myself."

"These colonials," Smythe says by way of preparation.

"Shut up, John. Alan, I'm telling you. If you ever do a thing like that again . . ." I think of Mackeson dead, his body 175 pounds of inert, useless offal. His death would strand us, and a stranded tank is a coffin. "You should know better, Alan. You just ought to know better."

"Well, now . . ."

"No," I say. "Close the plate. Close it and get us back up and hull down." I will talk to him later. It will be yet another lecture full of personal history.

Mackeson closes the plate in front of his face. No one speaks as he backs us up. They don't understand my outburst. Outbursts are not insouciant. But neither Smythe nor Mackeson knows about open hatches. Not even after France and another year of this shit. They think the words will pull them through. Gallantry. Decency. Honor. Courage. The Regiment. The motto on the capbadge: "Death Before Dishonor". They won't understand until death comes, swift and slithering; until they learn that to be a good soldier is just another job; that it's *just* like working in a slaughterhouse.

"I'll tell you about open hatches, Alan," I shout down the intercom. I am not insouciant or disparaging, calm or fatalistic. The price of open hatches, like the price of bad equipment, caution, idiot orders, ignorance, and sloth is high, and it is always the same price, paid in different currencies: death by fire, death by shell splinter, death by suffocation, death by explosion.

In Spain I escaped a burning T26B, a Russian copy of the Vickers six-ton Type B. Fire flooded the fighting compartment, lapped like water rising in a sinking ship at my boots, rose higher still to touch my trousers. Miles, the driver, was another enthusiast. He liked—what? To take the sun? To show his eagerness? To be someone? To complete the curve of his life? A nice California boy without common sense or fear enough. He died when a hot liquid slug, a round from a Star or a Carcano or a Mauser thrust like fire through his temple. The T26B veered,

Miles's damaged nervous system jerking his hands against the controls. I shouted down at him again and again until I realized there would never be an answer from Miles. Then, for no reason except that it was *Russian*, the T26B began to burn. I struggled from the turret hatch, my legs on fire. Mejia, the loader, drowned in the pool of flame inside the fighting compartment.

For three weeks worried Spanish and expat doctors in Barcelona murmured at the burns on my legs and moved on to murmur at the blinded, the amputated, the paralyzed. Recuperation was seven weeks of bedlam, a journey through a Calvinist allegory with pain for a traveling companion; a short vacation gorged with meaning: a seven-week reminder that the grim reaper is never far away when you are inside an armored fighting vehicle.

From that disaster I recall the horror of Miles's head bloodied and thrown back, his hands plucking at the controls. My kit was burned: from the fire I brought nothing but the scars on my legs. A conversation piece. Even before I had my trousers off I worried whether Susan would consider me. In the bedroom I worried more: her flesh, white and unblemished, glistened in the dark. She giggled as I undressed, gasped when she saw my legs; and then apologized. I do not deserve apologies: my legs are slick and ugly, mottled pink and purple. They are part of this century's comedy. Gezira Island, Cairo at Christmas, 1940. I cursed as I jumped on one leg getting my trousers off. I should have been in America like all good Americans. But I was in Cairo with my burned legs, wearing the badges of a British armored regiment, my lust and loneliness no less acute than that of any Brit. Nothing in Cairo—nothing in the world—was tolerable, except Susan's hand on mine and her lips against my cheek. She made me tell her about the burns: how I burned, how I suffered. She seemed very interested in medical information for someone who works in an obscure office with staff officers from each of the services. Each time I look at my legs I remember the burning T26B. I should not have been surprised disaster overtook me. After all, the T26B was typical of Russia's Spanish effort. The T26B was Russian mismanagement and incompetence built to a Vickers pattern. Still Marschal admired the T26B. He had a natural affinity for it, for he was as worthless as the T26B and was a killer to boot. Sanctimonious, studied, pompous, he listened to Alan Carl's criticisms and called for the devoted Communists who served as battle police in the international brigades.

I owed Marschal for Alan Carl's murder and for my burns. I canceled my debt in the winter of 1938 when the Republic had *for sure* gone bust. Dysentery griping my intestines, my underwear full of stinking filth, I found Marschal alone in a sidestreet in a dirty village through which we were retreating. Full of Spanish brandy, he swayed as he pissed through the light of a streetlamp into a scum of dirty snow against a stone wall. He murmured to himself, ran a peasant song up and down his thick dirty throat. I stepped up behind him. He deserved what I was about to give him for many reasons, but he deserved it most of all because he was a negligent soldier and violated the most basic rule of warfare: he turned his back on the enemy. He was reaching for a high keening note when I shot him in the back of the head with a .45 Webley revolver like the one in the shoulder holster under my left arm. He fell forward, the urine still running out of him, the back of his head gone, his face flung away by the heavy slug. A peculiar falling whistle fled up his throat.

I abandoned him, his shattered head hidden in the pissy snow, and marched seventy-five miles northeast, my buttocks smeared with excrement, the armored claws of strong crabs working at my bowels. Feverish and more thirsty than I have ever been in the desert, I ate snow and marched to France and freedom. Waiting at the border, diarrhea warm as blood ran down the backs of my legs. French customs took my rifle, pistol and ammunition and while French immigration processed my application to enter

France as a tourist I rehearsed my Spanish lesson. I learned it well and I can repeat it now. Don't discuss. Don't hesitate. And always shoot them in the back.

I lay in hospital in Perpignan for five weeks before my guts were well enough to travel. Deported from France, I was relieved of my passport at the dock in New York. Mr. Hoover placed my name on a list and reviewed the list each morning to refresh his memory. More democratic and, the reality of European turmoil confounding their meager expertise, unconcerned I might be planning the overthrow of constitutional government, the United States Army consulted me about more important and less topical matters than my thoughts about communism. Disinterested in political science and quick to recognize an approaching tempest, the officers with whom I met took care to absorb the lessons of armored warfare in Spain. As they said, it was all they had to go on; and they valued my knowledge of German tactics, German mechanics, German supply. After all, Khalkin Gol had not then been fought, and Spain was the only war in which armor had been used for something other than bashing through trench systems or chasing dissident tribesmen in northwest India. Ah, well.

"Alan. Remember this. Keep the hatch shut till I tell you."

"Well, ah . . ." Mackeson says.

"Allison," I cut in before Mackeson can ramble on, "load HE." I heave myself up onto the rim of the turret hatch as Allison closes the gun's breech. Raising the glasses, I look back up the track, examine each segment of the stony way with care. Nothing. I look again, shifting the glasses across the terrain, taking time with each successive view. Nothing. I swing around: from my high perch on the tank's turret I see six dozen or more of the green lice up and coming at the trot, their white knees pumping, rifles and machinepistols swinging at high port. Nicely trained. I have always believed in thorough training. On the other hand

I feel the sole of my boot against the breech of the 47mm gun and remember that sprinting about on some benign infantry training course is not war.

"Get up the ridge, Alan. Give Smythe room. They're coming."

"Crazy, aren't they?" Mackeson sounds as though he is going to a party. He puts the M13/40 in gear and we slide up to the crest as I drop back into the turret.

"This seems about right." Mackeson halts the tank and Smythe starts firing his guns. Squinting through the gun-slit, I survey the effects of his marksmanship. The roar of the Bredas fills the constricted space inside the fighting compartment: it sounds as though we are working in a sawmill. Dressed in khaki, the *Feldgrau* fall down in ranks, dying as they might have been taught to die at some tactical school in green warlike *Deutschland*. I fire the coaxial Breda, shifting the turret, pouring tracer among them as though I am a rich man throwing handfuls of coins to a flock of beggars. Smythe and I sweep the slope, the fire of our guns as imperturbable and implacable as an Act of God. The German soldiers die with precision. Dressed in khaki shorts, their weapons swinging, they jog toward us. They wanted the great adventure and now they have it. They do not fire their weapons as they come on. Smythe, methodical and a good shot too, kills many. Brought up northeast of London, he has told us his father disapproves of firearms and works in a government office. But Smythe has become a good soldier. He wouldn't twist the balls off a prisoner under his hand, but if circumstance gives him license he will shoot down boys from Milan and Munich, hum while he works his guns and take care with his expenditure of ammunition.

"Look," Mackeson says. "They're surrendering. The fuckin master race with its hands up."

And they are. A loose group of them, straggling and sweaty, their faces gaunt and terrorized, their uniforms dusty and awry, are tottering to their feet. They move with care, like drunkards. Most of them have stuck their arms up into the air. One works the slide of a pistol. The bullets leap out of the action, bright copper bits thrown up by the pistol's mechanism. Ostentatious. It is stupid to handle a weapon while you are tying to surrender. You could be killed for doing such a stupid thing. But perhaps that's what they teach them at Paderborn.

Two of them are hardcases: they hold on to their weapons and gesticulate in our direction, shouting at their cowed companions. One holds a Mauser rifle, a 98K, the other a Schmeisser machinepistol. Perhaps they're uncomfortable without them. After all, they've had a life of it. Guns, the system, the bright prospect of living through battle, uniforms and bands, orders and medal ribbons. Victory. They never expected to be shot in the back. I traverse the gun, lay the coaxial machinegun on them. The one who has ejected the cartridges from his pistol—an officer, I note—gestures and yells at the two recalcitrants. He moves his hands as though he is calling them safe at home. But they hold on to their guns and, this being no time for negotiations, I fire the coaxial Breda. Their folly drags three others down. A spray of blood like paint flicked from a brush scatters in an arc from the throat of the officer who did his duty and emptied the magazine of his pistol. The Germans left living throw themselves down, scrabble at the stony ground for shelter from the whining burst of 8mm machinegun bullets snapping in the air above them.

"Jesus," Mackeson says.

"They're not believers, Alan," I remind him.

Beside me in the dark of the fighting compartment, Allison says, "What's happening, Sarge? What is it?"

"We're being careful," I tell him. I fire the machinegun again as I traverse the turret and elevate the gun. Tracer and shot spatter the column of bent and burning vehicles and guns. More men die, their bodies thrown backward as though they have been struck by a heavy sea.

"For Christ's sake," Smythe says. He is admonishing me. "Didn't I tell you they don't believe?" But I cease firing: we will have no resupply of ammunition. Through the gunsight I see the silver thread on another *Offizier*'s collars glitter as he rises from the desert and semaphores his arms. I shift the turret, train the 47mm gun and the 8mm Breda on him.

"A member of the fuckin master race," Mackeson says. "Take a look at him."

I elevate the gun a degree and fire the Breda. Tracer flicks above the officer's head. He crouches, cringing but alive, gropes in his pocket, pulls out a thin streak of white handkerchief.

"Magician," Smythe says.

"Allison," I say as I stick my head out of the turret. "Get on the gun."

I stand chest high in the turret, jerk my fist up and down between the hard blue sky and the earth. "Get 'em up."

The officer—bareheaded, dark hair plastered on his forehead, narrow face full of fear and strain—takes a pace forward, hands pointing at the sky. I gesture and he puts his palms on top of his head and marches forward. The turret, and with it the 47mm gun and the coaxial Breda, shifts, follows the officer as he comes on.

"Get rid of the pistol," I shout. He stops as though he has forgotten something: to wear a prophylactic in Benghazi last week; a paper at the office; his cap; to protect his men; to wipe his ass. He dithers, shifts from foot to foot. Take his hands down or not? At last he drops his hands to his waist and the two glittery halves of his belt buckle flash as he unsnaps and drops the belt and holster.

"Stop him before he gets too close," Mackeson says. None of us likes anyone near the M13/40. We cannot depress the guns enough to defend ourselves against anyone who comes near.

The German has his hands back on his head. He sets out a second time, stops when the muzzle of the gun shifts toward him, comes on again when I beckon. As he approaches, I listen for the first time since I first fired the 47mm gun. I hear the crackling of flames. Someone is shouting in pain and fear. The M13/40's exhaust flutters and bubbles. The German officer's boots scrape and crunch. When he is fifty feet away I shout, "Halt." He stops, steps from foot to foot, hands on his head, eyes flicking to one side of the tank and then the other. He does not seem to be able to look at the machine that has cost him so much. "Speak English?" I ask.

"A little," the German cries back in a thin voice. He is a captain. "A little English."

"Get them lined up. All of them. Now." The German glances down the slope, looks up at me. He doesn't know what the hell.

"Forgot his English, didn't he?" Smythe says. "He ought to have brought that Eyetie leftenant with him."

"He's German," I say. "You can't expect him to know a lot of English."

I open my mouth to shout down at the officer again; but my throat, raw from the stench of burned powder and the rasp of sand and the heat, can only croak. I cough, whisper, "Water." Allison hands up a water bottle. I wave the officer forward as I drink. I spit out a mouthful of phlegm gritty with sand and a gray sludge of cordite and dust.

"No . . ." the German calls out, ". . . understand."

"Better get someone who can," I tell him. The German doesn't understand the words; but he understands tension and anger and interprets what I have said. His shoulders slump. It is a classic pose. In the way he stands I see defeat, exhaustion, the possibility of death. Despair.

"We're taking a chance here, Sarge," Mackeson says. "There must be fifty and more of them down there. And armed, every fuckin one of them."

"Fuck 'em," I say. I wave at the captain and shout, "Get someone. Who speaks. English."

He calls down the slope at the men lying on the ground behind the verge of the track beyond the ruined vehicles and guns. A lieutenant gets up and, hands up, runs forward across the road through the smoke pouring from the first burning Blitz. He trots up the slope with his eyes down. His step is awkward: he is doing his best to avoid putting a boot on the bodies that litter the ground like dirty papers. Halfway to his captain he lowers his hands and unbuckles his belt, flings it aside. He runs right up to the captain who now stands with his fists balled on his hips. The lieutenant comes almost to attention. He does not salute. It is politic of him not to perform the ritual of the *Hitlergruss.*

The captain nods up the hill at me standing like vengeance in the turret hatch of the M13/40. The lieutenant nods, trots farther up the slope with his hands on his head. When he is thirty feet away I shout a rough angry sound without meaning and he halts.

"I speak English," he says.

"Good on him," Smythe says. He swivels his Bredas toward the lieutenant.

"Get your men up the slope. No nearer than the captain. Tell them to leave their weapons on the sand. On this side of the track. Got it?"

"I understand." The lieutenant speaks to the captain and in his turn the captain begins to bellow in forceful German. Along the line of smoldering shattered vehicles and useless guns, German soldiers get up in ones and twos and begin to come forward. The captain hectors them, shouting and swinging his arms. He's back in form now: he's got something to do, orders to give, men to do his bidding. Moving against the grain of their training, the captain's troops shuffle up the slope, laying their weapons on the near side of the track: 98Ks. Equipment belts. Schmeissers. Grenades. All of it like a ragged line of refuse at the edge of the sea. Yet another shipwreck.

"Have them sit," I call to the lieutenant. He cups his

right hand behind his ear and comes a step farther up the slope. I shout the same message and he nods and speaks to the captain, who shouts at his troops and gesticulates with his arms. The men sit, shoulders hunched. Most of them are boys. A few are sergeants who move with ostentatious grudging movements to indicate they are not part of this surrender and that someone has taken advantage. I can see they think it would be a different story in a fair fight. They think of war as an extension of team sports. It is a disease soldiers have. They don't understand no one cheers, or that the losing team is put to the sword. "There aren't any fair fights out here," I yell down the slope. The lieutenant misunderstands: he thinks he is being ordered. He considers what I have said, realizes it is a simple declarative sentence and nods as though he understands.

None of the troops wear helmets. This must be another German innovation in desert warfare. If it is it is a poor one. I recall bloody whorls of brain exposed. Head wounds are difficult. Marschal treated his troops' head wounds with nine grams of lead, explaining in his heavy Slavic accent that they would have died anyway. But I know he felt a pleasurable tremor of anticipation each time he prepared to give the coup-de-grâce to one of his own men, the muzzle of the pistol a half inch from the skull. That tremor was a third good reason, in addition to Alan Carl and the T26B, why I executed him.

The Germans wait, glancing up the slope at the tank and the snout of the 47mm gun as they listen to their captain shout orders. Now they know what the French army felt like in June 1940.

"What the fuckin hell are we going do with them?" Smythe asks. He sounds bitter, as though he has been ordered to perform a tedious and filthy job. Yet it is a good question, to which there is only one answer. We will leave them to fend for themselves. They are big boys now.

"Tell them to get their boots off," I yell down the slope.

The lieutenant speaks to the captain and the captain yells at his troops and begins to wave his arms again. The troops look at me. I am an implacable menace in the turret of an M13/40. They grumble and shake their heads but they begin to pick at their bootlaces. "Slow," I say down the intercom. "John, give them a burst. Not close, now."

Smythe fires his guns before I finish speaking. The tracer speeds away down the slope, whizzing above the prisoners squatting on the sand. The hammering of the guns reverberates inside the tank.

"That should keep their fuckin heads down," Mackeson says. He is right: the troops are scrabbling at the ground again.

"And get their boots off," I say. When the shock passes the prisoners tug at their boots and throw them down the slope. The sergeants toss theirs away with studied disgust. Perhaps the sergeants remember Spain. In Spain, before prisoners were shot, they were required to remove their boots. Supply was difficult in Spain and boots wore out in weeks in that stony country.

"How many of them do you reckon, Peter?"

"I figure fifty or more."

"A quarter of a company, then."

"Think on the bright side," Mackeson says. "They started out ten minutes ago with a hundred men."

"And guns," Smythe said. "And tracks." Smythe is remembering how bad the odds were when this fracas started.

"Shut up and watch," I tell them. You must be cautious with soldiers, and particularly so with German soldiers. "And John," I tell Smythe, "stay on the guns. Kill them all if they fuck with us." I watch as the *Wehrmacht* tosses its boots down the slope. "Get them together," I yell. I make gathering motions with my arms. The *Wehrmacht* lieutenant peers up the slope at me, squinting in the morning sunlight. "The *boots*," I shout above the rumble of the M13/40's engine. "I want the boots in a heap. A pile. Got it?"

72

The lieutenant jerks his chin up and walks down the slope, glancing at me over his shoulder. Perhaps he fears I will shoot him in the back.

"We killed a lot of them, didn't we? About half, wouldn't you say?" Mackeson is interested in this kind of statistic. It encourages him to think he is chipping away at the monolithic block of the German army.

"Worried they'll take the boots off the dead?"

"The thought crossed my mind," Mackeson says.

"You ever see a corpse with boots on?"

"No."

"It's hard getting the boots off a corpse. It's even harder getting them off a burned corpse."

"Oh."

The lieutenant and two of his bootless men are constructing a squat cone of German army footwear.

"You, ah, really want me to shoot them if they do anything out of the ordinary, Sarge?" Smythe asks. He doesn't mind killing them. It's the cold-blood part that makes him squeamish.

"Yes," I say.

"There's nothing left for them to do, is there?" Mackeson says. He wants to reason with me.

"You wouldn't think so, would you?" I say.

"It's not over?" Allison says. He thinks he has seen the third act.

"Drink some water, Timothy," I say. Ordered, he obeys, lifting a canteen and drinking. Like any other manual labor, operating a tank is hot work.

The Germans glance at the muzzle of the 47mm gun each time Allison shifts the turret. The captain looks about him, shoulders back, fists on his hips, as though nothing final has happened to him, his men, his equipment, his well-laid plans. The lieutenant and his men finish piling boots. They have done a workmanlike job. They may even have completed a quartermaster's course in boot piling.

I glance up the track at the distance from which the

captain led his transport and guns. Nothing. I wipe sweat from my forehead, pick up the Zeiss glasses and look again. Nothing. I look a third time, shift the glasses, hold each view for instants while I stare at the gray and gold desert. Still nothing. Yet I look again, and again. I know there is something out there, sliding along like a warship at sea.

Through the glasses in the extreme distance I see a faint shifting of light against the horizon, dust stirring in the still air. I look away, swing the glasses back, see it again: a low shifting cloud coming on. Only a light wind brushes my neck and I know at once something is coming, a menace tacking toward us, beating up the distant dim cloud that obscures a narrow arc of the horizon.

A tremor passes through my hands and I think for an instant of snow falling on an icy road crowded with stalled vehicles, bloody stretchers set out on the ice with corpses on them, men shouting to get out of the trap. Through the cloud of fine sand and dust an arachnoid silhouette slides down the rutted track. Armored fighting vehicle God help us now. I glance at the captain standing on the slope with his hands on his hips, shoulders back, his face turned away. I guess his face is turned away so that I won't see him grin: he knows what's coming. I bring the glasses back up: behind the first AFV two others slip out of the drifting dust. All three are moving more than twenty miles a hour. I know how fast they are moving because I recognize the angular menace of the *PzKW III* and I know just how fast it can move on hard ground. I see the blunt thrust of their 50mm guns. As they come closer the radio aerials whipping at the rear of the turrets resolve themselves; and soon I see the three tank commanders bracing themselves in the turret hatches. Fear slides against me and I shout down the intercom, "Get us down there, Alan. Get us down the slope and up the track. Panzers coming."

"Jesus," Smythe breathes. "Let's *go*, then."

"Three of them," I say, just so they'll have the numbers.

"Is it bad, Sarge?" Allison asks.

I look down into gloom inside the turret at him. "What'n the fuck you think?"

"Load AP then?" he asks. The intercom processes Smythe's laugh into a barking yap. Mackeson, his voice cautionary and kind, says, "That's all right, Timothy. The thing you do with this thing here, with panzers, is run. I mean, you run if there's one of them. With three you bloody well *flee*."

Mackeson swings the M13/40 in a long curve down the slope toward the Germans, who don't know it yet but are halfway to liberation. I slither down into my seat inside the turret and close the hatch. You never know. One of these Germans may be a fanatic, or a man angered by being disarmed, or just a dutiful soldier. Or someone who might try to kill an enemy tank commander just to see if he can do it.

Through the periscope I see the prisoners staring. One, then two, then all of them turn to look west. They have heard the sound of Maybach engines. The sound of salvation.

"Get through them, Alan," I tell Mackeson. "Take a turn over the weapons and the boots and then get us the hell out of here."

"Jesus yes," Smythe seconds my motion.

"It's bad, isn't it, Sarge?" Allison says. His certainty is dreadful.

"Panzer Three," I recite. "Fifty-millimeter gun, five-man crew, well armored."

"And five miles an hour on us," Smythe shouts.

"On the road," Mackeson says. He sounds harried, as though he doesn't have time for a lot of conversation while he is driving the tank. "Five miles an hour on us on the road. Fifteen off."

"Oh," Allison says.

We are down among the prisoners, the M13/40's engine roaring like a beast. Mackeson swings us, runs the tank's starboard tread in a neat curve over the line of weapons laid out like ragged stitching on the desert. Something beneath us snaps. Then Mackeson has us onto the pile of boots, a gentle hill in the sand crushed flat.

I rotate the turret, train the gun and coaxial machine-gun back across the engine compartment. I don't like it: to turn one's back is the greatest danger, for the back of an armored fighting vehicle is thin-skinned and full of oil, gas and delicate machinery. Worse, the flat cans of gasoline we lifted from the Blinda this morning are strapped on the hatches above the engine compartment. Fortunately the Germans seem, for the moment, docile enough. I lay the 47mm gun on them. They are standing and sitting, listening for their friends in the *PzKW IIIs* and watching us heading northeast up the track. They are still wary. Perhaps they have yet to recall what I cannot forget: we are the last of the 2nd Armoured Division. In full retreat.

"Peter," Smythe calls up the intercom. His voice runs upward to a shout as he says, "I think . . ."

A swift mechanical hammering against the turret and hull. I recognize the insistent tapping of the machinegun bullets as I gulp hot air and dust, trying to see through the lurching gunslit. I flinch: my back is to the rattle of shot against the front of the M13/40's hull and the back of the turret. In front of me, receding as the tank speeds forward, the Germans stand or squat: as I watch they begin to crawl, the smarter, more aggressive ones taking the chance and sprinting toward the vehicles on the track. Looking for cover. Looking for weapons.

"What is it?" I ask. "What's going on?" I glance at Allison beside me. His face is blank, his head inches from the steel shell of the turret against which the machinegun rounds hammer.

"Fuckin MG34," Smythe says. These are the last words I am ever to hear John Smythe speak.

"It's down behind that 251," Mackeson says.

"Get it. Get the fucking thing, gunner," I yell at Smythe.

Smythe fires the twin Bredas in economical bursts. I hear the 8mm rounds rushing away, and then the hammering of his guns stops.

"Oh, for Christ's sake," Mackeson says.

"What is it?" I ask. I do not take my eye from the gunsight: there are too many Germans behind us. And behind us is the direction from which the *PzKW IIIs* are coming.

"John's . . ." Mackeson says. The M13/40 lurches as it rushes forward. Through the gunslit I see the sand on gray on brown vehicles and guns of the destroyed column, their angled metal surfaces burned and bent.

"What about Smythe?" I ask. This is a foolish useless question.

"Shot," Mackeson says.

"Where's the gun, Alan?"

"I said he's been shot."

"The gun. Where's the MG?" The tank bounds, heaving as Mackeson balances the tug of the starboard track turning on soft sand off the verge against the port track running on the hard rutted way.

"He's . . ." Mackeson says.

The German machinegun hesitates, begins again, firing longer bursts. The bullets tap against the M13/40's armor, steel knuckles rapping against our steel carapace, seeking entry. I know these German machinegunners are worried. The manufacturer can't have recommended such long bursts for the MG34. Extended bursts will damage the rifling.

"Oh, hell. Smythe is . . ."

I look through the gunslit along the guntube, lay its snout on the Germans running or lying down or sitting, their hands on their heads, obedient to the last order they were given. I fire the 47mm and the 8mm coaxial machinegun. The 47mm HE round explodes in a group of them sitting on the desert. I shift the turret, lay tracer on a group of running men. Some of them are bowled over.

I shift the turret again, follow the ones still running with a long thread of tracer, watch them fall. One gets up, staggers, his torso mashed and flayed. An optimist. He takes three paces and falls, a splash of khaki and red on the sand: more food for the flies. Allison shouts "Loaded" and I fire the gun. Another round of HE flashes into the bootless running men.

"What the hell are you firing at?" Mackeson asks.

"Germans," I say.

"Smythe's gone," Mackeson says, as though he has just discovered we are out of tinned meat.

"Yes." I go on firing at the soldiers I can see. They will be Smythe's memorial. An evanescent but appropriate monument. They are shapes, targets posed in different attitudes of effort. Once an identifiable man is distinct in the sight. An officer in starched khaki and desert boots, the silver furniture on his uniform bright. He looks confused, as though he didn't expect anything like this. I think of Marschal, my brutal, inept Russian tutor. Marschal was emphatic about prisoners. Prisoners were useful, and were to be used. Prisoners were like battle police or spades, spare parts, ammunition, tools, fuel, or high ground. The object, Marschal explained in broken English as he smiled at the callow American and British volunteers, is to win. You will make use of any means necessary to win, Marschal said. Any means, he repeated, showing us his steel teeth. Any means at all, including marching prisoners in front of your tanks.

I cut down the confused German officer, the long lash of tracer and shot throwing him away. I did not see his face. I wonder if he was the lieutenant who spoke English and who stacked boots so well.

"HE loaded," Allison screams, hitting me on the knee. I take a final swipe at the confusion behind me with the coaxial machinegun and rotate the turret, traversing the gun. I feel the weight of gasoline strapped to the engine hatches, though. The thought of it there weighs on me like the lid of a coffin.

"Where's the gun?"

"There," Mackeson says, and before I can curse his imprecision he says, "A hundred yards. Behind the first 251. Down behind the tracks. Firing from between the half-track and the PAK. Got it?"

I lay the gun.

"Got it."

Through the sight I see the first third of the column, a static line of vehicles and guns that still seems to threaten the northeast. For an instant the thought of unexploded rounds of 88mm ammunition littering the track frightens me. But they are less dangerous than turning our gasoline-laden back on a functioning machinegun. Smoke bleeds across the track and in the smoke I see the wink of the machinegun's muzzle. To my left a twisted 88 flashes by, the barrel askew, the Blitz in front of it smoking, the combustibles inside it consumed. I train the gun on the space between the destroyed PAK and the halftracked 251. Something moves in the smoke: men down in the dirt behind the burning halftrack, crouched behind and beside a machinegun on its bipod.

I fire the gun. Flame spreads across the ground where the machinegun and its crew lie.

"Got them," Mackeson says. "*Got* the bastards."

Perhaps. Through the gunslit above the sight I see movement close to the ground. Not dead. I traverse the turret and fire the coaxial machinegun with care, as though I am counting out money. The shape—more than one man, I see—humps and shifts toward the protection of the verge of the track.

"Get up there," I tell Mackeson. "Get right up close to them." I fire the gun as I speak, the stink of cordite all around me, the compartment full of smoke, the hammering of the Breda deafening. Sand whips from the earth where the Breda's bullets sweep, chips of rock rattle against the 251's steel sides, ricochets rebound from steel and stone, leap and rush this way and that with intricate illogic. It is as though some drunken sailor is operating the coaxial machinegun. "Get up there. Stop ten yards short."

"Almost there," Mackeson says.

I fire one more burst as Mackeson brings the AFV to a halt. I slip down from my seat, take the AA Breda from close beneath my feet. I fling open the halves of the turret hatch and follow the Breda's muzzle outside, shoving my head out into the light. I point the gun with its rakish clip jutting up and forward from the breech and shout bad German. Three Germans come from the cover of the half-track. They crouch as they come through the smoke, their hands in the air. They wear dirty sweatstained khaki uniforms. I point the Breda at them and they halt.

"*Kommen Sie hier,*" I call out. A sergeant and two lads—stripeless privates, teenage representatives of the new order—come forward. They are nervous and wary. They are fearful I will kill them as I would cut grass with a scythe.

"Fuckin motherless sons," Mackeson says. He is mad about Smythe's death. But no madder than I. I wonder what to do. This is a clear case. I feel the weight of the Breda in my hands. At this range the 8mm bullets would devastate these three Germans. No case is clearer than this one. Their officer surrendered them and they attacked us after the surrender. The burden of proof is on them to show they shouldn't be executed. But time is short, and a petit jury of one must decide. I breathe out and know that had I breathed in I would have killed all three of them with one burst and fuck the specifications that remind one it damages the Breda's barrel to fire more than six rounds at a go.

The German sergeant holds a hand to his stomach. Blood stains his uniform shirt. He is subdued, but even with their hands up the young ones are arrogant. They act as though they have nothing to fear. They remind me of juvenile delinquents from a Chicago slum. I could—I should—kill them all. I have every right. But expedience and caution carry the moment. The panzers are coming.

"Get up here," I say. They seem not to understand. I

jerk the muzzle of the Breda at them, jerk my head toward the cans of gas strapped to the M13/40's engine hatches. They may not know English but the motion of the Breda in my hands is as clear as *Hochdeutsch*. The sergeant understands but he does not like it. It is a lot of gasoline and he knows I want him and the other two to get up on top of it. But no one is asking him for his opinion. He steps forward, the other two follow him and then all three of them climb up the treads and hull and squat on the cans of gasoline on the slanted steel hatches. I hold the Breda on them and say, "Get us out of here, Alan."

Mackeson shifts up and drives the tank along the edge of the track, heading northeast, building up speed. "What're they like?" he asks.

"Who?" I say. I stare at the Germans. One of the privates grins at me as though he knows a secret he isn't going to share.

"The fuckin Germans."

"They're quiet. One of them seems to think the situation is amusing."

"Good on him," Mackeson says. He sounds dull and I know he is exhausted. We have gone almost two weeks without enough sleep or food. We are out in nowhere in Libya and none of the four of us—three of us, I amend—believe we will escape. We have endured the limited life of the M13/40's tracks, a dwindling supply of ammunition, little water, meager food, no news, no orders, not enough diesel and enemies in all directions. We are still trying but none of us think we will get far enough east.

The German sergeant sits on the cans of gasoline on the starboard engine hatch, hanging on with his hands, staring at the desert. Rivulets of sweat run through the gray dust powdered on his cheeks. One of the privates is silent, his face blank. The other grins and keeps on grinning. Arrogant and healthy, he sneers and says something to the others. The sergeant lifts one hand to his bleeding stomach and stares at the desert as though he were all alone. The young German with the blank face nods but he does not look up. Maybe he understands.

"What did you say?" I pitch my voice at the cheeky one's grin.

"I say," he tells me in perfect English, "that our army will be with us soon. You should give up, Englishman. We fought you. We fired on you and you should give up."

"You killed one of us." I tell him this to put him in the picture. I see the corners of the sergeant's mouth turn down.

"That is war," the young German says. He seems almost gay. He thinks he has all the theories straight, all the rules memorized.

"I know an Italian sergeant who thinks the same thing," I tell him. "And I'm not English." I shoot him through the chest, a three-round burst, just as Mackeson wrenches the M13/40 to starboard, running it up onto the track. The impact of the heavy bullets and the jounce of the tank spins the boy's corpse from the gasoline cans strapped to the steel hatches of the engine compartment. His body bounces on the tank's hull, flops down onto the track. The other two Germans stare as it falls, glance at me, turn their faces away, stare at the desert. It seems they have not thought of retribution. But they're quick, and I'm sure they'll learn what they must. I look beyond them. The ruined German column disappears behind a slope of shattered gray rock lying under a mantle of golden sand. I begin to think escape may be possible. Then I recall the radio aerials whipping from the turrets of the *PzKW IIIs* and begin to worry about aircraft sliding through the sky, sleek sharks armed with cannon, machineguns and bombs. But aircraft or no, we must halt soon, for we must find a place to bury what is left of Smythe.

† † †

What's this day then?" Mackeson asks. "I've lost track."
"It's a Sunday," Allison says.

"Sunday," Mackeson says. "Sunday in a heathen land full of wogs lurking over the wog horizon watching us and the fuckin Germans pounding on one another."

"It's April thirteenth, 1941," I tell them. I recall bright dresses and my grandfather pointing with a cane to help me find Easter eggs with coins pressed through the shells into the meat. "Easter Day."

"Easter," Mackeson murmurs. "Christ Jesus what a day for Smythe."

"It's no different from any other day," I tell him. "Forget Smythe."

"You want to forget him you can fuckin forget him," Mackeson says. His voice is harsh and uncharacteristic, rasping over his words. He glances at the two Germans sitting on the sand fifty feet from the camouflaged M13/40—we have drawn the patchwork netting over it, hoping that it will, from the air at least, be invisible—and I see him cringe, as though he knows they may not be living much longer.

None of us look at the short hump of disturbed sand where we have buried Smythe's shattered body. I have Smythe's identity disc in my pocket. It is a small metal disc and it seems even smaller because it is all that is left of him. Smythe's grave is not much and I doubt anyone will ever find this single soldier's resting place after we leave this defile; for even though I have marked on my map the place where Smythe will lie forever, I doubt any of us will live to hand the map to the adjutant.

If the adjutant is still living, that is. He was at Agedabia with the rest of the sportsmen. For him the metaphor was polo. Others used the vocabularies of rugby, soccer, cricket,

83

field sports. Soldiers are athletic and their analogies tend to be athletic. But there are no analogies that apply to what we do here in the desert. This is reality and it has no analogy: it cannot be explained. Like birth, sex, and death it must be experienced.

"Put John to one side, then," I tell Mackeson. This is another ploy. It is the old "do what you think best but remember your fallen comrade would want you to keep your mind on the job" gambit. Ordinarily it works: it permits the grieving party to separate the dead scab of grief from his need to go on living.

But Mackeson does not give up. "You saw him dead in his seat," he says in the same harsh voice that tells me he's not going to listen to reason because he doesn't want to. Allison is embarrassed and new to all this—Smythe is his first dead friend, even though they knew one another only for a matter of weeks—and he looks away.

"I saw him, Alan," I tell Mackeson. "We've seen others like him. You remember Mitchell and Gibbons. And Nelson. With the mine."

"Thought he was a fuckin expert, Nelson did."

"He's dead now." I don't have to remind him of this. Nelson died one of the worst deaths: he stepped on a badly fused antitank mine and became an unidentifiable shower of blood, bone bits and ragged chunks only a forensic surgeon might have sorted out.

"Sure he's dead," Mackeson says. "I know he's dead." He rubs his dirty hands together. For almost two weeks we have not had enough water to drink. Washing has been out of the question.

"All of us might end like Smythe, Alan. Or worse." From the corner of my eye I see Allison look at me. He is wondering what could be worse. He hasn't learned the detail of horror yet, but I think he is beginning to get the general outline. "So forget him. For now at least. It's Easter Day. Pray if you want. But fucking forget it. If you don't want to pray, hope the M13/40 is big enough."

"You saw him, Timothy," Mackeson appeals to Allison. He gives the Germans another quick look, as though they were already dead.

"He was a good type," Allison says. "I didn't really know him but I should think he would want us, well, I mean, I agree with the sergeant. We ought to put that aside for now. We can think about it when we get back to the Delta."

Mackeson glowers at the Germans and then surprises me by dropping Smythe. "Aye, then. Forget him now, remember him later."

"Right," I say. I am stupid with exhaustion and I say the most inappropriate thing possible: "Let's eat something, then." As I speak I feel acid rise to touch the back of my throat. I remember my hands sticky with the blood and fluids from Smythe's chest. I shudder at the thought of eating. Still, I know it is best to go on, even through pain and vomit. I don't really know what I ought to do. I never do in situations like this. But then I don't think General Wavell knows what to do right now either. So I suppose it is best just to go on the way one is supposed to.

"Right, Sarge," Allison says. I look at him. "It's all right to call you Sarge, isn't it? Instead of Sergeant?" Allison doesn't want to seem familiar. It is remarkable, now we are all so close to death or capture, that he retains his manners.

"Timothy, lad," Mackeson says, "you did well enough this morning, you can call him fuck you if you want."

Allison tries a smile. He is still uncertain about his role in the crew. The light wind full of sand and dust blows his fair hair from his forehead and I remind myself he is still a child, just out of school somewhere near London.

"Peter is fine," I say. "Or Sarge. Your choice."

"Do you really, ah, want to eat?" he asks. I think again of how young he is. Even Mackeson and I are young. Smythe was twenty-one: three years older than Allison. I am twenty-seven, Mackeson twenty-five. We are all children. Even the German sergeant sitting on the sand fifty feet away holding his right hand to his side is a child.

Mackeson looks away to the north, down the wadi in which we have hidden to bury Smythe. I feel an urge to get up and walk away and get into the M13/40 and close the hatches and sit in the dark but I say, "Yes. We'll eat. Standing orders: every soldier's got to keep his strength up. No fire, though. I don't care if there's no smoke from the gasoline. The shimmer in the air's enough to give us away."

"Tinned beef and water, then," Allison says.

I nod. Mackeson gets up and goes around the back of the tank as Allison gets into the M13/40 and comes out again with a couple of tins of captured Italian meat, a package of hard crackers and a canteen.

Allison displays his manners: he does not ask where Mackeson has gone. He opens one of the tins. I spread the greasy pressed meat—it is almost liquid in the heat and oozes tiny bubbles of fat—on a cracker. I pass the knife to Allison and bite into the dry cracker and messy meat. I am not hungry but I eat all of it. I try not to think of Smythe, alive and drinking beer in Cairo twelve weeks ago. I try much harder not to think of Smythe dead in the gunner's seat of the M13/40, his torn chest against the butts, sitting in his own excrement, his blood shifting in the heat through the spectrum toward the color of tar. Twenty-one years old. His chest was mashed like a soft bloody bundle of old clothes. It was impossible to tell how many rounds of 7.92mm ammunition came through his vision slit and, by a miracle, missed his face but shattered his chest. However many it was, it was more than enough. I think of the additional years I have been lucky enough to have. Even when Marschal showed me his steel teeth and the FBI's man in New York told me my passport was gone, that my name was on a list and that I had better watch it, it was better than what happened to Smythe.

Mackeson comes around the front of the tank, his fingers sweeping along the chest-high hull. He does not look at the Germans or at Allison or me when he sits down and takes my knife and spreads some of the slick ugly pink meat on a cracker and eats it in two big bites, showing his teeth. His face is long and wide and though he is not tall, he is wide through the chest and has long arms and a lot of muscle. He is a Scotsman from the city. I can never remember the name of the city. Mackeson refers to it as "somewhere that's not fucking here." He is offhand about it but he loves every square yard of pavement and recalls it with fondness. Dundee? No, Dundee is marmalade. Whatever, Mackeson is right to think well of it: even the worst part of Calcutta is better than this desert. And it does not matter that I cannot remember the name of Mackeson's hometown. I have his address in the tank and in my effects in Cairo, and I can almost see the house in which he and his wife live, for Mackeson talks about it in detail. He wants nothing more than to get back to it— "if it's still fuckin there," he says, "given the fuckin Germans and whatnot." I know he worries about his wife more than he does his house but he does not enunciate that worry. I think he believes it would be bad luck to do so.

I also have Allison's address in central London. His father, he has said, is "in government." To a Brit this amorphous categorization may mean something. Whatever. I do not need to know his father's occupation. All I need is his father's address, just in case.

Smythe's address is with Mackeson's and Allison's. If I ever get near a postbox I will write Smythe's parents. I am pretty good with this kind of fiction and I have found I can blend reality with decorum and provide solace. The letter I hope to write to Smythe's parents will be the seventh in a series.

As for myself, the regiment's records contain my particulars; and three people in Cairo know who I am and where to write if I do not come back from the desert.

As I reach for the knife in Mackeson's hand, I notice a fleck of vomit on his shirt just above his belt. I say nothing. I take the knife and smear greasy meat on another cracker.

"What are we going to do, Sarge?" Allison asks.

"Fuckin get the hell out of here to the Delta," Mackeson says.

"That's it," I say.

"But, Jesus," Allison says, "the distance is . . ." Mackeson and I look at him: we have not heard him curse before.

"It's still Easter, you know," Mackeson says.

"I'm sorry," Allison said.

"Alan's screwing with you," I say. "What he means is he doesn't know what's going to happen."

"Aye," Mackeson says. His eyes flick at the Germans, flick away.

"It's a hundred and ten miles to Tobruk," I say. "Mechili's ten or fifteen miles to the northeast. We'll pass to the south of it in an hour or so."

"We'd best pass well to the south of Mechili, Peter," Mackeson says. "I've no fuckin doubt it's swarming with fuckin Germans."

"We'll see it from a safe distance."

"A hundred and ten miles to Tobruk is more like two hundred on tracks," Mackeson says.

"Ten hours," Allison says.

"If we have the fuel," I remind him. "If we can go straight through. If the M13 holds up."

"You think we'll make it?" There it is: Allison has asked the bald question, the one with no answer. But he doesn't want an answer: he wants reassurance.

"To Tobruk? Yes," I say, drawling a little, imitating the manner of a Brit officer, "I should think we'll make it."

"On the other hand, we could end up anywhere," Mackeson says. "Behind wire, for example. Or nowhere. And what are we going to do about them, Peter?" he asks, raising his chin and pointing it at the two Germans. I look at the Germans. They look back. I have not decided about them.

"They look thirsty," Allison says. Allison must be trying to make conversation. It is a hundred degrees and the dry heat draws moisture from everything living almost as fast as it can be replaced.

"Tough," Mackeson says.

"We left those Italians . . ."

"Not a fuckin drop," Mackeson says. "Nothing at all. Except maybe a bullet each."

"We don't have to go into that right now." I try to sound smooth. Allison looks at Mackeson. Then he looks at me. He starts to say something, thinks better of it, and bites down on a cracker smeared with greasy tinned beef.

I look at the Germans. A veteran and a recruit in the army of the master race. I have seen men like these before. In Spain they were usually shot out of hand if taken prisoner. During the desperate retreat northeast to France preparing with diligence for its own calvary, they were always shot out of hand. I think about having to shoot them. I am not worried that they mean so little to me and I know that shooting them will not be difficult. I will simply shoot them, twice each, once in the lower back where you get that pain if you sit too long in an office, and once in the back of the head. But twice for each of them. This is part of the Spanish lesson: there's no sense not being sure. Always put in a last round. Check corpses, rifle the dead. Look for papers, pictures, maps, ciphers. Top up tanks and ammunition whenever possible. Eat well and watch ridgelines. Check for movement and boobytraps, change plugs and filters, check oil and fuel levels, beware of mines, keep hull down and keep a tight asshole: the fucking enemy's fucking everywhere and the least bit of negligence can lead to something unpleasant. Like an antitank round flashing through the tank's shell.

At least we are all right for now. Our decisions, which

89

mean nothing to the overall picture—the one they have in Cairo and Tripoli—are momentous only for us. But the need to decide is, for the moment at least, suspended. After all, we could have been with the rest of the 2nd Armoured. We could be dead right now, a stinking mess in the desert. Or prisoners inside the wire at Agedabia, waiting for transport to Italy in an unmarked prison ship.

Rommel ripped us up. He acted as he wrote he would act. Rommel was very popular among the advisers with steel teeth from Moscow. They read Rommel on infantry tactics and Guderian on tank warfare. But they never apologized for the gap between their theories and the inability of their armaments industry to provide the Republic with the tools required to put those theories into effect. Even Marschal should have been able to comprehend that to dig a grave a shovel is required. Perhaps his doctrine forbade him to understand this. That is another reason I shot him: because whatever the reality, his doctrine was always more important. Occasionally I wonder whether they took his body back to mother Russia and buried his ashes in the Kremlin wall. I think not. I hope not.

"We'll keep them for now," I tell Mackeson.

"And then we'll see. Right?" A part of Mackeson wants to shoot them. The rest of him doubts.

"Perhaps," I say. Unlike Mackeson, I have no doubts about what may have to be done. But it is senseless to plan too far ahead. If Smythe had not dissuaded me, the German who hid in the Blinda and the Italian sergeant might be dead right now, even though their deaths were not required just then. And it is need that must govern the tactics of small units. Is there a need? Must we shoot them here? Or will they be more useful if we let them live a while longer?

"A hundred and ten miles," Allison says. "That's not that far, is it?"

We look at him. Mackeson says, "Far? It's halfway around the fuckin earth, man. It's likely we'll be dead before we get there, see? If we make it it will be some kind of fuckin miracle they'll write up in your hometown paper out in the arse end of Sussex or wherever."

"London."

"London, then. *The Times,* if you want."

"Alan," I say. "You're spreading alarm and despondency. We'll make it."

"Oh, well, then. God's on our side, is he? All right then, Timothy," he tells Allison, "we'll make it."

I reach to take another cracker but something—ominous thoughts about the future, the memory of Smythe slouched dead in his own gore, the loose weight of his corpse when we lifted him from the gunner's seat—makes me draw my hand back. "It'll be all right," I tell them. "You'll see. The Germans are quick. They require themselves to be careless. And there are lots of places to hide out here."

"Straight, Sarge?" Allison asks.

"Would I bullshit a member of my crew?"

"Now that you mention it . . ." Mackeson says.

"Get knotted," I tell him.

"Really, though," Allison says.

"Really. Hiding's the easy part. It's a big place out here."

"What're we going to do for diesel if we run out?" Allison is thinking ahead. We have scrounged for two weeks, but it was easy to scrounge west of here, where the 2nd Armoured Division was wiped out. M13/40s littered the desert. But from here to the wire between Libya and Egypt pickings will be slim.

"We'll get it from the Italians," I say. But I am not confident. The M13/40 is one of the few vehicles in the desert that runs on diesel and it is unlikely that we will come across an unprotected tanktruck full of the fuel we need.

"There's something I don't understand," Allison says.

Mackeson is fiddling with a cracker. He raises his eyebrows at Allison as I take the cracker from his hand and bite into it. My mouth is dry and I work my jaws, grinding the dry slab of cracker into dry crumbs.

"About the prisoners," Allison says. "I think you're telling me something I don't quite get."

"It's easy," Mackeson says. "We either take these two buggers back with us or we shoot them."

Allison is silent. They didn't tell him this at his school, or even on Salisbury Plain.

"Right," Mackeson goes on. "You understand? Shoot them. Bang bang. As in what you were never told in fuckin England.

"It's not that dramatic," I say.

"You understand, though," Mackeson tells Allison. "Don't you?"

"No."

"Forget it," I say. "It's not that big a thing. We don't have to decide anything right now."

"I want to put Timothy here in the picture," Mackeson says. "He might need to understand."

"Understand what?" Allison asks. I know he is not going to like what Mackeson is going to tell him.

"Understand," Mackeson says, "that you were there when we killed all those Germans back there. It's an anonymous war, see? That's what they tell you. Machines, distance, all that. But it's not that anonymous. We shot up those Germans and then, when they were prisoners or near enough, a couple of them started in on us with that MG34, and we cut them up. We killed a lot of them who might have thought they were still prisoners. You're with me, Timothy? I'm right so far, aren't I, Peter?" I nod and glance at the two Germans. "If they catch us, after that, and given the two of them here, the Nazi sergeant and his bloody Hitler Youth type, and given that Peter here shot the third one who was up on the tank, there won't be a lot of debate, will there? I mean, we could argue the toss if they gave us the chance. But these two are *sure* to tell their comrades we executed the third one. If they get the chance, that is. And even without that, some of them back there might have thought they were still prisoners when we gunned them. So—and this is the important part—we'll have to get down on our knees and close our eyes out here in the fuckin desert. Because they'll shoot the three of us on the fuckin spot if they catch us and if these two here can still talk."

"It wouldn't be like that," Allison says. "There are other things . . ." He doesn't like the reality Mackeson has shown him.

"There aren't," I say. "We had a bunch of them with their hands up. Then some others"—I nod at the two Germans sitting out on the sand—"fired on us. We had the right to kill them. But the others, who probably thought they were still prisoners? Out here there isn't time for appeals. Will the Germans care if I tell them, gee, we were fleeing for our lives and I fired on your troops, even when some of them had their hands up, because I was afraid they might get their weapons and take a shot at the gas strapped on the back of the tank? They won't care one way or another. They won't care because they won't listen. No one has time to listen out here. They'll just shoot us if they find us and one of these two tells them I shot their *Kamerad* off the back of the tank."

"And so . . ." Allison begins.

"And so these prisoners, well before we're captured, may have to be shot." I try to swallow the sludge of cracker in my mouth. "They know who we are. It's just like everything else out here. You assess, you decide and then you act. You commit. If you're lucky you live. If you're not lucky, you don't. You never have enough information to know whether what you decide to do is going to work. But you have to do something. So you deal with the problems as they come along. These two Germans may become a problem. Just now we don't have to decide about them. Still, we may have to decide later. It's a shame, but there it is."

"Oh, aye," Mackeson says. "A fuckin shame."

"That's it, then?" Allison asks. "We kill them when the right time comes?"

"No," I tell him. "Not at all. We kill them when the wrong time comes. Or maybe we don't kill them at all."

"But you said we'd . . ."

"Yes. However, you never know."

"We ought to get out of here," Mackeson says.

"Yes," I say. I look up at the slopes of the wadi. They are littered with shale, loose stones, sand. These slopes constrict our horizon. We should not be here. It is a mistake to hide up a wadi if you cannot see. "Timothy, get inside the hull. I want you on the Bredas."

"Sergeant, I . . ."

"I know." Smythe's seat is crusted with an inch or more of coagulated blood and fluid. A crusty square pie, all that is left of him above ground. "Put a rag down, cover it up with something."

"Shall I?" Allison says.

"Anything you want. But get inside the hull; I want someone behind the guns. We've all been out here in the open long enough."

Allison looks at the prisoners. He swigs water from the canteen and gets up and goes under the netting and climbs up on the M13/40 and slips into the hull hatch.

"What are we going to do with them, then?" Mackeson asks. He does not look at the Germans.

"As I said: I don't know. You know as much about it as I do."

"No. I've been in the army two years. I've only been in the war two weeks, if you don't count fighting the Italians. In France, all we did was run."

"You know all you need to know, then."

"No. France doesn't count. You were in Spain. What's it about? I haven't been against the Germans before, not before the last two weeks."

"You kill them before they kill you. There's nothing more to it. They're better than the Italians, but even the best of them are mindless. Soldiers are like that."

"And these two? They're prisoners, and there's something in that, whatever we told Allison about shooting them."

"They killed Smythe, Alan. I'll bet the *Feldwebel* there was behind the sights on that MG and I'll tell you for free he's lucky he and the private aren't dead right now. They're alive because it was better to have them tied to the back of the tank than not. Now that he's surrendered, he's relying on us to obey the rules and keep him and the private alive. But those rules don't apply. Not out here, not in a retreat. Out here the rules that apply are the ones that will get us back to the Delta. That's what's real. Look at the sun, Alan. Feel the sand."

"Aye. I see that. But there ought to be, I don't know . . ."

"Neither do I. Think about it. You could be alive ten years from today. Easter, 1951. Or you could be one of the honored dead. Fuck it, I want to be alive in 1951."

"Going to be a bitter old man, are you?"

"Right now I believe in armor and guns with a high muzzle velocity. In ten years I may mellow."

"Armor and guns? That's it?"

"That's all there is right now, Alan." I get up. We are beginning one of those useless, profound discussions that never make a difference and only seem to mean something when one is drunk. "Let's go, let's get out of here. I'll get the net off. You warm it up."

"You'd shoot them, then. Like we told Allison."

"Yes. They'll be dead anyway, Alan. If the war goes on. And let me tell you, it's going to go on."

"We'll all be dead, you mean?"

"No. We're good enough. They have tactics, machines, the advantage for the moment. We've got other resources, though, and we'll get through."

"I don't see the other resources. Not the last two weeks I haven't."

"We killed a lot of Germans this morning, Alan. They're not perfect."

"I still don't see it. We're losing."

"For now. You'll find out about the Germans. They're very good at war. But they'll make errors, and their hearts won't be in it forever. They're sentimental; they long to go home after a good fight. They long for dark beer and wet pussy . . ."

"I'm with them there."

". . . and when they've fought, they'll want it to be over. They don't understand. Remember what I said. In the end most of them will be dead."

"Sure," Mackeson says. He digs the toe of his boot into the sand. "And we'll be around to see it, will we? Or will we be dead too, like Smythe?"

"We'll get through."

"You sound like a fuckin speech in the Commons."

"I suppose. When you've got the engine running get them up on the engine hatches. One each side, facing outward. And keep them quiet. One word out of them . . ."

". . . and I should shoot them both."

"They'd shoot you in the back right now, Alan, if they could. If they thought they could get away with it."

"Well, they'd best not fuck with me then." He goes to the M13/40, slides into the tank and starts the engine. I undo the netting and bundle it up. Mackeson reappears. "Allison's all right," he says. I nod and continue folding the netting. Mackeson pulls one of the Walther pistols we took from the Blinda out of his belt and snaps the safety off with his thumb. I watch him walk toward the two Germans. They do not look happy when they see the weapon in his hand. When he gestures at them with the pistol they look even more unhappy. Mackeson points toward the tank with his free hand and they look relieved. The two of them get up, the older one swaying and staggering, his face white. I knew he was wounded, but I had not thought it was that bad. He takes two paces, falls on the sand and rolls onto his right side. The younger one moves to help him. He stops when Mackeson points the Walther at him and gestures him away. Mackeson keeps the pistol pointed at him until he has moved off twenty feet. I walk across to witness this small drama.

"He looks unwell," Mackeson says.

"His wound. See his shirt down by the belt." The stain, dark brown against the khaki shirt, the edges blood red, seems a little larger than when I last noticed it. "Roll him over." Mackeson rolls the German over as gently as he can. The sergeant is unconscious but he groans when Mackeson moves him. He is balding and his sweaty face is pale. Mackeson unbuttons the bloody shirt and unbuckles his belt. Two small blue-lipped mouths pucker and suck just above his waist close to his right hip. It must be shrapnel: bullets from the 8mm Bredas would have torn him apart.

"In the gut," Mackeson confirms.

"He might be all right. You never know."

"In this case, you know," Mackeson says. "He's gone, isn't he?"

"Probably."

"What're we going to do with him?"

"Let's get him inside the hull on the floor of the fighting compartment. The private will be enough up back."

"I thought you were thinking about shooting him. Now you're having him inside the tank. Next you'll be hoping for a doctor for him. What the fuck's it all mean?"

"I'll explain it to you some time." Mackeson is right: it is illogical that I am helping a *Feldwebel* I might have killed had he not been wounded.

"You want me to carry this bugger? I couldna lift the wounded pig if I wanted to."

I wave the tense young private over. He comes, shoulders slumped, and stands, shifting his weight from foot to foot. "Lift him up," I tell the private. He hesitates and I take the Webley out of my shoulder holster and point it at him. "Lift him up, I said. Mackeson, you take his legs. The private will take his shoulders. I'll keep him covered."

"I should bloody well hope so."

The boy lifts the sergeant's shoulders, holding him under the armpits, grunting as he lifts the heavy man's slack body.

"Get him inside the tank," I tell the German private. "Got it?" The boy nods but I am not sure he understands. I tell him the same thing in bad German and he nods again. Mackeson heaves the sergeant's legs up and the two of them, Scotsman and German, crab their way toward the M13/40, the sergeant between them. I look up at it fifty yards away and see the Bredas swiveling this way and that. Allison, sitting in Smythe's bloody seat, is trying out the guns.

"Treat him this way cause he's a fuckin sergeant like yourself?" Mackeson pants.

"Sure. If he were a corporal, Alan—like you—I'd of shot him as soon as I saw he was wounded."

"I bet the fuck you would've, too," Mackeson grunts. To the German private struggling with the heavier half of the *Feldwebel* he says, "Get it up you useless twit. Lift him for the sake of dear Jesus."

I call out to Allison to get inside the hull hatch to help with the wounded German. Allison sticks his head out of the hatch and says, "Sunstroke?"

"Gutshot," I tell him. He reaches out and pulls the German up and inside as Mackeson and the German private lift and shove. The loose body slithers through the hatch into the small dark interior of the tank. Watching the three of them handling the *Feldwebel* I think how crowded it will be inside the fighting compartment.

"Loosen his clothes, bathe his face and chest, and give him a shot of morphia," I tell Allison.

"Morphia?" Allison's face is a pale oval in the shadow inside the hatch.

"Morphia." Mackeson gestures the private up onto the cans of gasoline strapped onto the engine hatches.

"Get us out of here, Alan," I say as I get up on the turret.

"Aye," he says. He slithers through the hull hatch. I face backward, pointing the muzzle of my revolver at the private. He examines the rivets in the steel at his feet.

"Want a drink?" I ask him. Shoulders slumped, chest heaving, he nods.

"I'll bet you do, you young piece of shit." I hand him a canteen and his eyes flick at me. His hand trembles with fear and exhaustion. I ask him his name and he tells me: Jürgen Frei. He adds that he's eighteen years old.

"Older than I thought," I tell him. He hands me back the waterbottle. It is empty. "Know any English?"

"A little. I was, in a restaurant, a waiter. A *Kellner*."

"A waiter. Very nice."

Mackeson puts the M13/40 into gear and the engine roars as we drive off. "In Berlin," the boy says, raising his voice. "Berlin."

"Wonderful. A waiter in Berlin. Think you'll ever get back to Berlin?" He looks away and says, *"Weiss nicht."*

"Neither do I." I hold the pistol in my right hand and slip the headset on with my left. "Driver?"

"Up the track?" Mackeson asks.

"Yes. But slowly. I want a good look at it before we get out in the open."

"Aye."

"Timothy. You all right?"

"Yes." I think of him sitting in the sticky congealed pool of Smythe's blood, the stink of it like butchered meat.

"We'll get there," I say, to reassure Allison and Mackeson. I doubt they are comforted; but then, perhaps I am trying to reassure myself.

† † †

We go on, always to the northeast, Mackeson shifting up and down among his gears. Allison is silent. I understand his taciturnity: he is sitting in Smythe's position and I am sure his fear of dying as Smythe did is tinged with disgust at the bits of Smythe left behind on the seat. The German boy sits in the hot sun and whirling dust on the cans of gasoline we took from the Blinda. He holds on with both hands, face turned down, his cap blown away, sweat streaking the powdered dust on his thin sunburned neck. He cannot have been in Africa more than a week. Beneath my feet in the dim interior of the fighting compartment, the German sergeant sprawls on the metal deck, his head resting on a folded blanket. He is unconscious and I am sure he will die soon.

I sit on the turret, legs dangling through the hatch. I scan the horizon with the dead Italian major's binoculars, moving them in small arcs over the long flats and the occasional hills, looking for movement, dust, the shimmer of heat rising from engines, the glint of sunlight on metal or glass.

I see nothing, but still I am cautious and afraid and I go on looking. I am thirsty and tired. We were two days out in the desert before we found the wadi where we hid and, this morning, watched the Blindas whiz toward us. During those two days Mackeson worked on the engine, which had done something incomprehensible and Italian to itself. Only Mackeson understood what had to be done and while he worked on the engine, we kept watch and labored to change the worn pins that lock each track plate to the next. All the pins were worn and we carried only two dozen replacements. We changed those that seemed weakest and prayed the others would hold. The M13/40 is, as Mackeson reminds us, a weak machine. But it is all

100

we have and it is better than the T26B, or the M11/39, another Italian attempt one would call an armored fighting vehicle only in jest.

The two days we lost to repairs left us west of everyone except German and Italian reinforcements coming from Tripoli. Our side—Brits, Indians, Australians, New Zealanders—are far to the east. I suppose even the bulk of the Germans are ahead of us now, for the battle has moved over us and beyond. The Blindas must have come up at such speed because they *knew* the Allied forces had retreated far to the east, to Tobruk and beyond. The guns and transport we shot up this morning must have been reinforcements, a second effort. I am considering asking the private on the rear of the tank about the column's movements when Allison speaks for the first time since we left the site of Smythe's grave.

"Something, Sarge. Beside the track. A thousand yards. See it?"

I swing around, stare up the track through the glasses. Two wiry men in khaki shorts, both of them brown and hawkfaced, .303 Enfields in their hands, are standing beside the track next to a *Kübelwagen*—The *Wehrmacht*'s jeep—with two German officers. They have bayonets on their rifles and they are menacing the Germans with them. The Germans have their hands up.

"What the fuckin hell is this, then?" Mackeson asks.

"Reinforcements," I tell him.

"Indians, aren't they?" Allison asks.

"Yes." I know there are Indian troops in the desert. They have their own camps, their odd foods and religious rites I will never understand. They have a code of service I will also never understand. They fight, and relish fighting, and die with gallantry and regularity when their Brit officers tell them to. Yet their Brit officers seem disinterested in tactics or victory. They seem intent only on dying a proper death at the end of a proper life. They seem to be fools, and foolish too. Still their troops fight well, and that may be all that matters out here.

101

"We're five of us now," Mackeson says. "Where're we going to put four more?"

"We'll get rid of the private and the sergeant."

After a moment of silence Mackeson says: "Get rid of them?"

"Not that," I say. "I'm going to offload the sergeant and the Hitler Youth type and take on the officers."

"More Germans," Mackeson says.

"Sure. But if a German gunner looks through his fine German optics and sees them up on the back with silver thread on their collars he might be less inclined to bang away. You think?"

"Agreed."

"Get us off the track and stop thirty feet short. And Timothy. Keep them covered until we know where we are."

"Right."

Mackeson pulls the M13/40 off the track and we halt. I wave at the two Indians and they nod. They level their bayonets at the German officers and the Germans walk toward the tank. They are sullen. When they are twenty feet from the tank Allison swivels the twin Bredas at them and they stop. The Indians come on. I see the stripes on the taller one's sleeve: a corporal. The other one is a private.

"Get a couple of them, did you?" I say. I sound as though we have been out shooting game birds.

"Oh, yes, Sergeant," the Corporal says. "Hallo. You have one too, I see."

"Two. One inside. Wounded."

"They came down this track in their command car. As you see. We stopped them with our rifles. They were very mad."

"Who're you with?"

"Ha," the private says. "We're with no one. The regiment was destroyed two weeks ago. Until yesterday we were with a company of Scotsmen from your Second Armoured Division."

"That's us," I say. "The Second Armoured."

"It's nobody's Second Armoured now," Mackeson says down the intercom.

"What were they doing out here on their own?" I ask the Indians. The Germans are standing in front of the tank with their hands up.

"Anyone's guess, I should say, Sergeant. Whatever, I ɔelieve they are now bloody sorry they were out here at all." The Indian speaks careful but fluent English. His voice sing-songs as he speaks. Like most of the Indians I have seen, he is a small wiry man and I am sure that when he talks, his hands usually make short, deft movements. But now he holds his .303 Enfield with the long glittering bayonet on the end of it pointed toward the Germans and his hands are still. The Germans glance from the bayonet to the tank.

"Let's get the sergeant out, Allison. Corporal, get those two over here to help."

Allison opens the hull hatch. I jerk my head and the two German officers come forward and help Allison get the groaning unconscious German sergeant out of the tank. They lay him on the ground and stand so that their shadows fall across him.

"Is there a radio in the *Kübelwagen*?"

"Yes," the Indian corporal says. "It's built in. A nice set."

I consider their radio: we are without communications, and it would be helpful to have theirs. But we can't take it out of the command car, and the German sergeant is going to need transport right now if he is to have a chance to live. I weigh one contingency against the other and decide.

"Bash it up, would you?" The Indian private swings off toward the German command car, reversing his rifle as he goes, getting ready. I tell the German private to help the Indian corporal get the wounded German to the *Kübelwagen*. As they lift the sergeant I hear glass shatter and see the Indian private pounding at something inside the command car with the butt of his rifle. The corporal and the German private hump the wounded sergeant to the command car and stretch him out in the back. When the three of them return, the Indian private says, "All nicely bashed up, Sergeant." The sullen German officers grimace. The German private waits to be told what to do.

"You can drive?" I ask him. He nods and I say, "Better go, then. Take the command car and go back down the track. The sergeant will have a chance if you go now and keep on going." The boy nods, turns, walks off toward the *Kübelwagen*. He takes ten steps before he stops, turns, salutes and says, *"Danke schön, Herr Feldwebel."* The German officers look at him, frown at his lack of decorum and turn their eyes to the hard blue sky. I nod and the private goes off and gets into the command car. He gets it going, turns it around and drives past us, heading west. He waves as he goes by. The German sergeant slumped in the back is unconscious, his face gray, his body shifting with each movement of the vehicle. I am pretty sure he is not going to make it.

I haul out my revolver and point it at the German officers. I seem to have hauled the thing out a lot this morning. I gesture at the Germans to climb up. They look startled and offended, as though it were beneath them to ride on the back of a tank. But they do what I want: their only alternative, after all, is somewhere down the barrel of the Webley in my fist.

"Corporal, Private. Come on up. We'd best be going." The corporal and the private unclip their bayonets, shove them into the scabbards on the backs of their small packs and climb up on the hull. "Alan," I tell Mackeson. "Let's get on." He revs the engine and we move off.

"Very kind of you, Sergeant," the corporal says. "It is good to be riding."

"It'll be tight. Can one of you load?"

"That would be me, Sergeant," the private says. "I was in tanks for a bit. Served as loader, gunner, the rest of it."

"Good. Names?"

"Mohammed, Private Sadruddin."

"Chowduri, Corporal Ramchan."

"You can call me Peter. Alan Mackeson's the driver, Timothy Allison's the machinegunner."

"Where's your loader, then, Sergeant?"

"Allison was loader. The gunner died this morning."

"Oh," Chowduri says. "Sorry."

"You couldn't have known," I say. "Look, Private Mohammed. Get inside and see if you can figure how to load the gun." The private slips through the hull hatch into the fighting compartment. He sits in Allison's seat. Down the intercom I tell Mackeson and Allison we have found a loader. I look at the German officers in their clean khaki uniforms holding onto the gasoline cans. A colonel and a captain. A nice catch, if only we had someone to whom we could deliver them. I tell them to empty their pockets. I see at once they will adopt the manner of lunkheaded morons and will misunderstand every word I say. I point the pistol at them, since it is probably the only language they will ever understand. I'm sure these officers haven't read Schiller, or Kant, or Spengler. I met a German officer in 1935 in Munich who had. Major Count Claus something: full of honor, doubts and a terrible dread of what was coming.

I tell the captain to get up. He sits, a lumpish thick man, petulant, his face a grimace of distaste and refusal. "Corporal Chowduri," I say, "see if you can persuade the *Hauptmann* to rise and empty his pockets." Light brown like a bar of fine chocolate, all his teeth white from eating vegetables and exercising every day, he climbs from the turret onto the gas cans strapped on the engine hatches, balancing against the tank's surging motion like a spider. He jams the muzzle of his Enfield in the captain's ribs and says, "Up, now. Get up and empty your pockets." He raises his voice above the engine's rumble and the rattle of the tracks. The German, mulish and pushy, refuses to rise. Chowduri places the muzzle of the rifle against the captain's grimacing lips. The captain rises in haste, his eyes staring along the barrel of the rifle in Chowduri's hand.

"I think the captain has decided to cooperate," Chowduri says over his shoulder. The captain rises to a crouch, hanging on with one hand. He is furious. This is unwise: one should not show anger when someone is shoving the muzzle of a .303 caliber rifle against one's mouth. The captain takes a single step closer the turret and I go over him, turning out his pockets. I throw the bits into the desert: cigarettes, wallet, identification papers. I pull a fighting knife with a *Hakenkreuz* on the hilt out of a sheath under his shirt, stick it in my belt and run my hands down the man's sweating body. Down his sides, down into his crotch. I am reminded of the Italian sergeant: the minor physical acts of war are always familiar. I feel something hard in his crotch. The captain grunts a protest but his eyes tell me I have found something important. I pull out his fighting knife and cut through his belt and shove his trousers down. A small automatic pistol is taped to the inside of his left thigh. Chowduri grimaces and says, "Oh, and an officer, too." I rip the tape away and hold the pistol up to look at it. I know this weapon: .11 caliber, half the diameter of a .22. I saw it in Spain. The Fascists used it to neck-shoot prisoners. It is the answer to the question of how little matériel need be expended to kill another human being. Properly handled, the pistol is lethal.

I speak into the intercom and the M13/40 slides to a halt. I get out of the turret and Chowduri edges out of my way as I step down onto the load of gasoline tins and push the captain, his pants down around his knees, off the side of the tank. He is a heavy man and his body thumps when it hits the ground. "Corporal Chowduri," I say just before I jump down off the tank, "keep the other one quiet."

"He'll be quite all right, Sergeant."

I kick the captain in the side of the chest with the toe of my boot. He grunts and brings his legs up to his chest and wraps his arms around his head. This is to show me he has been well trained. It is the prescribed defensive position against another kick. I kick his right hand, which is protecting his right temple. A sound of sticks breaking: the captain screams once when the bones in his hand snap. I step back. The captain lies on the ground, ministering to his pain. I look up at the colonel on the back of the tank. He is horrified at what he is seeing. He is probably a good deal tougher when he is rolling through Polish villages in a *PzKW III* with a 50mm gun in the turret and plenty of ammunition racked inside the hull. "You always carry concealed weapons when you surrender, Colonel?" I cough and spit, my mouth full of grit. "You'd better speak English, Colonel. The captain here needs someone to speak for him." I hold up the captain's small pistol so the colonel can see it.

"I speak English, yes. It is, you know, the duty of prisoners to escape."

"After murdering us all?"

"One would hope that situation could have been avoided."

"You have another gun, Colonel? Like this one?"

"No."

"Telling the truth?"

"Yes."

"Better be." I am furious, more angry than I have been in days. I turn and kick the captain again, holding the small slick gun in my right hand. The captain groans and rolls this way and that on the ground, his eyes shut, sweat on his forehead. I know he is somebody's son and that I should feel pity for him. He is another human being. But he would have killed us and bragged about it; and he is going to pay right now. I kick him again, in the head this time. Chowduri says, "I say, Sergeant, is that really . . . ?"

Chowduri stops speaking as I draw back the tiny slide on the tiny slick pistol the captain carried taped against his thigh and point the pistol at the side of the captain's head above the ear. I pull the trigger. The captain's body writhes as though he is fighting a huge snake, his hips twisting one way, his legs the other, his torso pounding the road. His mouth is open but he makes no sound. I step in again and hold the muzzle of the tiny slick pistol four inches from his temple and pull the trigger. The captain jerks once and is still.

Up on the tank the colonel glares but he regards me with care. I climb up on the M13/40's hull and point the tiny pistol at the colonel. "You said you don't have a gun on you, Colonel. That had better be the truth."

"It is."

"Get up. Get your shorts off. Chowduri, get down and drag the captain off the track a way."

"I cannot, Sergeant, it would be . . ."

"Of course. You've got a religious problem. You should learn to wash corpses. Like the Bapuji."

"You say you know of . . . ? You are . . . ?"

"Private Mohammed," I call down through the turret hatch. "Get up here and get this piece of shit off the track. Get it away and shove it behind some rocks."

The hatch in the portside of the hull clangs open and Mohammed slithers out. He takes the captain's corpse by the heels and pulls it across the track. The corpse's right shoe comes off in his hand and he shies it into the desert. He grips the captain's ankles and drags the body to the verge and on into the desert. The captain's head thumps on the stony ground. A thread of blood trails from the corner of the captain's mouth. Fifty yards from the track Mohammed heaves the corpse behind a pile of rocks and backs away, kicking sand over his footprints and the channel the captain's corpse dragged in the sand. This is an unnecessary effort: riding thermals above the desert, kites will scent the putrefaction below. Gliding in a loose column down the sky, these scavengers will become a beacon which will lead anyone who may wish to investigate straight to the captain's corpse.

The colonel unbuckles and Chowduri and I watch him begin to lower his trousers. He is hesitant, and I watch him balance survival against dignity. At last he decides and shoves his shorts down to his knees. A leather pouch tied with a leather thong about his waist bulges like a tumor beside his genitals.

"Cut that off him," I say.

"It is against the laws of war, Sergeant," the colonel says in English, "to treat prisoners in this way. You realize it is against the laws of war, and against the rules of your army. I have . . ."

"I've just killed your captain. You want me to kill you too?"

"But surely the British . . ."

"You expect a lot from the British, don't you? Let me tell you something: I'm not British."

"But still, from the dominions."

"Not the dominions."

"But still . . ."

"Yeah. 'But still.' " Chowduri slits the thong, lets the leather pouch drop into his hand, passes it to me. Through the intercom I say, "Alan, let's get out of here. Private Mohammed," I call, "get up here, we're going." He has been strolling toward the tank. Now he sprints, thin and brown, across the track, vaults, grasps handholds on the hull and turret and pulls himself up and into the port hatch as the M13/40 begins to move.

"It is a matter of law, Sergeant," the colonel is saying. He is a colonel and he knows how to talk to noncommissioned officers. "International law. Perhaps you don't understand." He's arguing a brief. Right out here in Libya. He's certainly a staff officer and he may be a lawyer. As the tank accelerates he crouches to find a handhold. It is hard to present a sound legal argument when you're crouching with your shorts around your ankles.

"I understand, Colonel," I call to him across the roar of the engine and the whine of the gears. "The rule is: if you surrender, you surrender your weapons. A prisoner possessing weapons may be shot."

"After a court martial. Only after a proper court martial." The colonel is a casuist: I'm sure he's a lawyer. He probably studied at the Inner Temple.

"In the field the ranking soldier's decision is authority enough. I'm the ranking soldier." His shoulders slump. He will not argue further. After all, he knows I'm right. I have the captain's weapon in my hand and its existence and the manner in which the captain concealed it constitute all the case I need. "I know this pistol, Colonel," I tell him. His eyebrows go right up. "I was in Spain. Remember Spain? I had a couple of good German friends in Spain. When they were captured, they were shot in the back of the neck with a pistol like this. I helped bury them. The wound is discrete and identifiable. You'll be lucky if you don't get worse than shot in the next few hours. Corporal Chowduri, tie this wordy bastard down."

Chowduri is balancing like an Asiatic dancer against the lurch and buck of the M13/40. "With what, Sergeant?" he asks. "Have you rope?"

I hand him a three-foot length of black electrical wire I folded into the thigh pocket of my overalls days before. Chowduri does not need to order the colonel to hold his wrists together. He knots the wire around the colonel's wrists and makes to tie the other end of the wire to the lifting ring on the turret. "Not the turret," I tell him. "He'd be a hell of a mess if we have to traverse the gun." Chowduri squats and pulls the colonel's hands down. The colonel is forced almost to his knees and he scrabbles his legs up under him to sit. Chowduri knots the free end of the wire to one of the ropes laced over the cans of gasoline. The colonel looks at me. He is as bitter as a boy who

cheats and expects praise from the adults he has emu-
lated.

I heft the worn leather pouch Chowduri cut from the
colonel's crotch. Ammunition? Trinkets? I glance back up
the track to gauge the amount of dust Mackeson is raising while my fingers work at the knot in the leather cord
that closes the pouch. Impatient, I pull the captain's fancy
knife out of my belt and slash through the leather bag.
Gold coins spill into my hand. They are Maria Theresa
dollars and gold sovereigns. Queen Victoria's stern visage
stares at me. Two fall through the turret hatch and bounce
jingling on the steel floor of the fighting compartment.

"Thought you were going to get to Cairo, did you?" I
ask the colonel. "Thought you might have to negotiate
with the Bedouin?" Before the colonel can answer I call
down the intercom. "Hey, guys, we've got a reasonable
number of gold coins here."

"Gold?" Allison asks without interest.

"Fuckin who cares?" Mackeson confirms Allison's
opinion.

"Private Mohammed," I say, passing the coins down
through the hatch, "put these in the equipment locker beside the radio. We'll share them out later."

"Later?" Mackeson says.

"We're all right," I say. "It's all downhill from Mechili
to the sea."

"Fuckin Mechili." Mackeson has always had a low
opinion of Arab towns. Even in Cairo he speaks of
Scotland.

"Are we going north, then?" Allison asks. "After we
get to Mechili?"

"What do I know? You could come up and ask the
colonel if you want." I think for an instant of what I have
said and then say, "Alan, pull up. Get us off the track
and up a wadi, first one you see."

"What the fuckin hell's going on?" Mackeson asks. "We
just get started and you want to stop again?" He likes a

111

nice quiet drive, none of this starting and stopping. "And remember those Panzer Threes, Peter. They're back there somewhere and they've got five miles an hour on us, don't you see."

"I see. But get us off the track. I want to ask the colonel a few questions."

The tank tilts as it runs over the verge down onto the desert. The rim of the turret hatch batters my right shoulder and Corporal Chowduri, grabbing a handhold, says, "Oh, my, take it easy now, you know." Through the intercom I hear Allison sigh. He sounds like an elderly man putting up with the idiot antics of his grown children. Mackeson runs us three hundred yards up a shallow winding wadi and stops.

"Finished with engines?" he asks. Occasionally Mackeson uses the vocabulary of the Royal Navy.

"Aye," I say. "Everyone stay inside the hull. Have some of that wonderful Italian chocolate and wait for me." Italian chocolate is tasteless: they have little sugar in Italy these days. I lift myself out of the turret. The steel is hot: the sun has been up for five hours and it is almost directly overhead now. "Chowduri, get inside. Use the glasses, keep watch. You understand?"

"Of course. Out here, the least motion is, well . . ."

"Yes."

I untie the colonel's tether but I do not release his hands. "Off the tank, Fritz," I say. He hesitates. "Jump or be pushed," I tell him. He jumps. He is young for a colonel and in good shape. He lands well, breaking the force of the jump with his ankles and knees.

"Where are we . . . ?" he begins but I tell him to shut up and to walk in front of me. He is reluctant. No one likes to start a journey if they don't know where they're going. Once again I pull the Webley out of its holster. From inside the M13/40 I hear Mackeson say, "Now, Peter, where the fuckin hell are you going with him?"

"I'll be back," I say. I do not say "We'll be back." I

hope the colonel notices the difference. I prod him with the muzzle of the revolver and he starts walking deeper into the wadi. He is composed but apprehensive. He seems ready for anything. He can't be more than thirty-five. Still, it's early days for this war, as the Brits say every time they suffer another disaster. Give us a couple of years and the fieldmarshals will be forty and the colonels twenty-three. Give us time enough and the children will be shooting the last batch of prisoners with their MG34s.

"Move faster," I say. But the colonel keeps on, treading one steady pace after another. He is not going to be rushed. I kick him, hard, in the buttocks and he squeaks and falls. He cannot use his arms to break his fall because his wrists are tied together. The electrical wire cuts into his wrists and blood spatters on the stones and sand. He hoicks himself to his knees and stands. His cheek is cut, his cap is gone and his blouse is in disarray. The second button down from his collar is missing and blood slides down his chin. Trying to keep his back straight but shivering because he thinks he knows what is going to happen to him—he probably has a broad experience of situations such as this—he turns and walks up the wadi more quickly, as though he has figured out where he is going. I remember the joke I heard when I was a child, about first getting the donkey's attention. "Keep going," I tell him. "Let's get well away from the tank."

The colonel walks twenty paces before he says, "What is going to happen, Sergeant? I am your prisoner." I kick him again, in the lower back with my heavy British boot and he goes down on the shale, falling on one side. His shirt is torn and blood seeps from abrasions on his knees and shins. "Get up," I tell him. Trembling with pain and fear but still trying to recall his staff-college training—or is it his training at the *Panzerschule* at Paderborn?—he gets up. "Up the wadi," I tell him again, standing well away from him. After all, he's got to be desperate enough to try anything.

We go on up the wadi until we are around a bend in the crooked geological illogic of the stony slash in the earth. I kick the colonel in the back of the right knee. He falls for a third time. Blood flows from the crosscuts on his knees.

"Keep down," I tell him. I step behind him and his back stiffens. We are two thirds of the way from Tripoli to Cairo but it is clear the colonel believes he is on his way to nowhere. "Keep still," I say, and he stiffens even more. "You understand, don't you, Colonel? You know the answer, don't you?" The colonel grunts, his mouth against the earth.

"Get up," I say. The colonel groans. "Get up," I tell him a second time.

The colonel rolls over and forces himself to his knees. His uniform is torn and filthy, crumpled and bloody. "Ever been to Lichterfelde, Colonel?" The colonel closes his eyes and groans. He thinks I know something about him. But I have only heard a rumor that in a prison barracks at Lichterfelde the German army trains troops who are fodder for penal regiments. Their jobs are the worst there are: bomb disposal, mine disposal, frontal infantry assaults. I had a German friend who fought for the Republic and who, when the fighting ended, disappeared back to Germany and was swallowed up by the German legal and penal system. I hope he had the chance to kill himself before he was sent to Lichterfelde.

"Speak English pretty well, don't you?" I ask. I am standing behind the colonel. He knows where I am, though, for he can see my shadow, and part of that shadow is the hard black outline of the Webley jutting from my fist.

"*Ja*," he says. "Yes. Some. I went on a course in England."

"England."

"Salisbury Plain."

"I'll bet."

"I liaised with the First British Armoured Division. 1935."

114

"Wonderful. Smart, aren't they? The British, I mean."

"Of course."

"Didn't listen, did they? To Guderian. Listened to their own experts."

"Yes."

"I don't want to talk about the British," I tell him. "Or Guderian. We've got a problem, Colonel. Right now I'm not interested in the *Panzerkeil,* or the *Schwerpunkt* or whatever. Right now I'm interested in your future. I'd like to have you tell me if you think you have one. Whether your opinion is correct will depend on what you tell me. What were you doing out here, away from everything? What were your orders?"

"You know I cannot tell you that, Sergeant." He hunches his shoulders as though he knows what's coming.

"Can't? Can *not?*" I slide the captain's fancy knife from its scabbard in my belt and swipe it across the colonel's khaki back. He should be grateful: if I were serious I would have shot him dead. He screams, a short bark of surprise and pain. For an instant he is silent and then he howls as though he has gone mad. He sees some terrifying thing in front of him. It is my shadow, falling on the sand.

"Ah, ah," I say, pressing the point of the knife against the back of his neck. "That's not what I want to hear."

"I cannot."

"I'll butcher you if you don't."

"No."

"Colonel, Colonel," I say as I cut him again, another light long swipe across his bloody khaki-shirted back. "I want to hear about dispositions and plans. I want to hear about compass bearings, objectives, capacities. You know: all those things a good staff officer holds so dear."

"This is unbelievable." He says it as though he has some right.

"Unbelievable? Come on, Colonel. I know you're used to wielding the knife and letting the other one do the screaming. But this is different. Now you're at risk. Your army may win this battle. It may even win the war. But I don't think you'll be marching in the victory parade." He says nothing and I press the point of the knife into the soft spot beneath his earlobe between his jaw and his neck. "Right now the best you can expect is three inches of steel in your brain. You understand?"

"Please, Sergeant, you must control yourself."

"Control myself. Here? Now? This is for keeps, Fritz. And you think I should control myself? A *very* interesting concept. Perhaps you could do a staff paper on it. Call it 'Control in Combat Conditions.' What about it? Do you think that would interest the rest of the staff?" The colonel is silent. "You could get up and run. If you ran I would kill you with the revolver. The choice is yours." He says nothing. "Isn't the choice yours?"

"Yes," he hisses. His torso quivers: he is waiting for the knife.

"Why don't you run? After all, you said it is your duty to try to escape. And if you ran you would die and wouldn't have to tell. Wouldn't you?"

"Yes."

"Then why don't you run? Come on," I say, shoving the muzzle of the Webley against his spine. "Up you get. On your feet." The colonel struggles to his feet. "Go ahead, then. Run, you shit. Run and die. Do your duty."

"I . . ." the colonel says. "I . . ."

"That's the crux of it, isn't it?"

"What is 'crux'?"

"What's your name, Colonel?"

"Steiger, Rudolph."

"Steiger Rudolph. I'd have thought Rudolph Steiger would have sounded better but then you never know what parents will call their children. You have parents?"

"Yes."

"And?"

"In Hamburg."

"I'm surprised you're not in the *Kriegsmarine*."

He says nothing.

"They're old?"

"Yes."

"They're happy to see you in uniform, are they?"

The colonel pants, three deep breaths, and says, "No."

"Of course. What parent wants to see their son come home in a box?"

"A box?"

"A coffin. You understand 'coffin'?"

"Yes."

"Or not come home at all."

"Yes."

"I don't have time to fuck with you, Colonel. What's it going to be? What's coming up the track?"

"I cannot."

Once I was four years old and played with a wooden toy train and wore an outsize ballcap and knelt in the grass in Lincoln Park to examine a ladybug on a thin spear of grass. But that is long ago and now I cannot remember my childhood. Now I am in my twenties and full of fear. I start in on the colonel, the son of parents in Hamburg who didn't like him in uniform and don't want him to come home in a box. I go after him: I use the knife, the barrel of the Webley and my boots until his face is bloodied and bruised and his back is threaded with shallow cuts that resemble a map of the rail net outside Frankfurt.

"You'll have more scars than Rohm," I tell him. "You couldn't have done this well if you'd taken eight years for a doctorate at Heidelburg."

"Uh," the colonel says: all his sage answers memorized at Paderborn and the Bendlerstrasse have been leached out of him through the long shallow cuts on his back. "Uh."

"Not much of an answer for a staff officer, Colonel. Last chance, now. Speak, or you'll forever hold your peace." To emphasize what I say I put the point of the knife against his temple, an inch from the corner of his right eye.

"Kill me then. Kill me." Stubborn and brave. I would

117

have told him anything he wanted if he'd put me through this. Even with tears on his face and blood on his back he has a certain courage. I remember again that I was once satisfied with a toy train and the adventure of Lincoln Park. Out in the lake sailboats leaned from the wind, heading this way and that. I wonder how I came this way. I cannot say, for I cannot remember where this journey began. I am desolate, bored and in despair: for myself, for the colonel, for Allison and Mackeson and the Indians. For Smythe dead. Even for the Germans I killed this morning. Even for the German captain I executed. Certainly for the Italian lieutenant blinded by the mine that exploded beneath the Blinda in which he had sallied forth to embrace his war.

I end it. Even though I have been as brutal as the colonel might have been—though not as brutal as Marschal, or the communists who crucified priests in Spain—I have learned nothing. I give the colonel a last light kick: a swipe with the side of my boot. A coda for this particular piece of the horror. "All right," the colonel shrieks as he feels my boot. "I will. Stop. I will tell but stop." I wonder why this final kick makes him betray himself. He pants and bleeds, the sound of his voice rising and falling with the rush of air in and out of his lungs. He is *in terrorem* and in his panic he is hyperventilating.

"For your parents," I tell him. "You'll tell me for your parents."

"Yes. For them. Yes."

"Hamburg," I murmur. And I think: a single last kick. A gentle thump against his ribs. You never fucking know anything.

"They are coming. We are advancing east up the track. To form a block southeast of Tobruk. We are ordered to block whatever forces appear from the east."

"You're doing well, Colonel. What's going on?"

"I don't know. This is all the information I have. I swear it."

"What were you doing way out in the desert all alone? The captain on one side, that is?"

"I . . ."

"Hmmmm?" I show him the knife. His eyes glitter and follow the blade spattered with blood.

"I was waiting for instructions."

"Instructions? How?"

"They were to be dropped from a Storch. It did not arrive."

"Why not the radio?"

"The staff distrusts the radio. They do not like it."

"Rommel?"

"He believes it insecure."

"What about Mechili?"

"Mechili?" The colonel nods and swallows. "Mechili was taken a week ago yesterday. You have been out of touch?"

"Right out of the fucking picture," I tell him. I remember the last ten days: out of touch, fleeing and falling back, scrounging in the rubbish heap of the battlefield for spareparts and fuel, hiding for days from dust on the horizon and *Stukas* stooping like hawks in the distance.

"How far east have you gotten?" I do not want his answer to this question, but I must know.

"We took Bardia yesterday."

"Bardia?" I say. "Bardia?" Bardia is eighty miles east of Tobruk, almost on the Egyptian border. We are a hundred and ten miles west southwest of Tobruk. We are in trouble, much worse trouble than I had thought. We will not make it to Egypt.

"And Tobruk?" I think of Tobruk, the only decent port between Alexandria and Benghazi.

"We have bypassed Tobruk. It is heavily defended. Australians are there." The colonel doesn't like the sound of Australians. Everyone in the desert knows about the Australians: they are implacable enemies far from home and they *always* fight to the death.

"And your intentions?"

"I don't know." I show him the knife again, shove the muzzle of the Webley against his neck. "All right. All right. Tobruk is to be assaulted."

I remember the deep caves at Tobruk. The Italians, their minds turning always to the defense, transformed them into bunkers. I know Tobruk cannot be held without re-supply: Tobruk is useless except for its port, a water distillation plant and tracks leading out into the desert. I assume the distillation plant has been destroyed. The tracks are of use only to the Germans. The garrison defending the place must be resupplied from the sea. It is the end in Spain all over again, with the Royal Navy on our side this time.

"When?"

"I don't know," the colonel says. "I *don't*," he repeats when he sees the knife.

"What's coming down the track behind us?"

"There is a column of guns and vehicles. I was—we were—supposed to join up with it at a crossroads eight kilometers east of where we were stopped."

"That's it?"

"I know nothing else. The general likes to have all his forces always at the front."

"You don't have to worry about the column," I tell him.

"I do not understand."

"Where do you think the sergeant and the private came from? The ones I sent back in your *Kübelwagen?*"

"You mean . . . ?"

"Think about it." He nods and nods, as though he has at last understood something that has puzzled him. "On your feet," I tell him. He struggles up, bent at the waist, his hands to his stomach. He staggers and falls. His back is a mess: I have sliced away at him and the long shallow cuts bleed and bleed. He gets up on his hands and knees. His face is flushed and sweaty and snot runs out of his nose. He gets his feet under himself and heaves upward and stands swaying back and forth. Apparently the pain of his wounds, superficial as they are, strike at his balance. He sways, stumbles, begins to fall. I do not jump forward to help him and he steadies himself. His balance isn't that bad after all. "A little tricky, Colonel," I tell him. "If you try anything like that again, I guarantee I'll kill you." He sees I am serious. "Get on, now. Back to the tank."

The colonel shambles, his uniform shirt slashed across the back, blood seeping on his white flesh. His knees are bloody and his boots scuffed. A regular fucking mess. I do not wonder what he would be like if he had me under his hand. I already know the answer to that, for I have seen what it means to be in the hands of the colonel's acquaintances. I recall snow, blood, and sprawled limbs: the by-product of executions carried out by the Fascists. One day I may go back to Spain. One day in August in a hundred fucking years. August or not, I will always be beset by the memory of snow tinted red. But I know I will never go back. Under no circumstances. Orders or not. Wavell himself could mount an attack on Barcelona and I would desert from the ship bearing me there. Better the sharks than to review the place of those horrors.

I shove the muzzle of the Webley into the colonel's back. "Get on. And no more tricks."

The colonel nods. He is concentrating on his pain. He breathes in harsh, repetitive snorts. When he spits his saliva is pink: his throat is full of blood.

We come around a bend in the wadi and I see Chowduri's head up out of the turret hatch. The other hatches and viewing ports are closed. The 47mm gun points at us; the headlights on either side of the hull stare like the eyes of an insect.

As we approach the M13/40 I hear Mackeson say, "Jesus Christ, Peter. What'n the fuckin hell have you done to him?"

"He wanted to tell me something to our advantage but

he needed encouragement. Besides, he'll live."

"Sure about that?" Mackeson asks. He has opened the plate in front of his face and peers out from the gloom inside the tank. Mackeson is another one like Smythe: he'll kill as many of them as you want so long as the rules are observed. But he doesn't like this: it's beyond the norms he has been taught.

"I'm sure. What is it, you disapprove of carving on someone with his hands tied?"

"Yes. Yes, I do."

"You'd rather try it when his hands are free?"

Mackeson has no answer to this: out here in the desert he lives with reality, and the rules are a long way away, at HQ Cairo. Or perhaps back in Scotland. To avoid an answer, he says: "So what the fuckin hell did you find out?"

I gesture for the colonel to get up on the back of the M13/40. "Tie him down, Chowduri. Find out? The Germans took Mechili a week ago yesterday."

"My Christ," Mackeson says.

"And they took Bardia yesterday. I wish to Christ the radio worked."

"We could have used the one in the *Kübelwagen,*" Mackeson says.

"The *Feldwebel* needed to get on, John. He would have died if we'd kept the command car."

"He probably died anyway. I'll be fucked if I understand you at all, Peter."

"Start thinking, Alan. Consider where we are. I might not be here this afternoon, and if I'm not you'll be in charge of this mess. You better start thinking right now about how you'd handle these situations."

"So what the hell do we do now?" he asks. Mackeson knows as well as I do it is almost two hundred miles to the Egyptian border.

"Tobruk's the only place open to us."

"Tobruk."

"The Germans bypassed it. The Australians are defending it, the colonel says."

"Good on them," Mackeson says. "Tobruk. You think we can make it to Tobruk?"

"I'm not that worried about getting there. What I'm worried about is getting into the place once we're in the neighborhood. The Germans have invested it and they're going to assault it."

"So we'd have to get through the Germans. And then get into Tobruk. Through the Australians. In an Italian tank. Fuckin hell."

"We've got regimental markings. The Australians will let us through."

"Regimental markings? You mean that fuckin patch of color? You think some AT gunner is going to look for regimental markings before he lets fly?"

"At least we don't have a kangaroo on the turret," I tell him. Captured M13/40s in service with the Australians have bounding kangaroos painted in white on either side of the turret. A very prominent means of identification: one the Germans would with ease recognize through their fine optical instruments. Mackeson knows this and nods.

"We'll go in with the gun reversed: that should tell the Australians something."

"With the gun reversed," Mackeson says. He cocks his head as though I have suggested an impossibility. "Thinking pretty far ahead, aren't you? I mean fuckin hell, we've got to *get* there first."

Chowduri finishes tying the colonel to the back of the tank. As he straightens his back stiffens and he says, "Aircraft." At first I do not understand: he speaks with the same tone he might use had he said "Sand" or "Water."

Mackeson slams the faceplate shut and I hear his hoarse voice call out, "Oh, Christ now."

I vault onto the hull of the M13/40, scramble up onto the turret. I take the fieldglasses from Chowduri and say,

"Where?" He points an arm northwest and I see three shapes moving against the sky. They are close to the earth and they are angling toward us. As I raise the glasses I tell Chowduri to get inside. He slips down through the hatch and flattens himself against the wall of the fighting compartment in front of Mohammed's knees. He says something to Mohammed I do not understand.

Through the glasses I see the aircraft are Savoia SM-79s: more Italian equipment. But Italian aircraft are better than Italian armor, and Italian pilots are good. I have seen the Savoia before: it was the standard bomber aircraft used by the Fascists in Spain. It is a trimotor and it carries more than two thousand pounds of bombs. It also carries five machine guns, but these do not worry me. Machinegun fire is not a problem unless the gunner is very lucky and is able to shy rounds through an open port. As in Smythe's case. But here we have warning and can button up like a tortoise. Unfortunately, no one can button up against bombs. A good pilot in an SM-79 can end our journey to the east right here.

The Savoias are in desert camouflage: beige covered with green mottling like a long cancerous vine grown across the aircraft's skin. These Savoias fly in formation, edging this way and that across the desert. They are low enough so that they must rise and fall with the slight changes in the geology beneath them.

They seem to be looking for something. I remember the Panzer IIIs coming on, remember their radio aerials whipping at the cloud of dust and sand thrown up by their tracks. I also remember that although it is more than two hundred miles to Egypt, the Savoia can cover that distance in an hour. These bombers are doubtless from one of the airfields near El Agheila and they will be able to loiter over the desert for two hours or more.

"Start engine?" Mackeson whispers in my ear. I am startled: I do not remember having put on the headset. Chowduri or Mohammed must have handed it up to me.

"Christ no," I say. "They might see the shimmer of heat from the exhaust."

"What about the colonel, then?" Mackeson is thinking about Steiger, Rudolph, from Hamburg. He is sitting out in the open, the silver thread on his collars flashing in the sunlight, flies buzzing at the blood on his back. If we are bombed and he is outside the hull he will have no chance at all. Indeed, since he is sitting on sixty gallons of gasoline his chances are zero.

"Fuck the colonel," I tell Mackeson. I have no time to think about the colonel's welfare. I don't even have time to worry about the rest of us. The Savoias slide and veer across the desert, their propellers reflecting the light like silver discs when they turn at a certain angle. If they catch us in this wadi we are all dead.

The Savoias are sleek, humpbacked and menacing. They are close enough so that I can see the machineguns protruding fore and aft from the hump above and behind the pilots and from the ventral position behind the bombbay. At least they are not very good aircraft for ground attack: only the Savoia's ventral machinegun can be fired downward as the aircraft sweeps over. This may make the pilots hesitate. After all, when they are directly overhead they are vulnerable to ground fire. Except for the bombs they would be no problem at all.

On the other hand they may not see us. They are passing from the northwest to the southeast and they may fly past without noticing us. After all, it is a very big desert and we are a very small object.

The formation passes to the east and is beginning a jink to the southeast when it regains its course and begins to rise from the low altitude at which it has been flying. I am beginning to relax when the three aircraft begin a sweeping turn to port. I watch as they complete a full one-hundred-and-eighty-degree turn, level off and begin losing altitude. They are heading northwest and I almost think they have missed us when the ominous arrowhead jinks to port and heads directly toward us, letting down until it is close above the desert.

For the first time I hear the sound of their engines: a high hammering overlaid with the humming of the propellers.

"They're coming for us," I say. I have the glasses up and I focus on the lead aircraft. Through the paneled Perspex of the windscreen I see the pilot turn his head and say something to the copilot. When they are a mile away I lower the glasses and raise my right arm and wave. Perhaps they will think we are Italian. This is doubtful, but worth a try. As I wave I see the starboard and port wingmen drop back and maneuver until they are in line astern of the lead aircraft. I also see the bombbay doors of all three aircraft flop open. It is a swift mechanical rearrangement of the aircraft's geometry that I have seen before, in Spain. I had hoped never to see it again.

They are right down on the desert now, thirty feet off the deck, roaring toward us: the noise is tremendous. I could hit any one of them with a pistol; but such a gesture would mean death for us all. If they are fully armed, the three of them are carrying more than three tons of bombs. That is a lot more ordnance than is required to hammer a single M13/40.

The first Savoia is three hundred yards away when it zooms upward. I see the bombs racked inside the open bombbay. The second and third Savoias, obedient and precise, zoom up after the first. Perhaps they really do think we are Italian. Or perhaps they have seen the colonel tied like a goat on the rear of the tank. Or perhaps they have had orders to go elsewhere.

The three of them gain altitude and angle into another turn. The second and third Savoias break away from the three-plane parade and begin orbiting above the desert. The first is coming back for another look. He wants to look us over with more care. To be sure we are the enemy before he bombs. He is very civilized and proper. But then this is not Spain, and he too may one day be a prisoner.

"He's looking us over." The leading SM-79 skirts our position. It is four hundred feet up and six hundred yards away: close enough for the crew to get a good look through glasses, but not close enough for them to be at risk from any weapon we have on board. The pilot is orbiting to port. He has fieldglasses up to his eyes and I wave at him and make exaggerated gestures. Behind the machinegun in the Savoia's waist a man wearing goggles and a tan flightsuit stares down. The muzzle of his gun tracks us as the aircraft swings around our position.

"They're trying to make up their minds," I say.

"Thank Christ we don't have those bloody great kangaroos on the turret," Mackeson says.

"I don't look like much of an Italian, though," I say. But who knows? I have never been to Italy and I do not know what an Italian is supposed to look like. I know these pilots would find life a lot simpler if all their enemies were Chinese.

Two orbits later the pilot makes up his mind. He puts a wing over and comes for us. He is competent and aggressive. The colonel tied down on the back of the tank must have decided him. Identifying the bloody prisoner from his uniform as a German, the pilot has deduced that we are the enemy. I see the bombardier lying full length in the ventral compartment beneath and behind the bombbay doors. When I see the bombardier I know the pilot has decided something else: he has decided the German prisoner is expendable. The colonel will be the first to go when the bombs come down.

"Start engine, Alan," I yell down the intercom. I slide down from the turret through the hatch into my seat, slamming my hip against the rim of the hatch as I disappear into the fighting compartment. Pain spreads from the blow of the bone buried beneath my flesh against the steel; but my fear is greater than any pain and I reach up to close the two halves of the hatchcover. Chowduri holds himself against the wall of the fighting compartment, staring and staring. The sound of aero engines grows louder. I have the hatch half closed before I realize it is ridiculous: if this Italian bombardier can drop a two-hundred-and-fifty-kilogram bomb on the turret it will not matter if the hatch is closed or open. I fling the hatchcovers open, stick my head up: the Savoia is eight hundred yards away. From the rear of the tank the colonel is screaming something in German. At his fate, at me, at the professionalism of the Italian pilot, I cannot tell which.

"Move, Alan," I yell. The M13/40 jerks forward and as we begin to slither over the desert I see the bombardier move his hand and a bomb—slim, finned, dark green—detaches itself from the SM-79's belly. The aircraft commander is a methodical man: he has told the bombardier not to salvo his bombs. He is going to try to pick us off without wasting ordnance. The bomb seems to move with deliberation, as though it will not be hurried. I know this is illusion. "Turn left," I shout. The tank spins to port, a brisk movement. I picture Mackeson working the levers and pedals that may save us. The Savoia zooms up and away: the bomb is falling fast now, ruled by physics and geometry. I duck my head inside the turret just as it flicks down against the earth.

A monstrous cracking like a tooth crushed in steel pliers. The tank jumps and rocks. Someone shouts down the intercom. Chowduri's mouth is open and he has his left hand up to his ear. Pressure presses, presses. I draw my jaws open in a snarling rictus. Mohammed's eyes and mouth are closed and he holds to the breech of the gun and the handle of the port hullhatch. Blood runs from his nose: he has forgotten to open his mouth. Through the hatch above me I see a flash of white light and a swirl of dust full of rockchips.

The M13/40 is still moving, zigging and zagging. "Turning right," Mackeson cries and I feel us sway and slew to starboard. He wants to get us out of the wadi into the clear where he can maneuver.

Silence expands: I hear the muttering of the tank's engine, the whine of gears. I cannot hear the colonel shouting. The thrumming sound of the Savoia's engines diminishes. "Everyone all right?" I ask. I hurry through the words: the Savoia will be coming back.

"All right," Allison says through the intercom. He is breathless and afraid. His reaction is normal. Chowduri's is not: he grins and says, "Better than the last time. The last time we were in the open and it was Stukas. With those bloody sirens." Mohammed says nothing: he nods and wipes blood from his nose with his forearm.

"Next time," I tell him, "keep your mouth open. To let the concussion through." He nods and wipes away more blood.

I poke my head halfway out of the hatch. The Savoia that has bombed us is a mile distant and is turning. The other two are farther away. They pass through one orbit after another. The first one sharpens his turn, starboard wing tip pointed at the hard blue sky. He is going to take another crack at us. The others will wait their turns. All three aircraft act as though they have all the time in the world. Compared to what we probably have left they may be right.

The SM-79 that has bombed us completes its turn. I recall the Savoia's speed is more than two hundred and fifty miles an hour. In one instant it is a distant, truncated cruciform shape against the sky. In the next its fuselage fattens and its wings thicken. It jinks left and right as it comes on. Details reveal themselves: panels of Perspex in the cockpit, the twitch of the machinegun in the hump above and behind the pilots, a dark smear of oil on the cowling of the center engine under the oriflamme. I cannot make out the picture this pilot has decided will be lucky enough to carry him through the war, but then I have never cared about Italian art and I do not ever want to be close enough to this Savoia to be able to examine this particular flightcrew's totem. Now the aircraft is even closer and I see the pilot and copilot sitting behind the

129

Perspex windshield, manipulating the controls of the technological marvel in which they ride down the sky, making the small adjustments they hope will end with a bomb cracking the carapace of the turncoat tank fleeing from them at twenty-two miles an hour. I wonder if they think of the destruction they will cause if they are good enough to nail us. I doubt it: in Spain Italian and German pilots cared for nothing.

I see a flicker of reflected light high in the heavens and recognize the sleek menacing shapes of a pair of Hurricanes. I realize that these Italian aircrews, at least, may not, just this once, be long gone after they have destroyed us; for the Hurricanes may deal them a death as impersonal and violent as the one they are trying to give us. The Hurricanes tilt against the sky: they are high up and far beyond the Savoia, too far to stop the SM-79's bomb run but close enough so that in the instant before I jerk my head back inside the turret and scream, "Right, Alan, turn right," I see the British rondels on their wings and fuselages.

Beneath me the tank spins with a vicious jerk, turning at right angles. Again there is the tremendous sound of the explosion, the high wind full of dust and rock, the bounce and lurch of the suspension, a muted shout down the intercom. The only difference between this blast and the last one is that Mohammed is holding his mouth wide open, showing me his uvula.

"Draw up, Alan. It's all right now," I tell the intercom, shouting so that Chowduri, who is not plugged in to the system, will hear me. "Two Hurricanes have arrived."

"Let 'em kill the Italian bastards," Mackeson grunts as he halts the tank.

"Yes," Allison says. "Kill them all." Allison is learning. Chowduri smiles as though someone has done something nice for him.

Mohammed grins and grimaces, wipes blood from his face, touches the back of my left hand with his fingers and says, "How did you arrange the aircraft, Sergeant?"

I poke my head out of the hatch. The sky is full of the roar and pulse of aero engines: mixed with the high pounding of the Savoias' radial Alfa-Romeos is the low mutter of in-line Rolls-Royce Merlins. But I can see no planes: the aircraft must be close to the desert beyond the rim of the wadi.

I am reaching for my fieldglasses when one of the Savoias—I cannot at first tell which one, and then I see the smear of oil on the cowling beneath the pilot's personal insignia—leaps over the edge of the wadi a quarter of a mile away, flying right down on the desert. These Italians have forgotten us now that the danger in their own dimension is greater. Tracer chugs from the machinegun at the rear of the hump above and behind the pilot and copilot. The gunner is firing at something I cannot see. Then a blast of machinegun fire comes the other way. Streams of .303 tracer sweep over the SM-79 and a Hurricane leaps over the rim of the wadi. For an instant the two aircraft seem tied together by long strings of tracer, then the Savoia is turning to port and losing altitude. But it has no altitude to lose: the desert is thirty feet beneath it. Turning degree by degree as it descends, it strikes the desert half a mile away. The explosion of bombs and fuel is awesome. I wonder whether the aircraft commander, in the instant before he was incinerated, wished he had ordered his bombs salvoed on the first pass.

"That's one gone," I say into the intercom.

"Bloody good," Mackeson says.

The Hurricane sweeps up and into a long turn to starboard, its wingtips pointed at the sky above and the desert below. The pilot makes the maneuver look easy. I can see into his cockpit: his head is turning this way and that. He is looking for another Savoia. For a Hurricane the metal and wood SM-79 is an easy kill: in Spain everyone in the Republic feared the SM-79. But now it is four years later. The Savoia is slower than it should be, and much slower than the Hurricane.

In the distance the second Hurricane is following another SM-79. Both aircraft fly just above the desert. They look as though they are thinking about landing, but they are going more than two hundred miles an hour, jinking this way and that, the Hurricane following the Savoia as though it is tied to the Italian bomber with wire. The Hurricane moves with precision, draws closer and closer still to the fleeing bomber until it is less than a hundred feet behind the Italian's empennage. The gunner in the hump on top of the Savoia is firing his machinegun. His effort is bootless: he hits nothing and the Hurricane flies right up behind the SM-79 and fires a three-second burst from its eight guns. The Italian bomber seems to hesitate, as though the pilot is trying to think what to do. The burst of fire chips pieces of wood and metal from the Savoia. The diligent Italian machinegunner's fire ceases. Oil spurts from the starboard engine and the Savoia begins to rise from the desert. Perhaps the pilot wishes to gain enough height to get rid of his bombs. Perhaps he wants to give the crew a chance to jump. Or perhaps he thinks he can escape if he gains enough altitude. Whatever he thinks, he is wrong. The Hurricane follows him right up in a graceful, serene arc, gaining on the bomber as they go. Then the Hurricane is no more than fifty feet behind the Savoia, and as I imagine the Italians' terror of what is about to happen to them the Hurricane pilot fires his guns and the SM-79 turns on its back and dives straight down into the desert. The full load of bombs it is carrying obliterates the aircraft. A propeller whirls spinning out of the fire and smoke. Even at this distance—we must be two miles from the crash—I feel the pressure of the explosion.

"Two," I say.

I turn to look for the other Hurricane and the third— the last—Savoia. They are two miles away but they are flying straight for us, the Hurricane behind and beneath the SM-79. The Savoia's bombbay doors are open and I have the sick feeling that this Italian pilot is going to try to be a hero. As I watch, the Hurricane fires its guns and the strands of tracer angle from the Hurricane's wings, glittering as they probe the Savoia's belly. The bullets strike multicolored sparks from the Italian bomber. It is like the Fourth of July. Then it is like the end of the world: the Savoia explodes in midair, the smooth geometry of its airframe torn apart. Flaming junk falls to the desert. Two bombs fall through the burning detritus, tumbling end over end. They strike the earth and explode half a mile away.

"That's all of them," I say.

Allison says, "Thank God for the RAF." The two Hurricanes approach in line astern. When they are almost upon us they both do that chilling slow victory roll pilots indulge in after battle to demonstrate their insouciance. Because he has shot down two of the Savoias, the leader repeats the gesture. The Hurricanes circle away and come back, flying fifty feet above the desert. They have throttled back and have lowered their flaps: as the leader passes he points at me, shrugs and raises both hands, palms up. I have seen this interrogatory gesture before: anyone who has ever dealt with a merchant in Cairo has seen it before. The pilot has flashed past before I can react but he and his trailing wingman come around again and I point northeast, toward Tobruk. The pilot nods and shows me his right fist with the thumb sticking up from it. I put both hands together over my head like a victorious boxer to show him our thanks. He waves back, raises his flaps and soars away, his wingman right behind him.

"How's the colonel?" Mackeson asks.

I have forgotten Steiger, Rudolph. I turn and look down from the turret. Steiger, Rudolph, lies full length on the cans of gasoline tied to the engine compartment hatches. His right leg is missing at the hip. He may have other wounds, but I do not look for them. He is dead and his blood is everywhere. I am surprised I do not smell gasoline, but none of the cans has been pierced by the debris thrown out by either of the two bombs aimed at us. It is astonishing: we seem to have suffered no damage at all.

"Are we running all right?" I ask Mackeson.

"The dials say everything's fine. And we sound all right." Mackeson believes mechanics is a matter of good sounds and bad.

I duck inside, rotate the turret, seesaw the gun up and down. Everything seems in order. I get out of the turret, take out the fancy knife I took from the captain before I killed him, cut the electrical wire that binds the colonel's wrists to the tank and shove his body off the side of the hull with my boot.

Mechili lies to the northwest. Through the fieldglasses I see gray buildings jumbled together under the midday sun. Vehicles move in a fog of dust but we have skirted the town well to the south and I cannot identify them. It does not matter: I know they are German. Colonel Steiger has told me so and I believe him. Occasionally aircraft rise from Mechili airfield, and when they turn against the sky I recognize them from the sweep and camber of their wings: Me-110s, Ju-87s, Savoias, Me-109s.

We do not wish to go anywhere near Mechili. This was the town from which 2nd Armoured Division and the rest of the Allied forces in Cyrenaica were commanded on the eve of Rommel's imaginative assault late in March. Now it is in German hands and the British command is far to the east. Back in Egypt, if Colonel Steiger is to be believed.

Wary, hull down and in silence, we circle to the south and east of Mechili and turn, with reluctance and caution, to the northeast. We are nervous: around any corner on any one of the tracks along which we travel may lie panzers, 88s, infantry. If they happen onto our path we may find ourselves an unwitting target. The fine white tendrils of our nerves tell us this is important; but our minds remind us that an antitank shell travels so fast we will die before we know the enemy gun has fired. First there is the crash of the shot against the tank's hull, then the havoc of its passage through our cramped world, and finally the crack of the gun firing. And in the havoc of our deaths I doubt we would hear the sound of the gun discharging. Yet however simple it is to understand the logic of the physics, chemistry and optics that may kill us, we are not comforted by our knowledge that a two-pound slug of almost-molten steel richocheting inside the tank will kill us before we know it is there.

We all understand, now that *Oberst* Rudolf Steiger (retired) has put us in the picture, that we are in the middle of an enormous battlefield, surrounded at a distance all around the compass by German and Italian troops, guns and armored fighting vehicles. Somewhere far to the east, beyond the horizon, lies Egypt; and somewhere in Egypt, our lines. To the northeast is Tobruk. Invested, its defenders compressed between the enemy and the sea, Tobruk is at risk. It is a fortress ringed by German guns. How we will enter the place if we can get near it is a mystery to which I must find the answer, for I am the tank commander and everyone on board looks to me to solve their problems.

By noon we are a dozen miles northeast of Mechili. Mackeson keeps us off the main track and I watch for dust, the glitter of light on metal, movement. The enemy may not be visible but we know he is out there somewhere. Each of us concentrates in silence, reviewing options, fearing possibilities.

We are to the west of a track leading northeast toward Tobruk, following a compass bearing, when I see, far ahead, vehicles cluttered on the desert beside the road. I peer and peer. They cannot be British. Not here, this far behind the Germans' lines. On the other hand, we are here; so perhaps others, also lost, are making for Tobruk. I tell the crew to get ready. Their acknowledgments tell me they are tense, exhausted, fearful. We are not in shape for any more fighting.

We are closer now. I identify Matildas and M13/40s, British trucks, Bren-gun carriers. There is even a Rolls-Royce armored car, the kind of thing fielded in the First World War. It is the sort of vehicle in which an unsuspecting gentleman might choose to go to war. It carries a single .303 machinegun in a manually operated turret of riveted boilerplate. Someone must have thought it was good enough in the battles against the Italians. Against the Germans it is pitiful.

I see no soldiers among the halted vehicles, but a column of kites turning in the sky tells me they are still there, faithful to their duty, faithful unto death.

The Matildas and M13/40s are out to the port flank, turrets turned to the west, the muzzles of their guns menacing the distance. The only sound in the great silence is the bubbling of our engine.

"A convoy," I tell the intercom. "It's been shot down." The kites become aware of us as we approach. The lazy funnel of scavengers widens and rises. Kites do not like the living. Through the fieldglasses I watch as one of the filthy birds hops from under a Bedford lorry with something in its beak, jogs along the track flapping its black wings, and rises into the air. Whatever it had in its beak falls to the earth when it is twenty feet up. I remind myself not to look under the Bedford lorry.

Now I can make out what happened here: a massacre, carried out from a distance by antitank guns. Here the convoy was brought under fire by guns firing from the west. I note again the Matildas, the thickest-skinned armored fighting vehicles in the war, and understand that only the 88 could have shot them down. I imagine the Matildas and the M13/40s spreading out to the left flank of the column when the firing began, their turrets rotating, the tank commanders looking for targets.

And seeing nothing. It looks as though they were all

shot down as they sought to join with the enemy. The vehicles and the M13/40s are blackened with fire. Since the kites are still tidying up, this disaster cannot be more than three days old.

On our left we pass the first of the destroyed tanks. I guess the German gunners went for the armor first and then shot down the soft vehicles. The M13/40s burned even though they run on diesel. The Matildas show less damage though their ends were no less dramatic. Soon I am close enough to see the holes punched in their turrets and hulls, the edges crenelated and blackened where the armor-piercing shot passed through into their fighting compartments. That is a problem with the Matilda: the armor is so thick that while an AP round may have enough force to find its way through one thickness of armor into the interior, it will not have enough to exit. For an instant I imagine an 88mm round richocheting among the armored surfaces inside a Matilda, slashing at the packed-in flesh of the tank's crew. My thought disgusts me and I try to forget it, but with the kites circling overhead I have difficulty. When I catch the first whiff of the sweetish smell of dead flesh rotting and remember that *something* fell from the kite's beak, I have even more difficulty.

"Get right in among them," I tell Mackeson. "This is as good a place to stop as any."

"It stinks," he says. He is pointing out something I haven't noticed.

"We'll be invisible when we're in among them."

"The M13/40 weighs fourteen tons." Mackeson is pedantic: he is pointing out something else I haven't noticed.

"Just get in among them, Alan. Hold your nose if you want."

"I want," he says.

I glance down into the fighting compartment. Chowduri and Mohammed are trying to stifle their disgust, but the stench twists their lips, wrinkles their noses.

We are beyond the shot-down burned-out tanks now, beyond the Rolls-Royce armored car, which placed itself among the tanks to defend the soft vehicles. A fine gesture, the kind the Brits appreciate. I'm sure the Germans who carried out this particular piece of the larger carnage were impressed to see a World War I weapon up against the 88s and the panzers. The tanks and the armored car failed their brief, though. The soft vehicles are in train, fifty feet apart and burned out. In one place bits of metal and pieces of machinery are strewn across the track. It looks like the remains of an ammunition truck. Perhaps there were two ammunition trucks. It is hard to tell: the pieces are too small. I start counting the truck tires scattered about but give it up. It is meaningless to know how many trucks were exploded. Whoever was here died: it does not look like any of the vehicles escaped to the northeast.

Mackeson places us close to a gaggle of transport destroyed by the German gunfire. We are not invisible but we are unobtrusive. Unless you were very close, or looked with care, you might mistake us for one of the vehicles shot down.

"Switch off," I tell Mackeson. I am worried about fuel, though I do not say so. There is no need: everyone on board knows we don't have enough diesel to make it to Tobruk. All we have is the gas from the Blindas. It would be nice if there were someone with whom we could work a trade, but commerce is slow in the desert this year.

I take a last careful look around the horizon before I get up out of the hatch and climb down from the M13/40's hull. The stench is powerful but a light wind blows from the northeast and we are upwind of the tanks. I figure it out after a moment's thought: a man killed inside a tank will rot before he is disposed of by the kites and rats and insects. These scavengers would hesitate to enter the confined space inside a tank, even if they could get in; and all the tanks I see are buttoned up: the only entry would be through the holes punched in the armor by the German antitank fire.

Whereas a truck and the men inside it are pretty much open to the elements. I don't expect to find much left of the men who were on board the wheeled transport. Still I brace myself. Death disturbs, and its remains are terrifying.

Mackeson raises his faceplate with a clang. The sound flees across the desert. Two mice leap from the cab of a lorry. I remind myself not to look inside: I do not want to see the final indignity. "Tea?" Mackeson asks. I stare at him. He does not turn his face away. He is solid and imperturbable. He would insist on mentioning tea in the midst of this sweet stench.

"If you want. But hurry. Let's check out some of this equipment. Chowduri, Mohammed, give me a hand." They slither out of the hull hatch and drop to the road. They look diffident. Diffident Indian soldiers. They even walk with diffidence. It is the presence of death that affects their gait. They were taught it was all some team sport and they have long realized their instructors were insane. "See if there's anything we can use," I say. "Take the trucks. I'll check the armor."

"Yes," Chowduri manages to say. He speaks with reluctance and he is right to do so. Repugnance at rifling the possessions of the dead is universal. Repugnance at what we smell is also universal.

"Check carefully," I say. "You never know what you'll find."

But it seems nothing remains that would be of use to us. The Germans must have taken it all after their attack. I scavenge among the tanks, a two-legged kite. I cannot enter: either their hatches were dogged down from the inside or they were fused shut by the heat of the conflagrations ignited inside them by the fire of the 88s. It has been a slaughter, a perfect battle from the point of view of the Germans, a pointless senseless waste by the Brits.

139

This was a mixed group of troops. The regimental signs on the tanks and lorries indicate elements of five different regiments had gathered for the retreat northeast. It is a wonder they were able to cooperate so well at the end; a wonder the tanks were able to turn in unison to face the enemy, to try to protect the defenseless soft vehicles from the distant guns.

I force myself to peer into the pistol port in the turret of one of the M13/40s. The stench is fearful: rotted roasted meat. In the gloom inside the turret I hear the faint buzzing of flies swirling around a piece of meat the size of a sheep. I know it is not: sheep do not travel in armored fighting vehicles. The meat seems to have been fused to the far wall, beyond the commander's seat. It is burned and crusted with black char. It has neither limbs nor a head. Along its vertical length a narrow red wound is open to the air. I pound my fist against the side of the turret and the flies buzz louder in the gloom, swirling up from the thing on which they feed. After a moment the buzzing subsides: the flies have returned to their feast. I turn away.

Chowduri shouts from the distance. He and Mohammed are standing beside one of the fired lorries, waving me on. They have found something. I walk away from the tank—a tank exactly like the one in which we travel and fight—but I cannot make myself turn away from the memory of the fearsome thing inside the turret which provides the flies with sustenance, even as they provide it with burial.

"Oh, God, Sergeant," Mohammed says as I come up. They are glancing into the cab of a Fordson three-quarter tonner, a light truck.

"What is it?" I ask as I approach.

"He's . . ." Chowduri says. "It's . . ." Chowduri is in shock, as though he has been shot.

"What the fuck is it?"

"A man, Sergeant," Mohammed says. "He's, ah, alive. We think."

"Think? Think? What the fuck does that mean?" I take the last steps up to the small truck. It has been scorched and has burned. I look inside the cab. Chowduri and Mohammed were right to hesitate over their definitions. Something lies across the seats. A sack of something, a thing part char and part red and part white. A fearsome thing. A head but no face, thighs but no legs below the knees that taper like wax candles to juts of white bone. The right hand is burned away, the left shriveled to a fist of charred bones. Fire has taken away the ears and lips and eyes. A torn scorched pair of shorts is all that remains of the desert uniform. "I see," I say. It is pretty weak.

"We think he still breathes," Chowduri says.

I look at the chest of the slumped burned man. It rises and falls with terrific difficulty and horrifying effort. The chest is naked, scorched black, burned red. On the flank the ribs have been exposed by fire. They are white and they gleam in the sunlight. They are slick and damp with a seep of fluid. Still the chest strains to rise once more, to suck in the breath of life. I hear a faint rasping. I identify it: air passing out of the throat roasted by fire. Chowduri and Mohammed hear it too. They turn their faces away.

"Get away," I tell them. They stare at me. Their eyes are round. They stare beyond me at the burned thing slumped across the Fordson's seats. They are as bewildered as I am that this man has somehow managed to go on living when he should not have. "Get away," I tell them, raising my voice. They turn like children, their military training gone, and shuffle away. They do not speak.

I turn back to the thing in the Fordson's seats. Still the chest rises, falls. The cycle of respiration is slow but steady, sliding now toward death, rising yet again toward life, traveling in limbo. On the seat beside the slumped thing is a heap of charred webbing. A revolver—a Webley like the one in my shoulder holster—has been seared in the fire and its bluing is iridescent. The weapon has fallen—

been pulled?—partway from the holster.

I glance up. Chowduri and Mohammed stand thirty paces away, glancing at me. "Get away," I tell them again, raising my voice. I wonder if the thing in the Fordson's seat can hear. I think not: it does not react when I speak, and the deliberate rise and fall of its chest does not accelerate.

I know what to do. I have always known what to do about things like this. I reach into my belt and grasp the butt of the .11 caliber automatic I stripped from the German captain's thick white thigh and with which I killed him. I slip the safety off, work the action. The two sounds—the click of the safety snapped down and the schk-chk of the slide working—are clean, distinct and, in this terrible silent place, loud. Still the thing in the Fordson's charred seat does not react to sounds it must know so well. Good, I think. Very good. Our luck still runs. I extend the small pistol toward the burned thing, taking up pressure on the trigger. But not this. Not this gun. You've had enough from the Germans, friend. Too much. I click up the safety of the small slick pistol, slide it into my belt, take the .45 Webley from the shoulder holster. Sweat runs down my forehead, stings my eyes. Or perhaps it is not sweat. I blink my eyes. It cannot be tears. I cannot afford tears. Not on this day.

I wonder who he is. I cannot identify anything about him. I know only that he is a human being as far *in extremis* as it is possible to go. The rest of him—his race, his nationality, his arm of the service—has been camouflaged by his burns. I cannot tell how tall he was. I cannot tell whether his eyes were dark or light, his hair fair or brown. Australian? British? Indian? Enlisted? Officer? I look again: even his identity disc is gone. I glance around the cab of the Fordson but I do not see it. I dismiss the identity disc: it does not matter. Not now, not out here. He will be noted as "missing, presumed killed."

I feel the cross-hatching on the hammer beneath my

thumb as I cock the Webley. I place the muzzle of the revolver an inch from a point halfway between what was his right ear and what was his right eye. I hear him draw breath, his lungs grasping for life like fingers clutching. I think of the Lord's Prayer. In this place, in the hot stinking cab of the Fordson, my eyes stinging, it seems only "forgive us our trespasses, as we forgive those who trespass against us" makes the slightest sense. And on this of all days. I squeeze the trigger of the Webley and the revolver fills the small space inside the Fordson's cab with a huge piercing noise that hurts my eardrums.

Half the head is tossed away. The burned chest heaves. I hear a hiss of breath from the man's chest. His effort is finished, his fight over.

A shadow passes over me. I glance up at the kite angling this way and that, waiting for us to pass on. I feel the weight of the Webley in my fist but I know it would be inutile to shoot at this villainous bird. Better to rob this filthy scavenging beast of what it craves.

"Mohammed," I call into the silence. "Bring two cans of gasoline from the tank." He nods, turns about, trots toward the M13/40. Allison and Mackeson are outside, standing in the track. They look toward me, wondering why I have shot. They are confused. Perhaps I will be able to avoid having to tell them what I have done.

Mohammed returns, a can of gasoline swinging in each hand, the muscles in his arms straining with the weight. He sets them down without looking into the Fordson and steps back. When he speaks it is with the formality I suspect he uses when he addresses his officers. "For what it is worth, Sergeant, I think you have done the right thing."

I nod as I unscrew the cap of the first can of gas.

"It was necessary," Mohammed says.

I nod again, and then try out my voice to see how it works. "I know. Thanks." I heft the can of gas. "Best get away now," I tell Mohammed. He nods, walks backward twenty paces. I pour gasoline in a thick stream onto the

Fordson's floor and over the seats. It puddles around the slumped corpse. I empty the can, put it down, unscrew the cap of the second one, pour most of it onto the seats, the corpse, the cab. I slosh gasoline from the Fordson's cab onto the ground, walking backward, pouring a glistening track of gasoline in the dust. When the can is empty I fling it back toward the Fordson.

"Best get back to the tank," I tell Mohammed. "Tell Mackeson to get us going. I'll be right there." Mohammed nods and trots off down the road to the M13/40. I take a box of matches from my coveralls, strike one, and throw it down on the gasoline-soaked ground. The fire is almost invisible in the bright sunlight. I step back as the fire rushes across the earth and leaps into the cab of the three-quarter tonner. Flames roar and a thin trail of smoke rises toward the heavens. The kites swing away from the disturbance beneath them. In the fire I see the last lump of the man's body burning. He should be safe from the kites, at least. If from nothing else. I nod at the fire once and again, blink my stinging eyes. I turn and jog back to the M13/40. Allison and Chowduri are up on the hull, looking in my direction. Mohammed is retying the ropes he undid to get at the gas. Mackeson has the engine running.

I climb onto the hull and slip into the turret, slip the headphones on and say, "Alan, get us out of here. Keep your eyes open."

"Of course," he says. "Something shot those AFVs down back there."

"Yes."

"You did the right thing," he says. The M13/40 rolls forward.

"Yes."

"I mean it. There was nothing else to do. Sometimes there isn't anything else to do."

"Right."

"Don't think about it."

144

"I won't." But I will.

"Something escaped," Mackeson tells me. "While you were, ah, back there I was looking over the track. See the tire marks? Looks like a heavy lorry. Articulated, I think. Look there, two hundred yards ahead. The marks go off the track, behind that hump. Follow them?"

"Yes."

"Might be something," Mackeson says.

"Yes." I cannot concentrate on the tire marks or on what Mackeson is saying. I am thinking of the man's chest rising toward life, falling toward death, never quite reaching either shore. Once I glance back. The fire is furious and spreads a shimmer of fierce heat upward. I see no smoke now and the heat has driven the kites away: if we are lucky no one will notice this anonymous soldier's funeral pyre.

The tire tracks lead us around a hump of stone and sand into the desert. Half a mile away, stopped at the foot of the hump's slope, is a Bedford prime mover with a fuel tanker at trail. I wonder for a moment what an articulated tanker truck is doing out in the desert. Usually they are found only at base or on RAF aerodromes.

"Keep your fingers crossed," Mackeson says. He hopes it is diesel. So do I: without it we will be on foot in another sixty miles. Perhaps we are in luck: in the desert only the Matilda and the M13/40 run on diesel; and the tanks shot down in the convoy behind us were Matildas and M13/40s. On the other hand, who knows? It could be a water tanker and we may be marching toward Tobruk in four hours.

When we are four hundred yards away Mackeson says, "Fuel for certain." At two hundred yards I see the red lettering on the back of the tanker truck. It reads: DIESEL

FUEL. Mackeson says, "Thank Christ."

"I wonder why they didn't take it with them?"

"The Germans' vehicles run on petrol," Mackeson says. He pulls the M13/40 up beside the tanker truck. I see no damage. "On the other hand, it's odd they didn't take it along for their Eyetie mates."

"What happened to the crew?" Chowduri asks.

"I don't see bodies," I tell him.

"See the tracks there," Allison says. He points beyond the Bedford. What happened is clear: a halftracked vehicle approached from the east, stopped, turned and headed northeast. Footprints leading from the tanker truck to the place where the halftrack squatted in the sand tell me the tanker truck's crew surrendered. Mackeson shuts the engine down. From the turret I look across at the tanker truck. It squats low on its suspension and I begin to hope it is fully loaded. "Alan," I say. "Check it out."

Mackeson slips out of the M13/40, goes to the panel at the back of the tanker truck, opens the doors. "The gauges read full up," he calls. "Can you credit it?" He turns a valve and a three-inch stream of fuel pours onto the desert. He shuts the valve, sniffs at it, looks up and says, "It's diesel all right."

"They must have left it intact, marked the position and intended to send someone back for it," I say. "Will it run?" Mackeson gets up into the cab, grinds the starter.

"Everything seems to work all right. It's only out of gas."

"Get the gas we're carrying into it and fill us up with diesel. Chowduri, can you drive?"

Chowduri hesitates. He is thinking about driving a loaded tanker truck. He is also thinking about the burned man in the cab of the Fordson. The glamour of the desert war is with the armored fighting vehicles; but however dangerous it is to go to war on tracks, it is a lot more dangerous to be in the army service corps and drive a tanker truck anywhere near anyone who can shoot at you.

146

This tanker holds many hundreds of gallons of fuel and even a pistol bullet will pierce the thin walls of the fuel tank. It is no fun to drive a tanker truck and it is not flashy; but the war runs on diesel and gasoline.

"Yes, Sergeant," Chowduri says. "I know how to drive a lorry."

"You'll drive, then. Mohammed, take the AA Breda and go with him. Follow four hundred yards behind us. Any trouble, get the hell out of it and run. Clear?"

"Clear," Mohammed says. Chowduri nods.

"Cheer up. With this much fuel it's clear sailing all the way to Tobruk."

"Yes, Sergeant," Chowduri says. He does not believe this any more than I do.

Mackeson and Allison are filling the M13/40 with diesel. Chowduri and Mohammed begin humping the neat German cans of gasoline to the Bedford. I stand in the turret and examine the desert all around us.

"When those cans are empty, fill them with diesel and rope them up behind, Alan." He raises an eyebrow at me, thinks about it, nods. He recognizes the logic: if the tanker truck is shot down, we will have a fuel reserve strapped behind.

When we have finished the fuel transfer and filled the cans and roped them behind the M13/40's turret, Chowduri and Mohammed get up in the Bedford's cab. The starter grinds and the engine fires. Chowduri waves as Mackeson starts the tank's engine. Mackeson sets off toward the northeast again. I glance behind: obedient and precise, Chowduri allows a gap of four hundred yards to open between us before he starts moving.

"I wouldn't have seen the tracks leading off if we hadn't stopped so long back there," Mackeson says.

"Chance," I tell him.

"No, really," Mackeson says. "I was looking around, waiting for you. I wouldn't have noticed them if you hadn't, well . . ."

"Something more than chance, then."

"I think so," Allison says.

"There's a meaning in there somewhere," Mackeson says.

I am silent. Perhaps Mackeson is right: perhaps there is a meaning. The convoy destroyed, the burned bodies lying beneath the planing shadows of the kites, the scorched half-man's chest expanding and contracting, allowing him life while he waited and waited. Was it death he waited for, or our arrival? What was the meaning of our search through the litter of battle and our discovery of him waiting in the Fordson, hanging on from one breath to the next, shifting in that narrow place between life and death? And what of Mackeson glancing through the slit in the steel plate in front of his face, examining the track until he noted the faint marks of the tanker truck's passage? Surely he would not have seen those faint traces had I not stopped to minister to the dying. As he said, there must be a meaning in this somewhere. Surely there is. But I cannot reason it out, and I no longer believe.

Our course is ever northeast. As the hands of my watch swing toward three, the sun shifts from the zenith of the sky toward the western horizon. We cross and recross the tracks of tanks and wheeled vehicles; but other than these traces scratched on the sand and stone surface of the desert, we see no sign of enemy or friend. We are, as we have been for most of the past two weeks, alone.

Twice we see aircraft. The first time a flight of four Ju-87s passes high above us, gaining altitude as they go, heading northeast, following our compass heading as though we were a navigation beacon along their track. The second sighting is more menacing: two Me-109s low on the horizon, heading west, jinking this way and that, hunting across the surface of the desert. Both times I call down to Mackeson to halt the tank as I wave at Chowduri and Mohammed in the Bedford tanker truck. They follow our lead, and more: each time they halt they dismount and jog off into the desert, just in case. After all, the planes might wing over and come screaming down with bombs or cannon like metal hawks hunting iron mice.

I estimate we are sixty miles from Tobruk. Were it night, I might be able to see the flash of guns firing along the northeastern horizon. But it is still afternoon and though shadows lean to the east, the brightness of the vivid yellowwhite sunlight is undiminished. Nor do I hear: the mutter of the M13/40's engine masks all sound. It even masked the engine roar of the Stukas and Me-109s that zigged and zagged across the sky.

At three we stop to refuel in a shallow wadi. Chowduri and Mohammed climb to the lip of the wadi with an Enfield rifle and the AA Breda machinegun in their brown hands. They stare all around the horizon and at last indicate with broad gestures that they see nothing. With the engines of the tank and the Bedford tractor shut down I hear nothing except the drift of sand blowing in the wind. The sand is almost dust: it has been ground again and again against the friable desert rock by the wind and the sound of its movement is ancient. No sound generated by man—violin, officer's voice, Maybach engine, artillery—is as old or enduring as the sound of sand shifting before the wind. I know that if I die in the desert, the sand will cover me. As Mackeson and Allison begin the refueling operation, I raise the fieldglasses to scan the horizon to the northeast and recall the Italian officer from whose corpse I took these German binoculars. The wind and the sand had been at work on him when I found him; for it was not until I moved his corpse with my boot that I saw the drifted sand had camouflaged the amputation of his leg.

While Mohammed and Chowduri stand guard and

Mackeson and Allison refuel the M13/40, I scan the arc of the horizon visible from the floor of the wadi and think of our predicament. The central aspect of our situation is that we do not matter to our army. We are a single tank, three quarters of a crew assisted by two passengers and a tanker truck. Though we might win another fight, we cannot win a battle and our utility to the defense of Egypt is nil. This realization of insufficiency creates the long lines of prisoners we have seen at a distance during the months and weeks past: first Italians, then Brits and Empire troops. For in every fight a moment comes when surrender appears to one side or the other to be a reasonable alternative to death. That moment is the instant in which one realizes that to continue to fight is to suffer and die to no purpose.

For us that moment came and went with the Germans' assault on Agedabia. In the shock and confusion of that fight an instant came when I balanced survival against duty and almost chose survival. I did not for the simplest of reasons: I know the Nazis and the *Fascisti*. I knew them in Spain, and I fear they know me. Somewhere, on a list in an office in Berlin or Rome, is my real name. And next to my name someone has placed a mark. For me, capture could be followed by disclosure of my identity; and disclosure means death. I am not unique among the Brits' foreign assistants: even Germans serve in the French Foreign legion in West Africa, and I have heard rumors that the Legion will soon arrive in the Western Desert.

I wonder, when time expands and I can think, how I got here. Who would have thought a lad from Chicago could have ended up in the Sahara in a captured Italian tank, fearful of anything that glitters or moves? The day before I went to Spain, a friend, Al Marks, told me Spain was the wrong fight; that war would shepherd us all toward the darkness in the years to come; that there was no need to rush. But I saw only the vista from the top of the hill. I ignored the worn slope, the streaks of blood in the grass, the bones in heaps in the shadows at the foot. I did not understand then why I went to Spain and I do not understand that decision, if decision it was, now. What possessed me? Perhaps someone else can answer. I know nothing, except that Al Marks was right: this war is expanding. It grows and fattens, inexorable and implacable. In the end it will gather the world into its process and the world will live in the dark for a time before the war degenerates and lets the light seep back into our lives. Into the lives of those of us who are left, that is.

Through the glasses I see the great desert, but I think of Chicago. The high sharp winter winds and the ice rising and falling at the edge of the lake. The glowing windows of restaurants along Clark Street; barbers in shops with tile floors, leather and chrome chairs and mirrors on every wall; antique streetlamps and bustle; and in the spring and summer, the expanse of Lincoln Park full of picnic parties, horses, ballgames and tranquillity.

Here we also have tranquillity, but it is false and momentary: beyond our ken gunners may be preparing our calvary; over the horizon armored fighting vehicles—Panzer IIIs, for Christ's sake—may be refueling and stocking ammunition from Bussing-NAG trucks. Our tranquillity is an illusion; but then perhaps my Chicago—the Chicago of 1935, the Chicago that existed before Spain erupted and the black uniforms of the Italian Fascists came into vogue—is illusion too. In Chicago the stockyards were out of sight and déclassé. Here the slaughter is up front and far more acceptable, so long as someone else is being slaughtered.

In the desert nothing moves. The empty sky above is bright blue. Yet they are out there somewhere, just as we are here. The purpose of what we do is, in biology and history, obvious; but inside our logical frontal lobes it is an insane horror to be endured, for escape is impossible. No one in an M13/40 with a tanker truck of diesel fuel can make it to Switzerland. And it is no more likely an

M13/40 with a tanker truck of diesel fuel can make it to Tobruk. The obstacles are too numerous, the dangers too acute. Antitank guns, infantry, field artillery, armored fighting vehicles, aircraft. And our own defenses, of course: they are as likely as the enemy's offensive tools to destroy us.

Still we must go on. Retreat is impossible, surrender dangerous, neutrality unacceptable. Our logistics dictate Tobruk is our only haven. But how do we break into a fortress? I have still not found the answer, and I am expected to do so. Allison, Mackeson, Chowduri and Mohammed rely on me for this decision above all others. Without radio we are speechless. To sneak in during the night? Impossible: the Australians defending the perimeter would look at one another and say, "At fuckin night? Give me a fuckin break, Bluey. Call fuckin artillery and tell them to fuckin shoot. Here, let me give you the fuckin coordinates." But in the day the Germans will have all the time they require to lay guns, plot trajectories, figure drift and speed. *"Was? Englischer Panzerkampfwagen? Ein Moment."* The clicking of range indicators, the hiss of a radio's carrier wave and then, when all the math is right: *"Losschiessen!"*

Not the day, then. And not the night. It is an insoluble riddle, yet it is one to which I must find an answer. And soon. We are doing well and at the speed at which we are pounding out the miles we will be near Tobruk by nightfall.

Abandon the M13/40 at the perimeter, then? Possible. But no steel shell? No carapace? No tracks and machinery? Everything is fucked up and without solution, like the battle just lost. But back in the Delta, Wavell can always call up another army and more tanks, while the dice in our fists can be thrown only once. Our croupier wears a black cowl and when I catch sight of his face I see not flesh but gleaming bone.

I never thought it would come to this. Not when I was

back in Chicago reading the papers and believing I should help against Fascism. Or was that what I thought? Did I think at all? Who can remember? All I can remember is that I did not, then in 1936, believe that I could exterminate someone like Marschal, or put a charred, remaindered man to rest, or kill the Italians and Germans I have killed, or run like a rabbit as I run now. But then no one answers any questions. They start with one thing and it leads to something else and soon they find themselves doing things they could not dream they would ever do.

Perhaps this is why I am in the desert. Because I could never have dreamed I would ever do such a thing.

"We're full up," Mackeson says. I lower the glasses and look down. His shirt is stained with diesel and he is sweating. "The stuff stinks."

"But makes us go," I remind him.

"Oh, sure," he says. He wipes his hands on a rag, rubs the diesel from his fingers.

"We're ready, then?"

"Yes. The Bedford's got another sixty miles before it runs out of gas."

"And we're all right for Tobruk?"

"We'll get there. If we—you, that is—can think of a way to get into the place."

"It'll be all right."

"All right? These are *Ger*mans. And inside there, there'll be Australians. You remember them? The 'shoot the buggers first and look into it later' school of warfare?"

"We'll be all right."

"I've your word on that?"

"Yes."

Mackeson grunts and grins, rubs his hands with the rag. It is useless: he will not be clean until he's back in the Delta and six times through the showers.

"We're ready, then," he says. Allison stands beside the tanker truck looking off into the desert. I wonder what he is looking for. A way out, perhaps. The seat of his trousers is stained dark. I remember Smythe dying and Smythe dead, the stink of his blood and excreta left behind him in the gunner's seat. To remind us all, if we needed a reminder.

I raise my voice. "Let's go, Timothy." I turn and call to Mohammed and Chowduri. They slide down the slope of the wadi's wall as Allison clambers into the tank and eases himself into the gunner's seat. His face tells me he is exhausted and troubled. I will keep an eye on him. He is new to the battle, so to speak, and has not had time to develop the fuck-it attitude we use to hold ourselves together in tight places.

Chowduri and Mohammed are professional soldiers. I guess they have been in Indian forces for ten years each. For them this is work, like running a lathe or driving a tractor. But Timothy is a civilian with six months training: the destruction, the chances we must take and the violence terrify him with their abnormality.

The Indians get up into the cab of the Bedford tanker and get the engine going. Chowduri, at the wheel, gives me the thumbs-up sign. I whisper down the intercom and Mackeson sets off. Chowduri, still obedient to my order, waits until we are four hundred yards to the front before he eases the Bedford forward.

We continue for half an hour, eastering. I sweep the desert with the glasses for the thousandth time that day. My vision is bounced about as the track dips and we follow it down into a low swale. It is nothing more than chance that I am staring through the binoculars at Chowduri and Mohammed in the Bedford when I see dust spring in a halo from the tanker truck. I drop the glasses and see diesel fuel pouring in streams as thick as my forearm from either side of the tank behind the prime mover. For a moment Chowduri and Mohammed go on staring through the windshield at me as though they are on a regimental exercise, driving from Delhi to Lucknow on a Saturday morning. But as I thought, they are professionals: the Bedford jerks to a halt, the doors fling open and Chowduri and Mohammed are down in the desert on opposite sides of the tractor, running hard, bent forward at the waist. Mohammed carries the Breda machinegun. They run straight away from the Bedford for fifty yards and then begin dodging right and left as they run on. They are lucky the tanker behind the Bedford tractor is loaded with diesel. They are also lucky the enemy gunners fired solid shot and that the walls of the fuel tank are thin. If the walls were a heavier-gauge steel and had slowed the shot, or if the load had been gasoline, they would have been incinerated before they could have gotten out of the tractor's cab; and I would have watched them burn.

† † †

I hardly need to shout at Mackeson to get hull down so that the tender parts of the M13/40—the tracks and bogies, the engine hatches under the cans of diesel fuel and the flanks, which are more thinly armored than the front of the hull and turret—will be protected. I have a problem, though: I cannot determine the direction from which the gunfire came. To the northwest or southeast of the track, for sure; for the shot went right through the tanker truck. But from which of these two directions? I cannot identify the gun's location. I saw no muzzleflash and though I heard the crack-clap of the gun firing after its shot struck the tanker, the sound seemed to come from every point on the compass. Yet I am the one who must decide the direction of this threat, for I am the one who gets to ride in the turret and tell the others what to do.

Mackeson slams at the M13/40's controls. We shift this way and that as he heads off the track, zigging and zagging southeast across the rolling, broken surface of the desert. I hope he has chosen the direction of our flight well: we may be driving toward the gun that fired on the tanker truck.

I hold the glasses up to my eyes with my right hand,

looking this way and that, hoping to catch a glimpse of the enemy. I must see them soon: they have already had more than enough time to reload. I cannot see Chowduri or Mohammed: they are hiding in the desert. Diesel pours from the tanker in shimmering streams. There is no fire: the shot did not ignite the fuel. I reason that the gunners used armor piercing. They should have chosen high explosive.

Mackeson jinks and zigs, the tracks clattering, the hull bouncing and shaking. "Where are they for Christ's sake?" he calls up the intercom.

I wish I could answer him but I know only that they are to one side of the axis along which we were traveling, or the other. I also know they made a mistake: they fired on the tanker truck first. They should have chosen us, for we are armed and can fight back; while the Bedford tractor and the tank it tows constitute a fat goose full of fuel. Then I recall that we dipped into a swale two moments before the gun fired. They must have switched targets when they lost sight of us. Loaded with AP, they fired at the tanker truck rather than not fire at all. They have made a mistake. Perhaps a fatal mistake.

I look and look through the glasses. Their bounce and shake blurs my vision. I realize I have no loader for the gun. My mistake, not to have kept Chowduri or Mohammed as loader. We may die because of this mistake.

The M13/40 clatters behind a hummock of sand and shale. The target we present is now much reduced. Only our turret, with a man—that's me—standing in the hatch, is visible from the northwest. Anyone to the southeast can take whatever shot he wants, though; for we have no protection in that direction. "Driver halt?" Mackeson asks. He sounds exasperated, as though he had feared everything would go wrong and has seen his fear justified.

"Yes," I tell him. "Driver halt." At least we have protection through one hundred and eighty degrees of the compass.

Through the glasses I see Mohammed squirming in the sand. He waves at me and gestures to the northwest, pushes the Breda out in front of him and fires a burst. The tracer points the way. I look: from the top of a low ridge of shale and sand a third of a mile away a gunbarrel protrudes. I catch my breath, look again. No turret. Thank Christ I see no turret: it is not a Panzer III. There would be nothing we could do, gun on gun, in a fight with a Panzer III. I look again: it is a PAK 37.

I glimpse men moving behind the gunshield. The gunbarrel shifts a few degrees, puffs smoke. The tanker truck takes another hit. This time they have chosen the right ammunition: high explosive. The diesel in the tanker truck ignites and flame sweeps everywhere, envelops the Bedford tractor, pours in streams from the tanker's sides.

"Timothy, get up here and load HE." I hear him scramble from Smythe's seat as I drop into the turret and swing the 47mm gun around. Through the gunsight I see a man in a peaked German cap standing behind the gunshield. He is looking at us through fieldglasses. He takes the glasses down from his face and shouts something to the men around him. I hear the breech of the gun close. I shift the turret and the gun swings through an arc of three degrees: this adjustment lays the 47mm gun's muzzle on the antitank gun's shield. I fire: the clap of the gun startles me as it always does but I keep my forehead against the rubber bumper of the gunsight.

The 47mm HE shot strikes the gunshield and explodes. the PAK 37 disappears behind a cloud of exploding gases, dust and chips of rock.

"Straight out of here and for them, Alan," I say. The M13/40 moves. "Left," I say. "More left. There. Straight on, now." Mackeson drives forward across the desert, working his way through the gears, building up speed. It will take us minutes to reach their position and overrun it. I stand up on my seat, my torso thrust up through the turret hatch. I do not need the fieldglasses. The smoke and dust thrown up by the 47mm shot is clearing. The 37mm gun has been flung onto its side. I see no movement.

"Straight on, Alan. As fast as you can. Like that time at Beda Fomm." At Beda Fomm on February 6 we drove right into the Italians' position firing left and right, killing dozens before the rest could throw down their arms and throw up their hands. Our Colonel complimented us. He said our assault displayed tactics reminiscent of Genghis Khan's campaigns. We thanked him, and when he left I began laughing and could not stop. Smythe and Mackeson kept saying, "Give over, Peter. Who the fuckin hell is Genghis Khan?"

The M13/40 accelerates and we roar across the desert, bouncing into depressions, roaring up out of them. Still I see no movement around the gun. If we are lucky we have killed them all.

Yet other enemies are sure to be at hand; antitank guns do not travel without support. Or if they do they do not engage the enemy. I duck down inside the turret, close the hatch over me. A hammering against the turret: rifle and machinegun fire. As I thought, infantry protect the PAK 37. I pray they were guarding only one gun.

"Timothy, get down on the guns." He slithers away, down into the gunner's seat. He begins to fire the twin 8mm Breda machineguns as I extract another round of HE from the rack against the wall and ram it into the breech of the 47mm. When I look through the sight I see the lines of tracer flowing from his guns toward the ridge close before us. He sweeps the tracer back and forth: the volume of the Germans' fire diminishes. I sight at a wink-winking machinegun muzzle and fire the 47mm gun again. The round explodes. Sand and pieces of men are flung upward. I trigger the coaxial 8mm Breda, working like a dentist with a drill, traversing the turret back and forth, hammering fresh clips of 8mm rounds into the coaxial Breda's breech.

Mackeson drives us roaring up the slope and into the gun position. I see wooden ammunition boxes, bits of the gun, bodies in khaki uniforms. "Turn left," I shout and Mackeson spins the M13/40 and drives along the ridge. The Germans' fire slackens but Allison and I keep on firing left and right. The Germans begin to run. We slaughter one group of darting men after another. "Bring us around," I shout and Mackeson spins the M13/40 and drives back along the ridge. Through the sight I see German soldiers raising their hands. Not many of them seem to be left. I release the trigger of the coaxial Breda. Allison keeps on firing and four men in a group with their hands up are swept away.

"Cease firing," I say. Allison fires one more burst before he stops killing them.

I rotate the turret three hundred and sixty degrees. The German infantry are getting together in a group, their hands up. I reckon we have impressed them. Then I notice Chowduri and Mohammed, chests heaving, covering the Germans, Mohammed with the AA Breda, Chowduri with his Enfield rifle. They have run all the way from where they lay in the desert, a third of a mile and more, mounted the slope and arrived to help with the prisoners. I am surprised neither of them has been killed.

I open the hatch and look out. Three unarmed Germans are standing near a Bussing-NAG lorry a hundred yards behind the destroyed antitank gun. They have their hands on their heads. Chowduri and Mohammed are shepherding the rest of the Germans toward the truck.

"Take the truck," I call out, "Leave the Germans and take the truck." Chowduri and Mohammed move the muzzles of their guns and the Germans shift in a group away from the truck. Chowduri climbs into the cab, Mohammed into the back. Mohammed points the Breda at the Germans from the gloom underneath the canvas roofed over the bed of the truck. Chowduri starts the engine and the truck trundles forward. The Germans stand in the desert with their hands up. They are at a distance and I cannot see their faces but I guess they are shocked and angry. I tell Mackeson to get us back down on the track and as he starts off I drop down into the turret and close the halves of the hatch over me. Even in defeat one of these Germans might try to kill me. Perhaps particularly in defeat one of them might try. In Spain they were vindictive more often than not.

† † †

A dozen miles closer our goal—we are just short of the junction of the Tarik el-Abd and the Tarik Capuzzo and it can be no more than forty miles from there to the fortifications at Tobruk—we pause to eat. We hide between a wall of rock to the northwest and a tumulus of sand to the southeast. Cans of beef and pressed vegetables are opened. Chowduri abjures the beef and eats the vegetables without enthusiasm. It is not much of a diet for a Hindu; but then, neither is greasy beef and water much of a diet for the rest of us. While I eat as much of this muck as I can and smoke an Italian cigarette, I listen to them talking.

"How did you get up that ridge so bloody fast?" Mackeson asks. "You were there as quick as we were."

"We were up and running just after the sergeant fired the gun. We could see the PAK was down." I goggle at them. A two-man infantry assault on a ridge defended by German infantry armed with MG34s and 98Ks? I would have hidden in the sand. But Chowduri and Mohammed are professionals.

"Nervy," Mackeson says. "*Fuckin* nervy."

"It seemed safer than lying about," Mohammed says. He is eating greasy meat from an olive-drab can with a metal spoon. He seems to like it more than Chowduri likes the pressed vegetables.

"I couldn't have done that," Allison says. "Not in a million years."

"It's safer on the ground," Chowduri says. "I don't like tanks. They're targets. Large targets. I mean, look at it." We look at the M13/40. It squats on the sand. It is yellowbrown and inelegant. And big. Not as big as a *PzKW III* or a Matilda, but big enough to shoot at.

"Oh, now," Mackeson says. "It's got us this far."

"It'll get us the rest of the way, too," I tell them.

"You'll guarantee that, Peter?" Allison asks.

I nod once and again. I think about getting them up and setting off northeast again. The shadows lie long and black on the sand to the east. It is four-thirty. If Tobruk is, as I think, forty miles away, we will need no more than four hours to get there. I have at last decided to approach at night. It will be dangerous, but the Germans can't see in the dark. Still the Australians defending Tobruk may be more dangerous than the Germans. I dread the Australians: they have a reputation for violence and energy, they are dug in and waiting and, I have no doubt, well-armed for the defense. They also have a reputation for taking no prisoners.

"They aren't as strong as they seem," Mohammed says. We look at him. "The Germans, I mean. Most of what's going on is flash. You notice how they charge about? Like that gun. I mean, a single gun with troops? That's a bit thin, don't you think? They count on movement. I think they're undermanned. And their supply lines have got to be just about as long as you can have them. Tripoli to Tobruk? That's a thousand miles and more."

I think about it. Mohammed is right: it is a long way to haul food, ammunition and gas. Their logistical tail is fantastically long, and the tip, the cutting edge of their forces, can't be very big. It may be big enough to inflict defeat on Wavell, but it can't, in finite terms, be very big. I consider how many AFVs the Germans could have out here. Not that many, and the part of the desert in which they are making their fight is huge. It stretches from the wire between Egypt and Cyrenaica west at least to where we are hiding and from the Mediterranean south a hundred miles. Anyone would need a tremendous armored force and lots of aircover just to survey that much ground. Perhaps Rommel's movement has frightened us so much we have forgotten to see the reality: that his forces are inadequate. I remember his book and the theses he expounded: surprise, violence, shock.

But who knows? None of this matters for us. We will either make it to Tobruk, or not. The larger picture is something they worry about in offices in Cairo and Alexandria and London. And Rome. And Berlin. Here in the desert I worry about the filters in the engine compartment, the amount of diesel we have, and the Germans—and the Australians. If it all goes our way we will make it. But trivial things can happen that may deflect us from our purpose: mechanical trouble, poor dead reckoning, a German gunner, an Australian sergeant who thinks we look Teutonic.

The shadows lengthen, stretching farther east. The desultory conversation goes on. My troops speak of where they live—two in Britain, two in India—and stare agog at one another's descriptions of home. They talk to camouflage the dread they feel at what we are going to try to do. Breaking through two sets of lines—one German, one Allied—and into a fortified perimeter around a coastal city is a daunting prospect and I hesitate to order them forward. But we have no option: it is Tobruk or nothing. For a time, before that fucking German gunner shot down the Bedford tanker truck, I thought about heading straight east for the border with Egypt. But I discarded the thought almost without consideration. Even with enough fuel we would not make it. We do not have enough water, or food, to go all that way. And the M13/40, even with Mackeson's diligent, loving care, has gone much farther since its last full maintenance check than it should have.

The tracks are worn and could go at any moment. The turret race could jam or the hydraulics break down. We have used the weapons hard and we have only a finite number of 47mm rounds on board. Worst of all, we have no replacement parts for the more intricate mechanisms in the M13/40's engine.

The German lorry yielded little. It is full of wooden crates of ammunition, some food and water, and the personal belongings of the troops who operated and defended the PAK 37 that shot down the tanker truck. It is full up with fuel but something has gone wrong with the transmission and we will have to abandon it here. They must have halted where they did, and unlimbered the gun, because the Bussing-NAG needed maintenance. I can think of no other reason the Germans would have established a gun position in the middle of nowhere.

So we must leave the lorry and go on as we have the last two weeks, in the M13/40. We could have traded our tank for the undamaged Blinda, or the *Kübelwagen,* or even the Bussing-NAG, were it mechanically sound. But aside from the fact that it would worry me to try to get through the Australian lines in any of those vehicles, we have developed a certain attachment for our turncoat Italian tank. It has gotten us this far, as Mackeson said; and as I told the four of them, it will take us the rest of the way.

"Almost time to get under way," I tell them. "Everyone finished?"

"God, yes," Mackeson says. He complains about the food but he eats all of it. Allison tosses the remainder of his portion down and kicks sand over it. While Chowduri finishes eating, Mohammed, Mackeson and Allison clean their spoons with sand. Chowduri has, as is his custom, eaten with his fingers.

"Let's mount up, then," I tell them. We shamble to the M13/40. Mackeson climbs up on the hull and slides through the hatch and down into the driver's compartment. Allison is about to follow him but I say, "Mo-hammed, can you be the machinegunner?"

"Of course," he says. "I know guns." I nod him into the tank and he slithers down into the gunner's seat in the righthand front of the hull. The twin Bredas shift through their narrow arc as he tests their movement.

"You're loader again, Tim," I say.

"A demotion?"

"I thought you'd be happy to get out of Smythe's seat." He nods, swings up into the tank through the port hull hatch. Chowduri gets up and stands behind the turret. I follow him up onto the hull and slip down through the turret hatch, slip on the headphones and tell Mackeson to get us going. The starter whines and grinds and the engine catches and roars.

Soon we are sliding along the track again and I am following the routine I have followed all day. I glass the horizon all around, searching for evidence of man; for man is far more dangerous than the scorpions and snakes that inhabit the Western Desert.

For an hour we go on. We cover ten or twelve miles of track: the ground is more broken here than it was to the southwest and our speed is uncertain. I do not know the geological reason, but the desert from Alexandria to Age-dabia seems to become rough as one gets closer to the sea. I know that to approach Tobruk we may have to descend the escarpment. I also know that only three roads lead from the escarpment down to the town at the edge of the sea. They lead to Egypt in the east, Benghazi in the west and El Adem in the south.

On the other hand, Colonel Steiger said the place is defended and I know that defense must be based upon the Italians' fortifications, which were constructed in a great arc around the city. Much of that fortified line was built on the escarpment. Thus I may not have to worry about descending the escarpment at night along one of the three available roads. Who knows? We will have to go cross-country and see what we find. We can make no plan, for

164

we have no information on which to base it other than my faulty recollection of the lie of the defense works the Italians threw up last year.

I sweep the glasses across the desert again. I am examining an arc of thirty degrees of the northwestern horizon when I hear a taut steel wire snap and feel the M13/40 shiver and jounce. Through the intercom I hear coughing. Someone draws an enormous breath.

"What is . . . ?"

But before Chowduri, who is clinging to the outside of the turret, can finish the sentence I hear the crack of the weapon that has fired at us and I comprehend we have been struck by gunfire. The M13/40 slews to the right, jerks to the left, turns on its treads to the right again and runs off the track across broken ground, jouncing and bucking. Allison brushes against my left leg as he slips from his seat down to the front of the fighting compartment to peer into the driver's and gunner's spaces. A keening scream rises up the intercom.

"Alan?" I dread calling out to him, for I fear he will not answer.

"Aye." I cannot tell if it is Mackeson.

"Chowduri, get in here." Chowduri leaps like a cat onto the bucking turret, slides past me through the hatch into the fighting compartment.

"Alan, for Christ's sake what's going on?"

"Hit." He speaks as though his teeth are clenched together. "I think Mohammed's . . ."

"Can you get us out of here?"

"I think I . . . Jesus." His voice shouts out the name.

"Half his right hand's gone," Allison says.

I stare through the glasses, searching for the gun. It is just like the last time, with the tanker truck: I see nothing. No muzzleflash, no glint of light against metal or glass, no movement. It is just like Spain. The fucking Germans. They weren't kidding around in Spain and they're not kidding around here.

The M13/40 slews and slips on the stony ground, slides

165

behind a long hummock of sand and shale which hides us from all the points on the western half of the compass: we are in luck once again.

"Get us stopped, Alan. Shut us down." The M13/40's engine stops before I finish speaking and I wonder if the power train is damaged. Mackeson mutters something I cannot understand.

"Ignition off," Allison says. He sounds at ease, as though we are jogging through a training exercise.

"Get to work on them, Timothy." I glance down through the turret hatch and see this order is senseless: Allison has the metal first-aid kit open and is removing packages of bandages, a tourniquet, a Syrette of morphia, a bottle of some pharmaceutical.

"Mohammed's dead," he says as he unwinds the tourniquet. He sounds as though he has just glanced at the sky and is filling me in on the weather.

"Mackeson?"

"Let me get a tourniquet on him."

"Chowduri, help out down there. Timothy, what's the damage?"

"His hand's torn up."

"I mean the tank." It is callous. But the M13/40 is our salvation: we are not going to cover thirty miles on foot.

"Oh. The driver's compartment seems all right. Smythe's guns are destroyed. The shot went right through and out the starboard side. And Mohammed's . . ."

"Right. Later." I leave them to minister to Mackeson and stand up on the tank's turret so that I can see over the hummock behind which we are hidden. I scan the desert to the west and northwest. I see nothing. All around the ground is broken. Hummocks of shattered rock and sand surface from the flat desert like the backs of breaching whales. I review the specifications of German guns. A PAK 37 fires from no more than two miles, an 88 from no more than five. The shot that struck us must have come from an 88, for only an 88's round has the velocity to pass through the port and starboard armor of the M13/40. I scan the desert to the west, staring and staring. Still I see nothing. I do not hear engines or tracks. If there is no armor, this attack is identical to the one in which the tanker truck was destroyed. Except that this time no one is out in the desert to show me the location of the gun that has fired on us.

Inside the fighting compartment Mackeson grunts. His pain is beginning. Glancing down I see Allison and Chowduri squatting on the floor of the fighting compartment shoulder to shoulder, working on Mackeson's right arm. Allison jabs a Syrette of morphia into the forearm and Mackeson grimaces at this lesser pain. This is a good sign: he is not in shock even though his face shines white in the gloom inside the tank.

"Chowduri, get in the driver's seat and get us . . ." I do not complete the order: through the glasses, to the northwest, I see the yellowwhite flash of a gunmuzzle. It is more than three miles away but before I can think what to do a rushing turbulence and a sound like two flat stones struck together flashes over my head. I duck and whirl: the shot strikes a rocky hillock eight hundred yards to our rear. Debris is thrown up through the expanding puff of smoke and flame. "Moving," I shout down at Chowduri. "Get us moving."

"You see them?"

"Yes. West-northwest. An 88." Mackeson groans. I cannot tell whether it is his pain or the mention of the 88 that elicits this sound.

"Bastards," Chowduri says down the intercom.

"If we keep hull down I doubt they can get a clear shot."

"What was that that just went over, then?" Allison asks.

"They saw me looking. But they missed." I think of an 8.8-centimeter shell striking me in the face. A fearsome horror.

"They could shift the gun," Allison says.

"They're not going to limber the gun while we're still out here. Not unless they're going straight the other way." Chowduri nods. He is aware of the limitations of guns: limbered, they are helpless. Unlimbered, they require infantry and, if possible, armor to protect them. But though infantry may screen this gun, I am confident they have no armored support, for I hear neither the distinctive mutter of Maybach engines nor the rushing light clatter of tracks.

Chowduri gets the engine running and tells me the gauges look good. With the exception of Mohammed and, perhaps, Mackeson, we have been very lucky: the shot struck too high to damage the tracks or drive train, too far forward to ignite the ammunition racked in the turret, and much too far forward to damage the power plant or ignite the fuel. This German gunner must be up there right now, standing at attention next to his gun while his officer bawls him out.

At my order Chowduri drives straight southeast, keeping the hummock behind which we hid between us and the gun that killed Mohammed and wounded Mackeson. As we drive forward the wind keens and whistles through the holes the 88 punched in the port and starboard armor.

We drive away from the gun for fifteen minutes before I deem it safe enough to stop. Allison helps Chowduri lift Mohammed's corpse from the tank. The chest is smashed and the throat slashed as though someone has been at him with a straight razor. Allison and Chowduri and I take turns with a shovel. The ground is less stony here than it was where we buried Smythe and we have soon opened a decent space. I take half of Mohammed's identity disc and put it in the same pocket where Smythe's lies. Each time I move they clink together. Chowduri lifts Mohammed's body and lowers it into the shallow pit. Allison covers his feet and legs with sand. When he hesitates I take the shovel from him and pour sand over Mohammed's face and hands. We cover the hump of sand with rocks. I know this is specious: the predators will consume him however many rocks we lay on his corpse. Still it is the right thing to do.

When we are finished we stand about glancing at the grave and trying to think of what to say. I have never buried a Muslim. Chowduri says something in his own language—Hindi?—and turns away. I see Allison's lips move. I glance at the tank and see Mackeson's shocked white face peering from the port hull hatch. He stares and stares. I guess he is thinking how very close he came to having sand poured over his own face.

I try to remember something from my youth, when I went to church each Sunday and carried a heavy onyx and gold cross at the head of an Episcopal procession. All I remember are the passages from Ecclesiastes about futility and loss. At last I say, "Good-bye," remembering this is a contraction of "God be with you."

A minute later Chowduri has us heading northeast again. As we proceed I mark the position of Mohammed's grave as best I can on the map, write down his name and the date next to the notation, "killed in action by 88mm gun." The halves of his identity disc and Smythe's jingle against one another in my pocket each time the M13/40 lurches. I move one of them to another pocket and glance back toward the place where we buried this Indian soldier. I cannot see his grave.

╬ ╬ ╬

For an hour we drive in silence north by northeast away from Mohammed's grave; until Allison, speaking as though he is interrupting a conversation the rest of us are having, says, "I don't think we'll make it."

"Bad luck to say it," Chowduri says. I note he does not say we are certain to arrive in Tobruk.

"We're all right," I tell them. "We've had luck and there's no reason we shouldn't have more. The Germans

169

aren't waiting for us. Besides, they've got to be as exhausted as we are. And they probably think they've mopped up behind their lines."

But Allison doubts. I can hear it in his voice when he says, "I don't believe that."

"They don't have time to worry about us. They're assaulting Tobruk."

"A mouse fleeing among the elephants' feet," Chowduri says.

"Make it," Mackeson mutters. He is sitting on the narrow floor of the fighting compartment, to the left of Timothy's feet, his legs crossed. His bandaged right hand lies in his lap and he nurses his flesh, brooding over his pain. He wears a headset so he can hear what we say. It is his only link to the activity inside the tank and beyond its steel walls. Mackeson knows he is helpless and must rely on us for his safety. This depresses him, for no one likes to have to rely, not out here. On the other hand, he is lucky it is not four years ago in Spain. If he had lost the use of his right hand in Spain, Marschal, honoring the Russian doctrine that a wounded soldier reduces a unit's efficiency more than a dead one, would have shot him in the neck.

From my perch on the turret I nod down through the hatch at Mackeson. I encourage him with the thumbs-up sign, as the Hurricane pilot did me. I do not, however, answer him. Neither do Chowduri or Allison. We have nothing to say to one another that comforts and is true, so we go on considering one fear and another, our thoughts unvoiced.

Just after five-thirty we jib to the north to skirt the juncture of the Tarik el-Abd and the Tarik Capuzzo. Then we are out in the desert again, away from the main tracks, heading north by northeast. Shadows stretch far toward the faint gloom against the eastern horizon. Soon we shall have to reduce our speed and begin to pick our way; for by the time it is full night we will be in among the Germans.

On the other hand, perhaps Mohammed was right. Perhaps the Germans *are* spread in a thin, deceptive layer across the desert. General Rommel's book taught me about concentration of force. So perhaps he will have his troops and guns off somewhere, and perhaps we will drive right through into the Australian lines. Perhaps it is going to be easy.

I do not believe this for an instant. It is going to be a difficult and terrifying evening and we are more likely to find wounds and death and have our mouths stuffed with dirt than we are to reach succor on the other side of the fortifications around Tobruk. Still there is no sense dwelling on what may happen. If we are to die tonight or be taken prisoner, we can do nothing about it. I cannot offer warranties to Chowduri, Allison or Mackeson. No one hands them out in war, and no one expects them. Warranties are not part of the deal.

So we drive on, a single armored fighting vehicle vectoring along a compass bearing for Tobruk. I intend to arrive at the fortifications at a point directly south of the port. We will still be up on the escarpment there, with the town's defenses spread in an arc before us to the northeast and northwest. If we find Germans we will edge east or west, seizing opportunities. If, that is, we find opportunities rather than dead ends.

All at once I sense, beneath the mutter of the M13/40's engine and the rushing squeal and clatter of its tracks, a murmur of sound from the northern horizon. At my order Chowduri closes down the engine. I am right: it is the fitful rumble of artillery at work. We are lucky to be heading north by northeast. We should be able to avoid the thumping guns. I think of mice scampering among elephants' feet, but the thought is inapposite: at best the M13/40 can do twelve or thirteen miles an hour off the road.

"Guns," Chowduri says. He whispers the word, as though the enemy artillerymen's sound detectors are trained in our direction. Chowduri is right to be concerned about guns: we do not wish to be anywhere near barrage and counter-barrage. I direct him to drive northeast and he has us moving almost before I have finished speaking.

"Fucking guns," Allison says. He sounds lethargic and I doubt he will be able to handle another fight, not after two weeks of scrounging, iron rations, rusty water, tension, intense effort and death. I am glad night is coming, for armored fighting vehicles do not do battle at night. The horizons are too close, the angles too sharp, deathly errors made with profitless frequency. Night fighting is the province of the infantry screen around the armor.

Unfortunately, we have no infantry screen, so I review the little I know of nightfighting with armor as I stare toward the sound of the guns to the north and northwest. I suspect that there, along the western and southwestern rim of Tobruk's defenses, a battle is taking shape. And if we should keep our luck, find our way into Tobruk and discover the defenders are overrun? Horror. But if they hold and we get through, then the two-week long night through which we have lived will be over and tomorrow will be another day.

"Something out there," Chowduri says. I look forward along the jut of the gun's barrel. "Ten degrees starboard," Chowduri tells me. I see nothing in the direction he has indicated except hillocks of sand and sand-swept rock. No. From among the hillocks a shimmer in the air, the telltale mark of burning fuel, wriggles upward. Someone is brewing tea. Or *Kaffee*.

"Make for them," I tell Chowduri. "Timothy, get Alan down into the gunner's seat." Mackeson must be gotten out of the way: in the cramped fighting compartment Allison and I will require all the available space if we must fight. It is impossible to load and lay the gun or to traverse the turret if three people are crammed into the spaces around the gun's breech and one of them is not agile enough to duck and slide out of the way of the other two.

Mackeson hears my order and does what he can to help while Allison shifts him down into Smythe's smashed position. The Bredas Smythe fired so well this morning, and Allison at noon, are useless: on its flashing passage through the compartment, just before Mohammed died, the 88mm round hammered the mechanisms of both machineguns out of true and jammed their ball mounting. They cannot be armed and they cannot be removed from their mounting without a cutting torch. Perhaps they will *look* threatening. Whatever: we are left with the 47mm cannon and the coaxial and AA 8mm Breda machineguns. Perhaps these will be enough.

Chowduri has the M13/40 running across low hillocks and rocky flats straight for the shimmer of rising heat. As we roar over a final hump of sand and shattered stone, I see a Bedford ambulance parked in a declivity in the sand. Its rear doors are open and I see motion inside it. As I look two Arabs in long gray robes run around the front of the Bedford. They are carrying webbing belts, an Enfield rifle, a German tunic and a pair of desert boots. An odd assortment of booty. I wonder whether anyone is inside the ambulance. I also wonder how many Arabs have come for the plunder.

I slide from my seat and reach down and take the AA Breda from where it is clipped against the wall of the fighting compartment. I slap my palm against the distinctive, rakish clip above the Breda's breech and slip the safety off. I thrust it, and my torso, from the turret hatch and fire a burst of four rounds over the Arabs' heads. They stop running and drop the things they are carrying. They raise their hands and I see they have cloths drawn across their faces. The movement inside the ambulance resolves itself into a third figure. He is carrying a knife in his right hand and a pair of desert boots and some khaki clothing in his left. He jumps down onto the sand and stands behind the two with their hands up.

Chowduri brakes the M13/40 and we slew to a halt

twenty feet from the ambulance. The three Arabs begin to run. I fire another burst above their heads and they stop. One of them says something and the one who jumped down from the ambulance drops the knife onto the sand and kicks it away with a bare foot.

"Tim, get up here and cover me." I climb out of the turret hatch and hand Allison the 8mm machinegun. He puts it to his shoulder and aims it at the three Arabs as I slip down the side of the M13/40 and jump down onto the sand. I pull my Webley out of the shoulder holster and circle away from the Arabs.

In front of the ambulance I find an Army Medical Corps corporal dead in the sand. His throat is slit and he has bled to death. Beside him a desert cooker—a ration tin filled with sand soaked with gasoline—burns, the flame so bright it is almost invisible in the sunlight. The dead corporal is disheveled and bearded. Even in death his face looks tired.

I go around the ambulance to the doors at the rear. The three Arabs stand with their hands up, glancing from the ambulance to Allison aiming the Breda at them. They are thirty feet from the muzzle of the Breda and they do not move. I climb up into the back. Pools of blackening blood shimmer on the floor. I reach to touch the wall and draw my hand away: the walls are spattered hip-high with blood. As I step into the gloom a thousand flies buzz upward.

Six men lie on stretchers on the floor of the Bedford. Two of the uniforms are Australian, two British, and two German: a representative sample of the forces bashing one another this way and that across the desert. All six are bandaged. The bandages are stained with dark crusts of old blood and bright spatters of new.

Both Brits, one Australian and one German are dead, their throats slit from ear to ear. The four dead have been stripped of their boots and tunics. Each of them has been blinded and their testicles severed. I hope they were dead before the Arabs mutilated them, but I know this is an unreasonable hope.

The two who are still alive—an Australian and a German—hiss curses at me. The German scrabbles at the floor with his right hand as though he is trying to find something he knows he has set down right next to him. The Australian has a bandage across his chest, the German one around his head. They are exhausted and in terror and they stare at me, their heads raised, curses hissing from them as I come toward them from the back of the ambulance.

I shove the Webley into its holster and say, "You're all right now." The Australian's eyes glitter and he lowers his head to the stretcher.

"Thank Christ," he says. "We heard the engine but we . . . We thought you were . . . I mean, we didn't know you weren't one of them." I turn and look toward the rear of the ambulance. Against the sunlight flooding through the open doors my silhouette must have been as ominous as that of any Arab.

"What happened?"

"The fuckin Arabs killed all fuckin four of them," the Australian chokes out. "The fuckin bastards stripped their boots and tunics. Giggled, they did. Laughed while they did *that* to them, the fuckin wog bastards. Then they slit their throats. While we watched."

I turn to the German. He is thin and exhausted and his stubble of blond beard is dirty. *"Sprechen Sie Englisch?"*

"Ja, a little."

"You're going to be all right," I tell him.

"My thanks. They were about to kill us too."

"Don't worry about them. You're all right now. The medical corporal is dead."

"Bill's dead?" the Australian asks. "The man driving?"

"Gott," the German says.

"I'm sorry."

"God fuck 'em for it. Bill kept us up and running the last five days. And they killed him."

"Sorry," I say. "How did you get this far?"

"Marching. The four of us. Been marching ten days

175

steady. Found Fritz here along the way, with his mate there, the one they killed. Their car broke down. Took them prisoner. Then a fuckin plane came over two, maybe three days ago. Italian. Strafed the fuckin hell out of us. Then along came Bill in the ambulance and fixes us up best he can. And now this."

"It's going to be all right."

"I want those Arabs," the Australian says. He tries to sit up but he cannot. He lies back, groaning.

"Shot in the chest?"

"Shoulder. Bill said shoulder. Said we'd be all right provided he could get us to hospital. He was brewing up and fixing dinner, like, when they came. I want them," he says. He tries again to raise himself but I know his wound will force him down.

"Sorry," I say.

"Give us your revolver then and bring them to the door," he says. He is determined to see them dead. No matter what, he wants to kill them. I hope the Australians defending Tobruk are less determined.

"You're not up to it."

"Fuck it, I can . . ." But his head drops back and he sighs as he slips into unconsciousness.

"His name is Lister," the German says. "Sidney Lister. An Australian. I think he will be all right."

"And you?"

"Lieutenant Claus Pohl. A graze. I am a little light-headed. I don't think it's serious."

"It happened as he said? They mutilated and killed those four?"

" 'Mutilated'? I don't know the word. You mean, what was done to . . ." Lieutenant Pohl nods. "Animals," he says. "How can they be such animals?"

"Perhaps they've taken lessons from the rest of us," I tell him. "The Italians were here for thirty years, teaching them how to do this and how to do that."

He shakes his head and says, "We do not give lessons

like this. Neither do you." I think of Marschal, and the Italians and Germans in Spain, but I say nothing.

"Can you get up?"

Pohl nods and stands: he is shaky on his feet but he shuffles down the length of the ambulance, one hand against the wall for support. When he lifts his feet his boots make small tacky sounds in the blood on the floor. At the rear I help him down into the sand. The three Arabs stare and stare at him as though they had killed him and he had somehow come back to life.

As Pohl walks toward them the Arab who jumped down from the back of the ambulance with the knife in one hand and the boots and tunic in the other cries out, a high-pitched, piercing ululation escaping from behind the rag drawn across his face. He must be smarter than the others: he knows what's going to happen now.

When we are five feet from them Pohl says, "May I have your . . . ?" but there's no need for him to ask: I already have the Webley out. I reverse it and Pohl takes it by the butt and cocks it. He points it at one of the two Arabs who ran around the ambulance and pulls the trigger. The heavy .45 slug takes the Arab in the middle of the chest. He is thrown back and down, bowled over into death, blood spattered down the front of the dirty robe he wears. "That is for Pfferman," he says. He points the pistol at the second one and kills him too. Another good shot, right through the chest. The third begins to run, the ululations barking and yapping out of him. He is a smaller man, a lithe thin man and more agile: Pohl fires twice and misses both times.

"Kill him, Timothy," I call out. Allison fires a five-shot burst from the Breda. It catches the running man in the back, tears off his left arm, shatters his torso, stirs his ribs and innards together, and throws him down on the desert. In the silence I stare and stare: three more bloody bundles. I remember an old Arab in Tobruk who made me eat half a melon from a garden beside his house and who told me in fluent Italian how bad the Italians were and how glad he was the British had come.

"There were only the three of them?"

"I think so," Pohl says. He reverses the revolver and passes it to me butt first. "My thanks, Sergeant," he says.

"You're welcome."

"What the hell's going on?" Allison asks.

"They mutilated four wounded in the ambulance." Timothy swallows and clutches the Breda. "Then they killed them."

"Bastards," he says. "Fucking bastards."

I hear the rustling gulp of an enormous breath drawn. I hold up my hand for quiet. I hear the sound again and walk past the corpses, reloading the Webley in my fist as I go. Something is there, beyond this hummock and the next. I slither up the short slope of sand, peer over. Three camels step side to side, their eyes rolling: they do not like gunfire. They are laden with booty: rifles, helmets, clothing, an automobile headlight, packs, waxy ration boxes. The Arabs were scavengers. Like the kites, but less humane. The kites do not, as a rule, mutilate and kill. I stand up and walk down the slope. I glance over the loads of motley equipment their owners coveted. It is useless, the junky detritus of battles lost, regiments destroyed, men killed or taken prisoner. I would just as soon kill them, and so deny their use to others; but their carcasses would attract kites, and we have a grave to dig. I untether them one after the other and they bound away with hoarse grunts, the cheap booty tied to their backs rattling.

I return over hillocks of sand and shale to the M13/40 and the ambulance. Timothy stands on the turret, glassing the desert all around.

"Anything?"

"Nothing, Peter. Nothing anywhere. What was it you found?"

"Three camels." Allison grimaces, as though the camels were as responsible as their masters for what has happened here.

Lieutenant Pohl is standing over the third Arab, the one who tried to run faster than the Breda's burst of 8mm. "This one is a woman," he says. He says it as though he cannot believe that it could be a woman. I glance at the corpse lying face up: the filthy blood-soaked robe is parted, the halves thrown away by the Breda's blast. Black nipples protrude from large dark aureoles on the shattered bloody chest. The crotch is smoothly female where there should have been a penis and testicles. I nod. I am not surprised. Nothing surprises me. In the end, the children will mutilate and kill too. Everything imaginable has become mundane, normal, boring.

"Corporal Chowduri." He opens the driver's faceplate and looks out. "Check the ambulance. See if it runs, and see how much fuel it's got."

"Right, Sergeant."

"We're heading for Tobruk, Lieutenant. You understand?" Pohl nods. "We're going to try to get through the lines. Dangerous. We could leave you off on this side if you want."

"Many thanks. If you could do that, I would appreciate it a great deal."

"Might be better to be a prisoner."

"I think not. It seems it would be best to be among one's own kind."

"Your choice. We'd have to leave you in the desert, you know. And near the lines. All right with you?"

"Yes. All right. Shall we make a grave?"

"Timothy, let's get the shovel." I recall digging Mohammed's grave. And Smythe's. Now we must excavate another small piece of the desert. I wonder who will bury the last one of us.

"One grave? or four? Or should it be seven?" It is a reasonable practical question: it seems Allison is becoming harder as the late afternoon goes on.

"One's enough. And make it big enough for four only." I jerk my thumb at the scavengers we have killed. "We'll leave them for the kites and the rats."

"*Ja,*" the Lieutenant says. He nods. "One grave for the four of them."

Lister is still unconscious when I step up into the ambulance. I lift the four corpses one by one out of the ambulance and carry them to where Timothy is digging. The flesh of their backs and naked legs is cold and clammy against my hands and forearms. They have been bled white, as though they were slaughtered for food. I lay them side by side on the earth and take their identity discs. I hand the German's disc to Lieutenant Pohl. He nods and puts it in the breast pocket of his blouse.

The sand here is soft and Timothy soon opens a hole large enough for the four of them. Together we shift the bodies into it. I mark the spot on my map and show it to Pohl. He examines it, nodding again and again as he memorizes the terrain and the distances from this four-man grave to the Tarik el-Abd and the Tarik Capuzzo. He hands the map back to me, murmurs something and gets down on his knees next to the grave. I think he is going to pray; but instead of clasping his hands together he begins pushing sand over the dead German and the Brit lying next to him. Allison and I kneel down to help him.

Chowduri loiters about while we perform this Christian duty. When we have finished piling rocks on the four faint humps beneath the sand he approaches and murmurs, "Ambulance is all right. Full up with gas, too. These, ah, *swine* doubtless had no idea of the value of the thing."

"We'll take it. Get Mackeson across and into the back. Wait a minute, though." I take the shovel and go to the ambulance. Lister is conscious. "Going to bring one of our wounded in here with you, mate," I tell him. He nods but he does not speak: the experience of finding himself alive after being so close to death seems to have exhausted him more than his long march in the desert or his wounds.

I collect the clothes I find—the clothes the Arabs stripped from the dead—and throw them down on the floor of the ambulance. I shift them back and forth with my boots, sopping up blood. I kick them out the back and take the shovel and toss a dozen shovelfuls of sand into the ambulance. Lister nods and says, "Good on you, mate." I climb up into the ambulance and kick the sand about, covering the blood. It does not make much difference: the flies still buzz and hum, performing the function God assigned them, and the stink is as bad as it was before. Still I know I will not be able to stop thinking of the four dead men, and of the way they died, if I do not try to cover their blood. As I finish Chowduri appears with Mackeson. Delirious, Mackeson mutters to himself. I cannot understand his words. I help Chowduri get him up into the ambulance and onto Lieutenant Pohl's stretcher. I tell Mackeson everything is going to be fine but he does not answer me. Lister says, "Don't worry, mate. I'll watch out for him."

I take the shovel and Chowduri and I go back to Allison and Lieutenant Pohl. They are speaking to one another as though they were from the same town.

"Tim, you take the ambulance. Chowduri, you'll drive the tank."

"We could leave the tank and go all together in the ambulance," Allison says.

"We'll take the '40," I tell him. "Two vehicles are better than one. And it seems like bad luck to leave it. Besides, we may have to fight again. And let me have the Breda, Timothy. If there's trouble, I doubt they'll shoot up an ambulance. But if you're captured, you don't want to have to explain driving an ambulance with a Breda beside you. Right?"

"Right."

"Lieutenant Pohl, you can ride in the tank or the ambulance. Your choice."

"I will ride in the tank, Sergeant. Perhaps I can be of assistance. I know the M13/40."

"You can ride up in the turret or in the gunner's seat. The machineguns are jammed."

"You realize that if there is a fight I cannot help you?"

"We're hoping for clear sailing."

"We can only hope that will be the case."

"Let's get out of here," Allison says. He seems less nervous and more decisive than he has been all day. It is as though killing the Arab has taught him something he wanted to know. I wonder if he knows the one he killed was a woman. We get into the tank and the ambulance and set off through the dusk to the northeast. Night is coming. Soon I will have to begin calling instructions down the intercom to Chowduri. Or perhaps we will drive with lights on, taking a risk, gambling detection against speed. Right now I cannot think of what to do. I am as tired as Lieutenant Pohl looks. He lolls against the steel wall of the fighting compartment, the bandage on his head a stained, dirty white blot in the gloom. Once he looks up, touches my leg and calls out, "My thanks." I do not know whether he thanks me for saving his life or for letting him use the Webley. I wonder for a moment which it is but I cannot decide. I look out over the desert: night is sweeping toward us from the east. To the west the last, smallest arc of the sun flashes orange light across the sand and slips below the horizon.

A delicate crescent of silver moon ascends the night sky as Chowduri drives northeast, then north northeast, then north. As we slide forward over the desert I listen for unfamiliar mechanical sounds—the rattle of tracks, the throb of heavy engines—but I hear only the mutter of the M13/40's diesel, the faint squeak and chatter of its tracks and the resonant pounding of artillery to the northwest. In the hour or so since we left four more men behind I have made but one decision, and that a bold one: we drive with our headlights on. In the jerk and swerve of the beams I see sand and rock and, occasionally, tracks carved on the gritty surface of the desert by other armored fighting vehicles. Allison follows four hundred yards behind, the ambulance's headlights full on, the red crosses on the sides, roof and back illuminated. He, Mackeson and Lister are safe enough, though they may become prisoners if we come across Germans. Or if they come across us. After all, our lights are a beacon visible in the desert all the way to the horizon. Still we are safer now it is night than we were in sunlight. Antitank gunners cannot range at night; and the Germans may think our Italian tank one of theirs.

On the other hand, the Australians may deem us Italian.

Once Lieutenant Pohl calls up to me, asking for water. I gesture at a bottle hanging from a steel protrusion on the aft wall of the fighting compartment. He takes four small sips, recaps the bottle and calls out: "What when we meet our forces?" His grammar is defective but his meaning could not be more clear.

"We'll have to see."

"Could you surrender?"

"To you?" I have considered this. But it is pointless to surrender to Pohl: he may die with the rest of us before whoever kills us takes the time to determine who is whose prisoner.

"I meant to our forces. If we find them. If they find us, I mean."

"It depends."

Lieutenant Pohl nods. He is not satisfied, and he worries about the odds on which I may bet our lives. I watch as he considers his situation and begins to worry about the efficiency and nerve of German gunners should they be menaced by an Italian tank that might be British. Lieutenant Pohl has been wounded once and I can see he does not wish to risk another wound, or death. At least not tonight. On another day, weeks hence, he will take all the risks anyone asks of him; but not this night, with the horrid giggling of the Arabs echoing so close in his memory. I watch his face, try to gauge his thoughts. At last he folds his arms across his chest, closes his eyes and leans his bandaged head forward. The fingers of his left hand touch Pfferman's identity disc through the cloth of his breast pocket. He sighs and draws his fingertips away from this reminder of what might have been, this warning of what might be. His chin settles on his chest: he has, like the rest of us, decided to hell with it, there is nothing to do but go along and see where it leads.

Once we flash past a Matilda shot down by the Germans. The barrel of its two-pounder gun is shredded and burnt and the armored skirt that covers its bogies is punctured in half a dozen places. Only an 88 could have so savaged a Matilda. We do not stop. Whoever might have lived through this disaster is gone by now—dead, imprisoned or, like ourselves, in flight.

The horizon to the northwest pulses with brilliant flashes of red, white and yellow light. It is German or Allied artillery fire and it presages an attack. But who will attack, and who defend? I doubt the Australians, fought out and hunkered down inside Tobruk's defensive perimeter, contemplate an assault. Rommel has the momentum now and he will have the honor of the attack, and the glory of it too if it is successful. I wonder if he recalls how well the Australians did against the Turks at the Dardanelles; and if he recollects, I wonder whether the memory of that attempt might make him pause.

Unlikely. His book tells me he believes stasis in war is a mortal sin.

Twice Chowduri and I speak through the intercom about our compass heading: straight north on the map, but twenty degrees of magnetic declination west by northwest on the compass. Chowduri and I sound knowledgeable and scientific but our navigational abilities are modest. Who knows? The desert may be full of iron, and compasses in tanks are notorious for their unreliability. Most of my science, and his, is the fear that chases us forward and the hope that pulls us on. Of course the geography is easy, and this gives us confidence: to the north is the sea, and at the edge of the sea is Tobruk, the only place west of the Frontier still in Allied hands.

I am grateful for the gunfire in the northwest, for it tells me with more certainty than I divine from map and compass that we are at least driving in the right direction.

As we progress we pass more evidence of battle: patches of the desert blackened by fire, shattered vehicles, articles of clothing, hummocks of sand the length of a man, signboards set up at the edge of the track with strange German regimental identification marks on them. These are indications of the successive waves of destruction washed up by the waste of battle. A tactician or an archaeologist might be able to sift some meaning from it: here elements of the 2nd Armoured Division stood, fought, and died; here trucked infantry ran out of gas, were attacked by Ju-87s, and lost five men on the march; and here, helpless against gunnery's most ingenious development since the introduction of the rifled bore, a single 88-millimeter gun shot down six Allied tanks one after the other from a range of five thousand meters, and did so in forty seconds.

We pass through these successive junkyards of outmoded technology, pass by men killed and buried by bad tactics and querulous strategy. I wonder whether this war will ever end. I think not. More likely it will rise from its own debris, take on unheard-of horrific forms mounted in strange vehicles and armed with fearsome weapons and go on and on, snorting beneath a raging sky, careening toward a bitter end.

I lurch as though I have drunk too much or have been beaten and something has slipped inside my skull. I know it is exhaustion that seeks to pull me down. For two weeks and more, tides of enervation and fear-induced euphoria have pulled me this way, pushed the other. It is dangerous to be this tired, and I know I must think of nothing but fighting the M13/40. I must not consider the end of the war, or even the end of this part of it. I must not care about Susan or all of Cairo or London either or even Chicago. I must not even care about Tobruk. All I must do is what the remnants of all defeated armies have always done: flee before the advancing banners, flee from the triumphant bugles, flee and hide, find refuge where I can rest, revictual, refuel, rearm, remunition and return to fight again.

I become aware of the cold night air rushing against my face and I know time is passing with the irregular motion of a damaged but unstoppable machine. My watch has somehow broken and I cannot guess the hour. The knowledge that I cannot terrifies me. I have failed—failed to concentrate, failed to think, failed to scheme. Fear surges through me and the skin on the backs of my grubby hands tingles as I stare at the darkness flowing toward me from beyond the aura thrown out by the headlamps. I look and look for the man behind the gun in the angular tracked vehicle hidden in the darkness who will kill me if he sees me before I see him.

I remind myself it is absurd to peer into the dark like this. We are driving with lights on and therefore anyone out in the dark desert will see us before we see them. The intention, bold and fearful, of my decision to drive with headlamps full on was to puzzle; to make the German gunner hesitate; to persuade the commander of the *PzKW III* to take counsel before he fires.

"Nothing living out here," Chowduri says, as though he is commenting on my fear. "The battle's moved on. To the northwest, it looks like. I haven't seen anyone."

"Let's keep looking," I say, as though Chowduri, whose eyes are four feet off the ground and who can see an arc of no more than a hundred degrees in front of him, is responsible to see the enemy first.

"Here comes more transport," he answers. I have been staring down into the interior of the M13/40 through the turret hatch. I look up. Chowduri is right. A line of abandoned vehicles stands in the desert. Chowduri has first caught sight of this minor débâcle through the driver's vision slit.

We sweep past eight lorries parked hood to tailgate. They are empty and undamaged. When our headlights fall on them their masked taillights wink at us and as we rumble past I see the windshields are intact. I wonder what happened, and where their crews are. Out of fuel and taken prisoner? Out of fuel and pressed on north on foot toward Allied lines? Dead in the sand? Hiding in the desert three hundred yards away, fearful of the mutter of the M13/40's engine?

Who knows? I cannot count the number of the fates they may have met; and I have no time to investigate even the most likely one of them.

The moon has risen to its zenith and the desert in all directions beyond the glow of the tank's headlights is tinged with silver. I glance behind. Allison steers the ambulance in our wake, keeping a safe distance between us and himself. We, after all, will be the target for any gunner lying out in the silvery darkness. We are an easy target. Our machineguns are jammed and I have no loader. Our headlights may make the enemy hesitate for an instant but light will not stop an AT round. We are at sea in this waterless desert, traveling in a pool of yellow light. Whether the Germans we may meet will conduct themselves according to what is referred to as the "rules of civilized warfare" is up to them. I will be able to do nothing if they decide to kill us.

The M13/40 halts and as it rocks on its suspension I wonder why Chowduri has stopped. I have not told him to, and in my exhaustion all I can think is that he should not halt without my order. Halted, we are the easiest of targets. But Chowduri tells me nothing. I glance down into the fighting compartment. I cannot see Chowduri's back, but Lieutenant Pohl has come awake. He is groggy and I fear his head wound is worse than he believes. His pale face makes me suspect concussion. For an instant I consider my worry for an enemy's medical problem. But enemy or no, we saved his life; and now, I suppose, we're responsible for it.

I look up, see dark shapes spread across the track at the far edge of the headlamps' glare. I cannot make them out.

"Chowduri, what is . . ." I begin.

"They're dead," he interrupts, and I realize the shapes at which I stare are the bodies of men. They lie on their backs side by side. I count seven of them. None of them seem to have arms. I know this must be an illusion created by the blend of shadows thrown down by the tank's headlamps. I look again and see their arms are tied behind them. Cold shifts up my forearms. I do not want to know what has happened here.

"What is it that?" Lieutenant Pohl asks. He slurs his words as though he is having trouble moving his mouth.

"I don't know. Chowduri?"

"They're dead." All day long people have been telling me things I already know. Now Chowduri is doing it.

"Stay inside," I say. I glance back: Allison has halted the ambulance. He must wonder what we are doing. I get out of the hatch and slide down the front of the turret and jump to the ground. I march forward a hundred paces through the bright yellow space the headlamps have carved from the desert night. The mutter of the M13/40's engine diminishes. As though to compensate, the dull thump of the guns firing in the northwest becomes more distinct. I glance in that direction, watch for a moment the bright flashes of exploding artillery shells. I almost think I can hear the men targeted by this barrage panting as they press themselves closer to the earth.

I look down at the corpses. They are British. Each man's elbows are tied together behind his back with a short length of cord. Their faces are distorted, the features pushed this way and thataway from where they had always been. It is as though their skulls are of a more malleable substance than bone.

I look again. Each of them has been shot in the back of the head with a heavy-caliber weapon. I guess 8 or 9 millimeter. Italian or German. Probably German, for the Italians are not certain we will not, some day, take them all prisoner. The passage of the heavy rounds has collapsed the geometry of the men's crania and shoved their features one toward another.

I sway. Exhaustion? Fear? Disgust? I sense something alien near me and bound a pace to the right. Beside me Lieutenant Pohl stares and stares.

"Our troops," I say.

"Executed," he corrects me. "And for what?"

I have no answer for Lieutenant Pohl. Everyone has been demanding answers from me all day long, and I haven't had any answers for anyone for five years. I gave Al Marks my last answers in Chicago on the day before I left for Spain.

"I don't know," I tell him.

"This is a crime." He sounds like a lawyer. I recall Colonel Steiger outlining his brief.

"No more a crime than the rest of it."

"No. This is different. From the war, I mean." He wants to be precise about such a serious thing.

"Perhaps." I remember Spain and think of this morning, when the German sergeant hiding inside the Blinda might have killed us all. But Pohl is right: this is worse than war. I wonder if Marschal is somewhere out here in the desert. Impossible: I killed him myself, and did so just as someone killed these men. Still, Pohl is right: whoever did this is a criminal.

"These are your soldiers," Lieutenant Pohl says. He is stubborn. He wants me to help him with what happened here. To understand what he thinks, what he feels. "The men who did this are no better than those Arabs."

"I thought you understood," I say. "None of us are."

He raises his eyebrows. "Better than those Arabs."

"I would shoot whoever did this myself."

"Of course. Hanging. Shooting." I do not raise my voice. I speak of hanging and shooting with the same ease with which I might speak of golf. "If we could find them."

I glance behind me at the M13/40 and the ambulance in the distance. I hope the Germans do not lay wanton fire on ambulances. I do not know. I do not know much about the Germans, and things are said to have changed in Germany during the past eight years. Once, I suppose—people have said—the German army acted with honor. But I have heard stories about the Germans' conduct in France. Confused stories about executions of British prisoners that make one fear and wonder. These corpses seem to bear those rumors out, to give the bare bones rotting flesh, so to speak. And of course Spain reminds me there *must* have been changes in Germany. And I have heard still other rumors, of camps on the wide Polish plain and in the forests of Pomerania.

On the other hand, I have heard more than rumors about British troops who executed German prisoners just before the evacuation at Dunkirk. Much more than rumors. A captain from the War Office gave a quonset hut full of us a detailed emphatic lecture before we left England in November 1940. He did not speak of war, or the Middle East, or our enemy. His brief was the rights of prisoners and the duties of their captors. He hectored and admonished, repeating again and again the rules of the game we were about to play. More than once he slewed close to detail and revelation. But each time he approached the horror he hesitated and drew back.

Now we are here in the desert, seven Brit soldiers dead at our feet.

"Ah, *Gott*," Lieutenant Pohl says. I glance at him. He is more affected by these corpses than am I. He hasn't had enough of the war yet. When he gets enough of it he will understand that each day makes this kind of horror more comprehensible. With enough time all of us will find good reason to execute prisoners. This morning I sat in the wadi with Mackeson and Allison and listened and nodded as Mackeson reviewed our options. Lieutenant Pohl's problem is easy to understand: he doesn't know what he's gotten himself into.

"I thought you understood," I tell him again. I sound like a math teacher who has discovered his students don't comprehend the word *hypotenuse*.

"I understand," he says. "And I shall report this." Reports must be given a lot of weight in the German army.

"A report," I say. "Of course." Lieutenant Pohl can file all the reports he wants about these murders. I'll file one myself if I make it to Tobruk. If I make it to Tobruk I'll file any kind of a report they want. But no report is going to help us now. Somewhere up the track, somewhere in this desert, is someone who does things like this—and I don't mean shooting prisoners. For it is not the execution of these Brit soldiers that chills the flesh on my arms. It is the display of their bodies on the track that reaches out a fearsome hand to touch me. One can understand the execution, however murderous; but the need to display the corpses is insane.

"I don't understand why they were laid out like this," I lie. Perhaps I want to hear what Pohl thinks. Perhaps the dark frightens me and I want to hear myself speak.

"It is *Schweinerei*," he tells me. His voice is full of impatience, as though *everyone* ought to understand why these corpses have been laid out side by side like mackerel on a slab.

"Or a warning not to come this way," I say.

"No, whoever has did this"—Pohl's English is breaking up—"is no more than a swine."

"Whatever." I step forward and bend over the first body, part the shirt at the cold neck. Blood crusts his unshaven jaw. The man's identity disc is missing. I move to the next corpse, and the next: all their identity discs are gone.

191

Around the fifth man's neck is a bit of broken cord. Whoever took their discs snatched them away, but this dead soldier did not surrender his as easily as the others. I touch their clothing. Their paybooks are missing too. They are anonymous. Seven more for this century's heap of the anonymous dead.

But why take their discs and paybooks? Why hide the identities of those killed? Another desert mystery. Another senseless anecdote of war. To disguise the crime? To hide their identities might not save the killer. Or perhaps their discs and paybooks were taken as trophies? It is a puzzle, one more in an endless series.

"We must bury them."

"No," I tell Lieutenant Pohl. "There's no time. And if we leave them here someone with rank in your army might find out about them and issue orders."

"It is better to bury them," Pohl says. I'm sure now that he has been concussed.

"We've got to get on."

"Burial is better." He is insistent. We are becoming a debating society. Right out here in the Western Desert. "Burial is more Christian," Pohl says. He is marshaling his heavy arguments.

"I doubt He cares," I say. "The church might, but I doubt He does."

Pohl's shoulders slump. He nods. He has been hoping Christ could be found outside the church door. He nods again. "Perhaps you are right, Sergeant." He nods again and again, his agreement with me strengthening. "Yes, you are right." He turns away, turns back, draws himself up. His eyes glitter in the light thrown out by the M13/40's headlamps. The bandage around his head looks almost clean.

"It doesn't matter, Lieutenant. I know you wouldn't do such a thing." I do not tell him I am not so sure about myself.

"That is not the point," he tells me, lifting his hands to show me I am talking about the wrong subject. He is right.

192

I know it is not the point. But what is the point? That he is sorry and embarrassed for the *Wehrmacht?* We are standing in the cold desert night teetering on the edge of a discussion about law, philosophy and the brutality of man. But we have no time for discussion. We are surrounded, and however far away the *Wehrmacht's* anti-tank guns and armored fighting vehicles may be, they may also be near at hand. Who knows? Even the evil bastard who murdered these defenseless Brit soldiers may be lurking in the dark beyond the fat cone of light thrown from the tank's headlamps. We have no time: not for burial and certainly not for debate. This is the central problem with warfare, and particularly with mechanized warfare: there is no time to debate important issues. We fight and advance, defend and flee, all before we can consider what we do or why we do it. Even when we die, the instruments of our destruction move faster than the speed of sound and I have no doubt that one day those instruments will move faster than the speed of light. Though I guess they will never move faster than our fearful thoughts.

"Let's go, Lieutenant. It's not safe, standing around out here."

"*Ja,*" Pohl says. He puts a hand to his face, his fingertips against the edge of the bandage around his head. "So we leave them?"

"That's the problem, Pohl. There aren't any fucking options. You understand? Sometimes the dead have to be left. Sometimes even the living must be left. You get it? That's what all of this is about."

"All what?"

"Let's go, Lieutenant."

"Perhaps I should wait here, for our forces to come. To explain."

"We're fifteen or twenty miles from anywhere out here, Pohl. You'd die when the sun comes up tomorrow. You'd be dead before lunch. There's no point in staying. They're dead. That's the end of it."

"But I . . ." he says. His voice is plaintive, as though

he had never believed life might end like this, with your elbows tied behind your back and a bullet through your skull. "But I . . ." he says. "There must be something . . ." He says no more. He glances at the faces of the murdered men and closes his mouth. I can see he understands at last: that nothing can be done; and that while salvation and a better life after this one may await these men, resurrection is impossible.

"All right, then," Pohl says. He takes a step backward, stumbles, catches himself. "All right. We go. But I will report this."

"Let's get out of here. Standing around like this, none of us may get to report anything."

We return to the tank. Behind the driver's faceplate Chowduri is chanting something I cannot quite make out. More Hindi, I suppose. I climb up the face of the M13/40, slide down into my seat inside the turret and slip on my headset. Chowduri is reciting the Church of England's version of the Nicene Creed. I wait until he finishes, and four heartbeats more. Then I order him forward. It is not until we are rushing through the cold night air again, the corpses minutes behind us, that I wonder whether Chowduri recited the Creed for those murdered soldiers, or for himself and the rest of us still living.

We are closer now. Much closer. All around I note evidence of the Germans' presence; and I know that beyond the Germans, Australians crouch inside the fortified perimeter at Tobruk, violence in their hearts, weapons in their hands.

Once in the distance a pale purple flower trailing a stalk of gray smoke rises into the night sky, its flower's heart burning yellow. Signal flare. Minutes later, far to port—so far I cannot hear the gun firing—a burst of machinegun tracer rips low across the desert. Fired north to south, I note. Australian. An instant later I see the white flash of a shell's detonation close to the machinegun's position and hear the crack of an antitank gun firing.

I revise my theory that antitank gunners cannot range in the dark and I consider whether to douse the headlamps. For one side or the other may already have us fixed in their gunsights, the gun's breech closed on a load of propellant and tungsten-cored steel. Yet I reject the idea of continuing our trek in darkness. I could not communicate with the ambulance to tell Allison my intentions and in the dark he might lose me; or catch up and find me, his headlights obliging the cursing German and Australian gunners and illuminating the whole of the M13/40 long enough for them to touch us off.

Better to go on as we have begun, the dice scattered on the green baize.

"Something's coming," Chowduri says. These are his first words since he recited the Nicene Creed half an hour ago. What? I wonder. And *where?* Then I hear it too: the rumble of an engine, the swishing clatter of a track-laying vehicle heading our way.

I know this vehicle is German or, if we are lucky, Italian. It cannot be ours: we are still far behind the German lines. I glance down at Pohl sitting on the floor of the fighting compartment, below and in front of the loader's seat. If I rotate the turret he will have to take care neither the loader's seat nor my shins and feet strike him in the head.

"You recognize the sound, Lieutenant?"

He nods, swallows. *"Ein und fünfzig,"* he says. Realizing he has spoken German, he switches to English. "A two hundred and fifty and one. A halftracked vehicle, for reconnaissance mostly."

I'm grateful to hear what he has to say. A 251 halftrack is all right. I can deal with a 251. A single round of HE will suffice. A hit on the driving compartment and the

195

251 will explode and burn, as the other ones did this morning. And if the crew is stupid enough to come into the full glare of our headlamps, to come out of the dark into the light, then they and their machine will die without the honor or the dignity of having fought. I will murder them all.

If, that is, the 251 is alone out there in the dark, and is not being covered by an eight-wheeled armored car with a 2cm gun. Or by a Panzer III.

Pohl touches my leg. I look down. "You will fire on them?"

"If I have to."

"Is there anything else we can do?"

This is an interruption from the university classroom.

"No. You're not going to try anything, are you?"

"No," he says. "I was considering the ambulance. If we fire at this vehicle, the ambulance may be at risk."

I have forgotten the ambulance. I think of Allison at the wheel and Mackeson and Lister in the back. A fight now may kill them, even if they are four hundred yards behind. For if I lose the fight, our enemies may believe the ambulance was a decoy set out to lure German troops and vehicles onto our gun. And if they believe that, they may also believe Allison, if not Mackeson and Lister, deserves execution.

As I open my mouth to answer Pohl the 251 jounces into the throw of the M13/40's headlamps. The halftrack is moving at right angles to our course, tacking east. In its open armored bed behind the driving compartment I see a German in a garrison cap, his sleeves rolled up past his elbows. He is standing behind twin MG34s on a pedestal mounting, holding on to the guns' pistol grips with both hands. I begin to rotate the turret, swinging the 47mm gun's muzzle toward the 251's driving compartment. I know the man behind the machineguns cannot see me. I also know that whoever commands this German armored fighting vehicle is a fool. If I am the enemy he has placed his vehicle, his crew and his life in front of my gun.

The German machinegunner in the back of the half-track takes his right hand from the pistolgrip of the right-hand MG34 and waves, smiling through the light at me. "Flick the lights, Chowduri," I whisper down the inter-com. He flicks the headlamps on and off three times and the German waves again and lifts his hat, smiling and showing me his teeth.

It is all very companionable and the ignorance of this halftrack's crew has saved their lives. I take my eyes from the gunsight and poke my head out of the turret. In the instant of sightlessness between removing my eyes from the sight and looking out of the turret hatch, a thick, slabbed shape has trundled into the glare of our head-lamps, following the halftrack out of the darkness into the light.

Through the intercom I hear Chowduri make a sound in his throat. The shape is squat and angled, the black-and-white Maltese Cross on the side of the turret clean and precise. The short menacing 50mm gun thrusts for-ward as the Panzer III slides through the light.

A man with brown hair longer than it should be stands in the tank commander's hatch. He wears a headset and as I watch he says something into the microphone in front of his lips and looks into our lights. I shrink down into the M13/40's turret hatch before I remember he cannot see me through the glare.

He waves, waves again. Jaunty and confident, his hair moving in the wind, he looks like everything Rommel would wish a panzer commander to be. Chowduri blinks our lights with enthusiasm, throwing the German's com-radely gesture back at him. The German waves again. I can almost hear him thinking stirring thoughts: the roar of engines, the menace of the crew behind the armored walls controlling the ponderous machine, the orders com-ing through, the bark of tank guns, the sweeping *Panzer-keil,* comrades tacking together across the desert toward

197

Cairo, an irresistible force sweeping the puny British before them, a chorus of "Wir fahren gegen England" in the earphones. France all over again!

With a final wave of its commander's arm, the Panzer III passes out of the aura of our headlamps, sliding like the monstrous beast it is into the darkness.

"Safe?" Chowduri asks.

"Not till we're in Tobruk and drinking tea, Chowduri."

"The Germans won't have lines," Chowduri says. "Private Mohammed was right. They're spread out. And their assault's to the northwest. They won't be thick on the ground in this sector." He sounds like he's sorting through a stack of reconnaissance photos.

"I hope to Christ you're right," I tell him.

"They are gone?" Pohl asks from below my feet.

"Yes. They guessed we were friendly." I shudder at the thought of the Panzer III trundling across the desert. It is a terrible weapon. Head to head it would destroy us without effort. I think again and again of its turret rotating, the muzzle of the 50mm gun swinging toward us.

But they could not believe we would be audacious enough to drive with our lights on. I wonder what they would have done had we had our lights off? I push the obvious answer away and consider another question: if driving with lights on fools the Germans, will it provoke the Australians?

As we drive north I note other signs of enemy activity. The crisscrossed scars left on the desert by wheeled and tracked vehicles appear with greater frequency. Once I hear engines in the dark beyond the perimeter of light in front of us. I strain to see but the muffled roar fades toward the west. Heading for the battle raging there. As the sound of the engines diminishes I hear a man calling, his voice rising in amiable inquiry. He sounds like a Brit officer calling for his batman. A moment later we sweep past a gun position, the long barrel of the PAK 37 parallel to the desert, the crew gathered around the breech. One of them waves and calls out in Italian. I wave back.

Perhaps our passage *will* be easy, a simple drive straight north. The exhaustion I have felt for the last hours slips from me, borne away by the cold night air rushing against my face. "We're all right," I tell Chowduri through the intercom. "The silly bastards seem to think we ought to be here."

"Fingers crossed," he says. He is not as certain of our future as am I. He still believes we haven't a chance. I glance behind us. The obedient ambulance follows, jouncing over the desert, rocking in our wake. For an instant I have a sense of a larger shape in the dark behind the ambulance, a predator stalking a defenseless weaker thing unaware of the danger behind its back. I look again. Nothing. I remind myself that I am tired, however euphoric our brush with the Panzer III has made me feel.

Even as I consider the degree of my weariness, I glance behind me again; and as I do I see the ambulance accelerate with a jerk. Its lights flash up and down as it bounds forward. And in the dark beyond it I see an ominous shifting shape.

Allison begins to flick the ambulance's headlamps on and off and fear thrusts at me like a sharp glittering knife. My spine shivers as a bony fleshless finger skips from the nape of my neck down my back, counting vertebrae, seeking the spot where the neat blade will fit. With dread I know I should have trusted my sense that some *thing* lurked, preparing to pounce, in the dark beyond Allison. But in my exhaustion I forgot my Spanish lesson. I think of Mackeson and Sidney Lister lying in pain inside the ambulance, wrapped in sopped and crusted bloody bandages, and I strain to see into the dark beyond the pool of light in which Allison is, now, driving as though he is fleeing a man wielding an ax. I strive to separate the M13/40's sounds from all others; strain to suppress the rumble of our engine, the clatter and swish of our tracks; strain to hear what *else* is out there. Out there, and coming for us.

Allison is a hundred yards away when headlamps flick on, cut broad bright corridors through the dark behind him. Two pairs, harsh and blue. And rushing toward us. The lamps are five feet off the ground, almost as high as a man's head. Not trucks, then: armored fighting vehicles. Even as I think this thought I hear the squeak and rattle of tracks and the mutter of engines. I reach with my left hand to the hydraulic control: to rotate the turret, to prepare to fight. But I have no loader, the hull machineguns are jammed and Pohl shouts, "I hear them. Panzers."

Pohl recognizes the sounds of his army's engines, and now the AFVs are closer I agree with his analysis. Engines by Maybach. Armor and guns by Krupp. Two Panzer IIIs. I let my hand slip from the hydraulic control. I will not traverse the gun. I will not fight. Armored warfare is a game of stealth in which the players must count the odds with care if they are to live. Our odds have grown too long: it is senseless to fight two Panzer IIIs, for they would slaughter us with the same ease with which we would destroy soft vehicles or dismounted infantry.

I am left with only one hope: that these panzers' crews will not kill us when we surrender.

"Chowduri," I mutter. "Pull up."

Obedient to my order, Chowduri halts the M13/40. He does not speak but through the intercom I hear him breathing as though he is running a long uphill race.

"It's finished?" Lieutenant Pohl asks. I glance down. His face is flushed as though he is running a fever and I see he is almost as afraid as I am of what these panzers may do.

"I suppose. Yes. Unless they fire."

"They will not fire. They are now inquisitive only. And

if you surrender . . ." He leaves this condition without a predicate.

The Panzer IIIs are closer now, their clattering tracks throwing dust into the light of their headlamps. I cannot see the tank commanders, but I know they can see me. I gaze at the flood of light full of noise grinding toward me. Prudent Allison has halted the ambulance. He is waiting, I suppose, though for God knows what. The panzers rush past the ambulance and now I can make out through the flood of light in front of each of them the threatening shape of their turrets and the jut of their 50mm guns.

These guns are laid, and as the panzers come on, their turrets shift to keep the muzzles of their 50mm guns trained on us.

So at last we lie between their calloused palms, and can but wait to see; as beasts wait for the glittering flash of the thick falling blade.

Still I remember my Spanish lesson: survival is—as, politics and the rest of the bullshit to one side, it has always been—everything. I see the muzzles of the guns thrust toward me and I shrink down into the turret, exposing only the slope of my shoulders and, since I must, above all else, *see* if I am to decide, my head.

Still my observations may be inutile: they may kill us all. All of us, that is, who have survived this *débâcle*, which began at Agedabia and may end in Cairo. But the end of Cairo doesn't matter. Cairo is a place. Cairo makes no difference. All that matters is the death of the *Feldgrau*, the destruction of their equipment, the crushing of their will to continue. These panzer commanders probably don't understand this. I'll wager they're like the Brits, and believe it is all some kind of fucking game you play to win or lose; and if you win, and are alive, you get to go home a hero.

Like the Brits, the Germans are wrong about this. They have not learned the Spanish lesson: their staff plans tell them war ends with the defeat of the enemy's armies. But their staff plans are antique. This is a new age, and antique ideas are useless. Their staff, and ours, have failed to understand that the last man, the last woman and in all likelihood the last child may have to be slaughtered before they will be able to drive their panzers down the Unter den Linden between ranks of cheering children and willowy lovelies.

I put my hand to my belt, touch the slick .11 caliber automatic the captain might have killed me with if I hadn't killed him with it first. I ease it from my belt and slip it beneath my shirt.

They will take the Webley and the M13/40 with its 47mm gun and the two 8mm Breda machineguns that still function, but they may forget to search me. With luck—better luck than the captain had—I may become commander of a *Panzerkampfwagen III*.

The blinding light of the panzers' headlights hurts my eyes: they are upon us, fifty feet away.

I slip the dagger I took from the captain out of my belt, slide it behind my back. I feel the *Hakenkreuz* on the hilt under the pad of my thumb. I flick the knife away into the dark. Taken prisoner, I don't want to be in possession of a souvenir of a German officer I have executed.

"Sergeant," Pohl says. "You should give me that gun. It would be better were you taken prisoner with it not under your shirt."

I have forgotten Lieutenant Pohl. He has seen me slip the neat automatic pistol beneath my shirt. "Or throw it into the dark," he says. Options. The lieutenant has options for everyone. Except for those Arabs. Lieutenant Pohl gave them no option at all. I take the small pistol from under my shirt and slip it behind my back as I did the captain's fancy dagger. With a sigh—relief? exasperation?—I throw it into the dark.

"*Viel* better," the lieutenant says. He is halfway back to his own army. He thinks he has done me a favor. I doubt it. With it I might have killed the crew of a Panzer

202

III. Without it I will be just another prisoner. Bread and brackish water, the days slipping from my hand. Wire on each horizon, guards armed and arrogant. The computation of prisoners, rations, chances. Unreliable information retailed as fact.

It looks as though I will never command a *PzKW III* now.

One of them—massive, flat, slabbed, dust brown and gray, the essence of menace—has halted fifty feet away. The other roars forward, throwing up sand and dust, jerks to a halt close beside us. Its 50mm gun and coaxial machinegun are trained on my chest. Theatrics: it would be smarter to lay these weapons on the hull of the M13/40 at the level of my knees. A shot there would kill us all and the coaxial machinegun could then rake the mixed debris of flesh and bits of machinery, to be sure. Still, training the gun on me is an effective threat: I see the rifling inside the muzzle of the guntube and think of my body torn this way and that into ragged pieces, my guts unraveled down my quivering legs, the jerking final breaths of this life spilling out my throat, faint yelps fleeing a few feet away across this enormous desert. And at that instant, no hope but that salvation's arms are wide enough.

$$\dagger \; \dagger \; \dagger$$

Our surrender is predictable. Our words and actions—and the Germans'—are the denominators of every battle ever fought. Yet the familiar formulae do not render this moment less terrifying.

"*Raus!*" shouts the *PzKW III*'s commander, standing up straight in the turret. I can see the gun in his fist—a Walther—and the captain's insignia on his khaki uniform shirt. He is another blond German and I wonder if he is like the rest of them: strict, intelligent, at ease with killing.

"We must get out," Lieutenant Pohl says. But I don't need a translator to understand the commander of this threatening panzer and I am already halfway out the hatch even as Pohl speaks.

He follows me out and the tank commander yells, *"Deutscher Soldat? Offizier?"*

"Leutnant," Lieutenant Pohl says. This is not redundant, for Lieutenant Pohl's badges of rank are difficult to make out: his uniform is scruffy, torn and spotted with blood and dirt.

The German up in the turret of his monster tank says, with a peculiar sibilance sliding through the syllables, *"Kommen Sie hierauf, Kamerad."* Pohl glances at me, raises his eyebrows as though we are still together in this instead of on different sides again. He jumps down from the M13/40.

As he walks across to the Panzer III I see glittering bits of silver hanging at the juncture of the barrel of the 50mm gun and the turret. I cannot make them out. I look at them again and again. They are familiar, but I cannot make them out.

Chowduri jumps down from the M13/40, stands next to me in the sand with his hands in front of him.

"What now?" he asks.

"Wait and see," I tell him. I glance back, at the ambulance. Through the glare of the lights I can see into the darkness only with difficulty; but I think Allison is out of the cab of the ambulance, standing with his hands raised, a man from the other panzer pointing a machinepistol at him.

Lieutenant Pohl is up on the hull of the *PzKW III*, moving his hands, talking to the captain commanding. I hope he is telling him about Pfferman's death and my Webley in his fist. The captain seems to be questioning him in detail. I hear the words *"Wo?"* and *"Wann?"* The captain is interested in where we've been and where we're going. He likes to know the tactical situation. I wonder why he is not farther away, to the northwest, where the artillery fire is beating against the darkness, pounding the earth.

"Look there," Chowduri whispers. I have not heard fear in Chowduri's voice before.

"What?"

"Beneath the gun. Against the turret." I look into the bright light flooding from the panzer's headlamps. "See them? I think they . . ." He cannot say more, something catches in his throat and I watch as he stares and stares at the glittering metal things hanging beneath the gun.

But Chowduri does not have to tell me what they are. I have figured it out. They are British identity discs. I wear one of them strung around my neck on a length of cord. The loop of cord of each of these discs has been slipped over the barrel of the panzer's 50mm gun. At this distance each disc seems identical. But I know each of these discs identifies a man. A soldier in British uniform. I remember the corpses on the track, their arms bound behind their backs, their features distorted by the massive trauma of gunshot wounds in the head.

Inside the panzer the gunner shifts the turret and the identity discs swing on their cords, jangling against the steel carapace. As they swing I note one of them is suspended from a length of clean white twine. I remember the corpse laid out on the track with the tattered bit of cord around its bloody neck. The one who had not, even in death, surrendered his identity without a fight.

I wish I had kept the small slick pistol. I consider the distance back up into the M13/40's turret. It is impossible. The machinegun in the hull of the panzer is trained on my chest. If I move I will be killed and Chowduri will be slaughtered with me.

Lieutenant Pohl is standing on the panzer's hull speaking long sentences full of complicated German words, as though he is defending a thesis at university. I hear him say something about "Arab animals" and remember the elderly Arab in Tobruk who required me to eat half a melon from his garden.

Allison comes out of the darkness into the light, his

arms raised, a sick grin on his face. A German in khaki shorts and shirt marches behind him, holding the muzzle of a machinepistol a foot from his back.

"A good try, at least," Allison says as he comes up. The German behind him stops ten feet away, to give the machinegunner in the hull of the Panzer III an unobstructed field of fire.

"See the identity discs under the gun," Chowduri says.

Like Chowduri, Allison stares and stares. I can see the instant when he realizes what it means. "Why, the . . ." he begins, but I tell him to shut up. The last thing we need is to let the captain up there in the *PzKW*'s turret realize we know he is a murderer, and I pray Lieutenant Pohl will not notice the discs.

The private who herded Allison across from the ambulance calls up to the captain, telling him about Mackeson and Lister. The captain nods, cocks his head to one side. He is calm. I am surprised he has not doused the lights of his panzer. After all, the Australians are out there somewhere.

I wish I had decided to fight. Or had kept the small pistol. I wish I had decided anything other than to surrender.

Lieutenant Pohl and the captain are deep in conversation when I see Pohl turn his face, the skin gray as wax. His neck bends. I pray hard that he will not see the identity discs swinging from the barrel of the 50mm gun. He turns his face to the captain again; starts; jerks to look at what he has seen but did not at first recognize. From his throat comes a sound—neither German nor English. It is a sound from the lexicon of horror. The lieutenant has seen the captain's trophies and the sight of them chokes him like sand pounded down his throat. A second sound, half moan, half sigh, escapes him. At last he finds his voice and shouts at the captain. The captain laughs and laughs. The sound of his laughter falling into the blinding light of the panzer's headlamps recalls for me the fearsome medieval paintings of purgatory. I see the captain's head thrown back, the teeth sparkling in his laughing mouth. His throat is exposed, the skin white: he has not been long in the desert. I wish I had not thrown away the ceremonial dagger I took just this morning from that other captain.

The captain climbs out of the tank's turret, laughing and laughing. Lieutenant Pohl shouts, stumbles out of his way, slumps against the turret. The captain jumps down from the panzer and saunters across the ten feet of sand between us and the tank. He is laughing, and between his laughs he says something again and again in German. At first I cannot make it out: the noises of the panzer's engine and the captain's bubbling laughter interfere. But at last I understand what he is saying: *"Ich bin Jäger."* "I am a hunter." Perhaps he is. He seems the outdoors type and I recall that in Germany they hunt driven game. He holds the Walther pistol in his fist, the muzzle pointed at the ground in front of him. Laughing and laughing, he calls to the private who herded Allison over. The private slings his machinepistol, climbs up on the panzer, reaches inside the turret hatch. When he jumps down from the side of the tank I see the lengths of cord he is holding. He does not look troubled about what he is going to do. Perhaps it is true about the Germans after all.

"You fuckin . . ." Allison begins. But the captain points the muzzle of the Walther at Allison's chest and laughs. The captain likes the feel of deciding about the helpless. Beside me Chowduri tenses. I put my hand on his hairless forearm.

"Don't give him an excuse," I say. Chowduri nods and the muscles in his arm relax.

The private comes forward, the lengths of cord swinging from his hand. I look at his face. Bovine, almost somnolent, the meaning of what he is about to do seems to have escaped him. Perhaps he is a half-wit? Whatever. I do not think we will live long enough to carry out the tests necessary to determine his mental capacity.

Lieutenant Pohl is speaking from his perch on the tank. His voice is weak and I am sure now that he has been concussed. No help for us there. The lieutenant doesn't even have a weapon, aside from the fact that killing a superior officer is a serious offense in any army. You need a good explanation if you kill an officer. Or even another enlisted man.

"You realize this is a crime?" I ask the captain. I was a soldier. Now I have become just another argumentative lawyer. Like Colonel Steiger. And Lieutenant Pohl. The lieutenant is speaking German and English, mumbling threats at the captain, promising he will report this to the authorities.

"Everything," the captain says in workmanlike accented English, "is a crime. Everything. The war is a crime. I see no difference. At home I hunt and hang trophies on the walls of my father's lodge. Do you think you are worth more than a roebuck, Sergeant?" He pauses. I am supposed to answer this question. It will make him feel better if I answer it. I say nothing. "You are not, Sergeant." He laughs, a long curl of bubbling laughter rising from his throat. "I can eat a roebuck when I have killed it. But I cannot eat you."

"You eat shit," Allison says. Allison has come a long way from London to this place and his vocabulary has kept pace with each step of that brutal journey.

The captain laughs and wags the muzzle of the pistol in his fist at Allison. "No, no," he says. "No, no. You are wrong. There you are wrong. I know you are wrong." The captain seems drunk, but I do not smell alcohol. Drugs? Or is it his power to kill us or not as he wishes that has created the curious elation I see in his eyes, hear in his voice?

He turns to the private holding the cords that will bind us. The private's eyes are dull: they do not react to the bright light of the panzer's headlamps. The captain speaks, gestures. The private comes forward, the cords in his right hand, his left swinging at his side. I wonder what he is thinking. When I look into his eyes I wonder if he is thinking at all. Up on the tank, Lieutenant Pohl is still muttering in anger. But he cannot help us: his wound has taken control. He is slumped against the turret, his face indistinct beyond the brightness of the lights, the dirty bandage on his head a gray smudge.

"You will be bound," the captain says. "For our protection." He laughs again.

"We know what you're doing," I tell him.

The captain laughs and laughs. He knows what he's doing too. He gestures at the private to get to work. The man slips two of the lengths of cord around his neck and, holding the third piece in both hands, steps behind us. I guess he thinks we will place our arms behind our backs for him; that we will be docile; that we will go where we're told.

Beside me Chowduri tenses and I know that at least one of us is not going to die like one of the captain's roebuck. Waiting for this professional soldier from India to move, I glance at Allison and see the grim, determined set of his face: he looks like a man setting out to run a distance so great no one can measure it.

In the dark beyond the bright pool of light in which we wait to be killed a horn honks twice. The two sharp sounds are peremptory. I hear the vehicle's engine. A truck. The captain turns his head, looks into the darkness. He squints, trying to see beyond the bright light. The vehicle trundles forward, picking its way across the desert toward us. Its lights flash twice. It cruises into the aura of light thrown out by the panzer's headlamps. It is large, boxy, brand-new and British. It is a mobile command post for division and army commanders built on a four by four Bedford QL truck which, I know, has gone into production only in the past few months. Behind it comes a 251 halftrack full of troops and, behind the 251, a Blitz lorry.

The British markings on the mobile command post have been painted over with German signs: a *croix formée* in black and white, a stenciled palm tree with a *Hakenkreuz*, and the German word *Mammut*.

Sitting up out of a hatch in the roof, a middle-aged man in a greatcoat and officer's hat stares down at us through goggles. As the vehicle halts, he lifts the goggles and disappears through the hatch, reappears from a door in the wooden command post built on the truck's bed. He strides straight toward us. As he approaches, the private who had been preparing to bind us steps forward to join his captain, flipping the cord he carries in his hands around his neck. The ends of the three cords dangle against his chest. When the man coming on is forty feet away the captain and the private jerk to attention. The captain calls out something and salutes. Not the *Hitlergruss,* but the traditional salute of the German army. From inside the Panzer III I hear men speaking. Lieutenant Pohl stops muttering and slides off the side of the tank. He staggers, shakes his head, comes to attention and salutes.

The officer from the command vehicle—for officer he surely is, even though I cannot see his badges of rank because the collar of his greatcoat is turned up—stops thirty feet away. He pops the captain, Lieutenant Pohl, and the private a quick salute. Then he puts his fists on his hips and looks us over for ten seconds before he waves the captain forward. Unbidden, Lieutenant Pohl follows, stumbling and pitching as though he is making his way along the deck of a ship in a high sea.

The captain stands at attention while the officer questions him. Lieutenant Pohl stands beside the captain, one shoulder sagging lower than the other. Occasionally he shivers.

The officer listens to the captain speak, turns, looks over his shoulder at us, turns back to the captain. When the captain finishes, the officer, hands still on his hips, turns his face to Lieutenant Pohl. Even at thirty feet I can hear

Pohl's slurred speech. I hope he has not forgotten the corpses in the road and the identity discs hanging from this *Jäger*'s panzer's barrel. And his promise to report in the proper quarter. Pohl rambles on. His feet step this way and that in the sand and he is unable to keep his hands at his sides. The officer listening to him looks him up and down as though he is displeased with Pohl's turn-out and impatient of his long explanation. At last, as though he is asking the officer to watch some clever trick, Pohl lifts an arm and points to the Panzer III in front of which we are standing.

The officer's shoulders come back and he raps out a question. Neither the captain nor Pohl answer. *"Ja?"* the officer asks the captain, his voice rising in anger. *"Ja?"* he shouts at the captain.

The officer turns on his heel and marches toward us. As he comes he calls orders into the night. Men leap over the sides of the halftrack. Some sprint across the sand toward us, others toward the ambulance and the second panzer fifty feet away. Two officers—a colonel and a major—jog forward, overtake the officer in the greatcoat marching toward us and slow to match his stride, one on either side of him and a pace behind. He acknowledges them with a curt nod but he does not miss a single springy step. He keeps on marching straight at us, an athletic, energetic man with a broad face beneath his hat. Allison, Chowduri and I wait for him to come up.

The three of us come to attention as he approaches. He flicks us a salute and marches straight on past. He halts in front of the panzer. He raps out an order and the major clambers up the front of the tank. Holding onto the barrel of the 50mm gun with one hand, he slips the cords from which the identity discs are suspended along the barrel past the muzzle. The discs clink together as he jumps down from the tank. He holds them up for the officer in the greatcoat to see. The officer reaches out for them, but the major jerks them back before he can touch them. The major says a few quiet words I do not understand, but I know what he is talking about for I can see the dark spatters of dried blood on the discs.

The officer in the greatcoat reaches out again, takes the discs in his right hand and looks at them one after the other. Once he glances over at us. Then he looks back across the sand at the captain and Lieutenant Pohl. Pohl has walked away from the captain and is sitting on the desert, his head in his hands. The captain is still at attention. A tough sergeant with a machinepistol cradled in his arms stands close by, watching the captain as though he is worried the captain may do something odd and might have to be restrained.

The officer in the greatcoat comes toward us. The major and the colonel are right behind him. When he halts in front of us, they halt, and when he speaks rapid German, the colonel translates, "The general asks which of you is senior."

I look into the general's face, glance at the identity discs in his hand, and say, "I am."

"Name? Rank?" The general asks in English.

I give him my name and rank. He nods and, nodding, glances to the side and catches sight of the private with the three lengths of cord around his neck. The general's face flushes and he barks and shouts at the private, strides across the six feet that separate them and yanks the cords from the private's neck. Shouting and demanding answers, he lashes the private across the face and chest with the cords. The private's eyes blink and a faint confusion alters the cast of his features. The general stops lashing the private with the cords. He turns and marches back to us, hands the cords to the major and raps out an order. The major calls out into the darkness and three soldiers, a sergeant with a pistol and two privates with rifles at trail, jog across the sand. They crowd the private, relieve him of his machinepistol, cage him with their weapons. The private still stands at attention, his face full of consternation. I understand his problem: ordered by his captain, he is beginning to understand that he has assisted in the commission of crimes. He cannot figure it out. He thought he was a good soldier. Now he knows he is not.

The sergeant with the pistol and the two privates with the rifles herd him away.

The general shouts out more orders and the captain marches across, striding out regulation paces, the sergeant with the machinepistol right behind him. The captain stops six paces from the general.

For three beats of the heart everyone is silent and then the general begins to shout as he steps forward shaking his fist at the captain. The identity discs in his hand jangle, the small tinny voices of the murdered. The general is exercising his voice, working himself into a rage. He pushes his flushed face toward the captain's and juts his jaw at the captain each time he shouts. He seems to be yelling questions. The colonel does not translate—he and the major are standing to one side, at ease, waiting for orders—and I understand very few of the general's words. But I know what he is saying.

Shouting, the words rushing out of him, the general begins to strike the captain across the face with the jangling identity discs once and again.

At last, his rage expended, he steps back. He transfers the identity discs from his right hand to his left and begins to unbutton his greatcoat from the collar down. At his neck is the black and silver *eisernes Kreuz*—the *croix formée*. Beneath it is a second medal, one I have not seen before—a Maltese Cross in blue enamel on a black and silver ribbon. I can see words impressed in gold in the blue enamel but I cannot make them out. The general flexes his knees, reaches down with the blunt fingers of his right hand, unbuttons the last, lowest button of his greatcoat. He sweeps the heavy leather skirt aside. At his waist a shiny black leather holster gleams.

I know this holster: inside it are a Luger pistol and an

extra clip of ammunition. The general unbuttons the flap of the holster and takes the pistol out, snaps the safety down with his thumb, brings the pistol up and aims at the captain as though he is going to try to qualify on the pistol range.

He shoots the captain in the chest. The 9mm slug lifts the captain onto his toes, throws him away into the desert. A sound slides up the captain's throat. It is not laughter.

The general paces forward and stands over the captain. He shakes the identity discs he holds in his left hand and I see the captain's eyelids slide open. He looks up, his eyes glittering, at the jangling identity discs. The general says something—a curse? another peremptory order? a final question? He points the pistol at the captain's face and fires. The captain's features flatten and his skill expands this way and that. The recognizable, human angles of bone, tendon, and flesh are dispersed. I have seen faces like this before. So has the captain. But the captain doesn't know this any more.

The general snaps the Luger's safety up, holsters it, about-turns and marches back to us. He is still angry. Angry at the captain, angry at himself. Like the rest of us, the colonel and the major wait for him to speak.

The general hands me the identity discs and says in English, "I apologize for my country and my army." He looks at me. He has expectations: that I should accept his apology; that I should compliment his sense of honor, his respect for law, the dimensions of his morality. He wants me to pull my forelock because—I can see the words traced in gold in the blue enamel of the Maltese Cross hanging from the black and silver ribbon around his neck now—he wears the *Pour le Mérite*. His memory extends backward to a time in which words like *honor* and *law* may have meant something. He is from the generation that fought the First World War. Bands, flags and the swagger of dress uniforms. The formality of the regimental mess. Followed, in the trenches, by appeals from his sovereign.

And of course the bitter slaughter, the flares in the night, the firefights and raids, the deaths of men and horses, the hammering of guns. All that, and now he wants absolution from me, a sergeant he believes is British.

Yet more than the rest of us he is responsible for what we have had to endure. He is a director of this corporate enterprise. A theorist and tactician. Because of his rank he is, more than the rest of us, liable. Had I a knife he might pay his bill right now. Still I know that one day he will pay for the responsibility he carries with such confidence on his squared shoulders. And on that raging day he will pay his life into a black mouth and swallowing throat.

"I apologize," he says again. His English is accented. He seems concerned that I understand.

"There's no need," I tell him. I can think of nothing else to say. It's the exhaustion that forms my words. And the cold, the tension and the day just past. Half my crew are dead or wounded and the passengers I have picked up are maimed or dead. All of it has exhausted me. All of it, but particularly the fact that this general's captain—had this general not come out of the night, a *deus ex machina* with medals around his neck plunked down here in the fucking Libyan desert—would have slaughtered us as he slaughtered roebuck a mile from his father's lodge in the Schwarzwald. Or wherever. Masuria? Who knows. Who the fuck cares.

The general nods and nods. He answers me in German. His English is good enough for orders, apologies, sentiments, but is not up to explanations. The colonel—tall, impeccable, tailored and fragrant—even out *here* he smells of cologne—translates. "It is important, Sergeant. To keep to the rules. To fight a fair fight. You must answer the general."

"Fair fight?"

"The rules of war," the colonel explains. Is he translating or handing me a gloss on the general's text?

215

"I was in Spain," I tell the general. The colonel doesn't need to translate this. Nor does the colonel understand the meaning of "Spain." But the general does. He frowns when I give him the name of that brutal country. He sees I must be an enthusiast. And since I am not with him, I must be a *socialist* enthusiast. One of the foreigners who fought against Fascism in Spain. Against the Right. Against the orderly and the strict. He categorizes me: I am one of the suspect. An undesirable. He breathes through his nose, nods, nods again. At last he seems to decide: whatever I was in the International Brigades, I'm a sergeant in the British army now and the code he has taught the laughing captain protects me. Just this one time I am glad someone in authority sticks to the words in the rule book.

But fuck the general's code. I would kill him in a moment if I could and live. In a moment. I look at his throat above the blue, black, gold, and silver ribbons and medals. The general shifts from one foot to the other and the tokens of the violent life he has lived jangle together. Like the identity discs in my hand. I glance at the French inscription on the Maltese Cross. A quaint, *recherché* divergence from the national language of the *Reich,* an embarrassment to the purity of *Nazionalsozialismus.* I wonder what the Brown Shirts thought of this man and his medal. But who cares what they thought? Bugger Rohm and his Brown Shirts are dead. I know the colonel standing at my elbow, leaning forward with all the unction of a head waiter, believes this general's medal is a wonderful thing. A French inscription on a German medal! *Unmöglich!* I glance at the major. I'm not so sure about the major. He seems less conscious of the paternity of his army, less sensitive to the traditions that have put him in uniform. He reminds me of Smythe. Smythe dead for ten hours now, Smythe with an education and an officer's patent.

I wonder how many French soldiers slaughtered at Verdun, and how many of their sons, fleeing like rabbits through the sunny days of May 1940, appreciated the

French inscription on this most famous of all the Kaiser's medals.

The general speaks English: "Spain was another place. I apologize again. For my soldiers and my country."

He wants absolution. I'm sure of it. He wants me to absolve him from the deaths of the men whose identity discs I hold in my hand. It is apparent the general and I differ about the meanings of soldiers' lives and soldiers' deaths. Tacky with blood, jangling with the tremor that runs through my arm and hand, these discs are, to him, important symbols. To me they are just circles of metal spattered with dead blood.

On the other hand, I owe the general, and chance, our lives—and Lieutenant Pohl's. For surely the captain the general executed would have murdered Lieutenant Pohl once he'd finished with us, for Lieutenant Pohl is that most obnoxious of all men who survive in wartime: a witness.

"Thank the general for me," I tell the colonel. The colonel has been worried. My desultory responses to the general's generous statements have produced a faint skein of creases at the corners of the colonel's eyes. I try to remember all my best Chicago manners. "Thank him for me and tell him I understand." With my thanks the creases disappear and the colonel breaks into a sunny smile. He translates and the general grunts, nods once and again. I wonder whether all the generals in the *Wehrmacht* nod and nod. At last he grins. He has forgotten the captain dead on the sand, someone's son shot by their son's commanding officer for deviations from the norm.

I wonder where to find this norm. Somewhere a mathematician, insouciant and brilliant, a realistic witty man in years no more than a child, his mind fresh and unpolluted, applies himself to this problem, matching it to the clean matrix of his thought. He will find an answer, I know he will. An expert at cryptanalysis, he will find a solution that will be just, succinct and intelligible. Yet his equation will be displayed only to a favored minority, its meaning passed from one discreet group of protected intellects to another, its confidentiality preserved, the papers stamped with the crimson marks of priority and secrecy. In the end, knowledge of the knowledge itself will become as secret as the specifications of a special weapon.

The general waits: he expects a further gift of words from the enemy sergeant whose life, and whose men's lives, he has saved. I give him the gift he wants: this is no time for philosophy. "Tell the general I thank him for our lives," I tell the colonel. "Tell him he's a soldier."

I have said something felicitous. The colonel beams and nods. He translates and the general gives me a quick smile that is almost lost in the colonel's beaming. The general seems almost embarrassed: perhaps he's waited all his life to hear my words? But is he gratified to hear me thank him for saving our lives, or that I have confirmed he is a soldier?

The general straightens his shoulders—memories or no, he hasn't much time—salutes, turns and marches off, distributing orders as he goes. As he marches into the dark, the colonel calls out and the major marches away at another angle. The ambulance is driven forward. The colonel tells Chowduri and Allison—they are junior enlisted, after all—to get in.

The crews of the two Panzer IIIs are routed out into the night and led away. It seems the general doesn't think they're up to much. Men from the halftrack come forward and mount the panzers and the M13/40. It is an interesting bit of information: the general's troops are cross-trained. I'm certain the general himself could crew any position inside either tank.

"You will take the ambulance to your lines, Sergeant. With your men, of course." The colonel is filling me in on our future. While he speaks, Lieutenant Pohl passes, assisted by a medical corpsman. The dirty smudged bandage on his head shows a fresh patch of red blood. He waves and smiles, says something I do not catch and is drawn away by the corpsman before he can explain himself. "You will drive forward," the colonel is saying, "and we will fire flares to identify you to your troops."

I consider his confident plan, remembering the Australians crouched out in the dark.

"How far to our lines did you say?"

"Three kilometers," the colonel says. "No more than three kilometers. We will fire flares when you are a kilometer from the defenses." He seems happy we are this close to Tobruk's defenses. I am not. After all, he'll be here with the general, firing flares and feeling honorable. We'll be out there in an ambulance with plywood walls, wondering if one Australian is telling another, "It's the fuckin Germans, innit? I say fuck 'em. Give 'em a fuckin burst with the MG, Bluie. I mean, a fuckin ambulance? You've got to fuckin hand it to them, though. Deceitful fuckin sods, aren't they?"

Of course, Bluie might decide to wait and see. Anyway we have no choice: the general and his troops have saved our lives, and now they get to dispose of them as they see fit. We will not remain the general's prisoners, as safe as that might be, for the general wants his story told. He wants us to return to our—to the Australians'—lines to tell all and sundry that the Germans *really do* obey the laws of war.

I will not tell the colonel the Australians do not care fuckall for the general's honor or the general's nice observance of his gentleman's code. On the other hand, I sense the major is more realistic and less traditional than the general or the colonel. The major reminds me of a woodcutter, a butcher, an engineer. For him, war is a job of work. He does not care about honor or any rule that has no tangible purpose. He does not believe in propaganda. He wants only to finish the job and he is, therefore, the most dangerous of these officers. He would keep us prisoner, for he knows that to permit us to leave is an affectation, perhaps a dangerous affectation. Whatever the general orders, I know the major will want to be off and away from this place as soon as the flares that will identify us to the Australians have been fired.

Still he is only a major, and the general's observance of the formalities may keep the general, the colonel, and particularly the major in place long enough for the Australians to drench this piece of desert with high explosive, once we give them the proper map reference.

"So," the colonel says, smiling at me as though we are out hoisting a couple of beers instead of standing around in this cold dry desert full of death and archaic rules. "You are agreed with the arrangements?"

"Is there a choice?"

"The *Herr General* wishes this, ah, *inc*ident to be reported to your command. To your army. You understand?"

"Sure. We'd fight harder if you executed prisoners in a regular way, wouldn't we?"

"That is of course part of the reason for the *Herr General*'s decision. But only the smallest part. His main concern is for your wounded. And of course you are no longer a threat to us."

"Of course. On the other hand you're hoping for a quick victory. As in France. And you wouldn't want us to fear surrender."

"That is of course part of the reasoning."

"You know the Australians, Colonel?"

"I have never met an Australian. But as you are aware," the colonel says, smiling at me and flicking his head toward the northwest where the guns are pounding the earth, "they are getting to know us right at this time." He grins as though he knows something I don't. Still, he hasn't met the Australians. For that matter, he hasn't met anyone I've known. I wonder how he will fare if he is required to fight Marschal's people. Bloody Marschal, dead and bloody in the snow, was a harder man than this colonel can think to be.

"I'm surprised you're here, Colonel. You and the general. Instead of up there." I nod toward the northwest.

The colonel smiles as though he is conversing with a child. "It will not be difficult. The fighting, there, is only nine kilometers away. And we do not attack quite yet."

"You're sending us back for only a few hours, then."

"That will, I regret to say, be the case."

I wonder how many men the colonel has killed. How many, that is, he could smell as he killed them.

"I'd best get to the ambulance, then. To save on time."

"Yes, of course. But, oh, Sergeant," the colonel says. "One thing. Your accent. You are of course Canadian?"

"From Toronto." I give him my best Canadian smile.

"I have never been to Toronto. But I knew your accent was Canadian. The difference in pronunciation, you see." He is very satisfied with his knowledge of English. I leave him with his assumption and a salute. He draws himself up, returns my salute.

I wonder where he will die. He's got a lot of choices. Here, in this waste only nomadic Arabs might call home. Or somewhere in the civilized shadowed streets of Europe, in a place no more than four hundred miles from the front door of his orderly home. Or perhaps the bombers will get him when he's at dinner with his orderly wife and orderly children. Then, just before his eyes melt, he'll have the honor of seeing his family burn to death. Or perhaps, if his leaders are as stupid as they seem, they will make the Napoleonic decision and he will die in Russia. This option seems unlikely, for the Nazis and the communists now embrace one another in treaty and propaganda release with a hearty appreciation of one another's methods. On the other hand, their agreement is a contract between murderers, and like all criminals they are sure to disagree. And when they disagree, they will bicker and wrangle. At last they will go for one another with sharp knives. Perhaps the only relevant question is whether the rats will attack the pigs before the pigs attack the rats.

The colonel still smiles. I'm sure he'll smile right up to the moment someone carves him up.

"Good-bye," he says. "And good luck. We shall see you soon."

"Thanks for the luck, Colonel." He is unconcerned I don't tell him I'm happy to hear we'll be seeing one another again.

I salute him a second time. He likes this. After all, his army seems to be winning. He can afford to feel at ease. He returns my second salute with a languid throw of his arm. I wonder how he will lose this arm. Fire, shell fragment? Machinegun burst, mechanical accident? Artillery fire, antitank round? The colonel smiles and smiles. He is unaware of the possibilities. But when they are in uniform and winning, people don't think about possibilities. I about turn and march off. Ten paces on I turn my head and say, "My regards to the general. And my thanks."

After all, I want to get us out of here and through the Australian lines. I think a good deal more of the Australians than the colonel does, for I fear them and he doesn't.

The general is somewhere inside his command vehicle. Behind it a signals truck has appeared: a spidery net of antennae juts from its roof. The general has left the details of our disposition to the colonel—and the major, who now approaches. He calls out to the colonel, points at the ambulance. Allison is in the driver's seat. He has the engine running. The major gestures at me, at the ambulance. He gives me a hard look but he does not speak. We are lucky the general was here, and the colonel. The major would not have permitted our departure. He would have imprisoned us for the duration. I look at his hard face and give him a salute as I walk past him. He frowns as he returns my salute.

In the ambulance Allison says, "They're letting us go?"

"The general wants his generosity known."

"Good on him."

"They'll fire flares when we're between here and the

lines at Tobruk. The Australians will identify us and let us through."

"We hope."

"Chowduri's in the back?"

"With Mackeson and the Australian. Lister. They were a little nervous there, when I left the ambulance."

"Let's get out of here." I wave an arm out the window as Allison puts the ambulance in gear. The colonel waves back. The major stands still and silent. Perhaps he fears I too am a woodcutter, a butcher, an engineer. I look around but I do not see the general or Lieutenant Pohl.

"I don't see Pohl." I catch a glimpse of the M13/40. Germans are clambering over it. I wish we had had the time to get our kit out of it. And perhaps even Colonel Steiger's gold coins. Now there is a chance we might be able to use them.

"I spoke to him," Allison says. "Thanked him for his efforts."

"You have the map?"

Allison hands me our map. It is tattered, and blood-stained on one corner—far to the southeast, near the Egyptian border. "We won't need the map," Allison says. "It's three kilometers and we're there."

"I want to know where we are now."

"Here? What for?"

"Our artillery will want the information just as soon as we arrive." I crease the spot on the map with my thumbnail. I am not certain it is the right spot, and if the major has anything to say about it this bit of desert will be deserted by the time we arrive inside our lines. But it will be worth a try.

"Isn't that a little, ah . . . ?" Allison has qualms. After all this, and especially after today, he still has qualms.

"Disrespectful? Ungenerous? He's a German general. If we can kill him it will assist us greatly."

"It just seems a little ungracious."

"So is all this shit we've been through, Allison. Tomorrow will be the same. Don't forget that. Now let's get out of here." Allison lets in the clutch and we begin to move. We leave the panzers and the command and communications vehicles behind. I glance back: German troops are clambering into the M13/40. I turn away: I do not wish to watch them repossess the tank that brought us from El Agheila so far to the west.

Soon we are all alone in the desert, heading north, the engine of the ambulance grinding. Perhaps part of the mechanism is worn and we will not make it. I wonder if the general's plan accounts for this possibility. Someone in the back is murmuring. Chowduri? Mackeson? Lister? Men from the four corners of the earth, swinging with me tonight from one danger toward the next. Perhaps we will survive. It all depends on the colonel's timing, and the Australians' anger. I begin to wonder whether the Australians will have the same elevated sense of propriety as the *Herr General.*

✝ ✝ ✝

In the sky above us three bluewhite flares ignite one after the other. The cold desert fills with cold light. "That's better," Allison says. "See where we're going now." He puts his foot down and we bound forward, hopeful, eager, trusting.

But Alf says, "It's the fuckin Germans, innit? I say fuck 'em. Give 'em a fuckin burst with the MG, Bluie. I mean, a fuckin ambulance? You've got to fuckin hand it to them, though. Deceitful fuckin sods, aren't they?"

"You think, Alf? I don't know. I mean an ambulance and all?"

"Fuckin fire, mate. What the fuckin hell are you going on for? Shoot the fuckers and worry about Chancery Court later."

Bluie fuckin fires. The tracer comes for us like a lance thrown out of the dark. It flashes low across the desert, a straight snake banded gold and black. "Oh, Jesus," Allison whispers beside me. He wrestles with the wheel, bouncing the ambulance this way and that, as though he might be quicker.

He isn't. The windshield shatters and the tracer and shot strike metal and scream away. This machinegunner has had a lot of practice somewhere back in the Delta. I hear a thumping pounding. Things—machinegun rounds? pieces of debris?—pound my left shoulder, the bicep, the forearm. The seatback presses against me. Or do I press against it? Lightheaded, I hear Allison muttering beside me. In the back someone shouts at someone else's curses.

We are still moving. I am surprised. Allison wrenches the wheel this way and that and yells, "Fucking Australians!" He flashes the lights on and off. I glance at my arm. Blood and yellowwhite fat seep. From the forearm, bone juts like a shattered stick. I hope the *Herr General* is watching this. I giggle. It's been a long fucking day, and it looks as though I have at last found the end of it.

Allison shouts, stands on the brakes. My face bounces from the dash. Blood runs down my cheek. I wonder what the *fuck* Allison thinks he's doing. The knees of my coveralls are drenched with blood. Saliva loops in an intense thread from my mouth onto my right knee. I am surprised I can see such detail. Then I remember the bright bluewhite light of the flares above us. My head is on my knees when machinegun fire hammers through the cab again. Slim river of fire full of red and gold flashes. Someone pulls at my shoulder and I scream. I slide a glance to the right. Chowduri, standing in the desert. I realize we must have halted. His face is determined, his eyes full of fear and regret. Regret? I open my mouth to speak and vomit spatters from my coughing throat onto my coveralls.

I glance up, above Chowduri's shoulder. The night is full of colored light, but I fear the darkness beyond. I feared the dark long before I went to Spain.

The fucking desert. What a place.

Chowduri speaks but I cannot hear him. I'm tired and he's pulling on me. Tired: I remember Mohammed's face just before someone pushed sand over it. Chowduri pulls at me again. I watch him whip a cord around my arm. Close to the shoulder. I can feel the cord cinch tight, right up in my armpit. My arm is mantled with blood, the back of my hand spattered red. My life's blood pouring out of *me*. I think of Steiger, Colonel Rudolf's body slipping from the M13/40's hull. Ah, me. Chowduri shouts. He strikes me on the cheek. Mackeson's face appears beyond Chowduri's shoulder. I have seen the expression on this good Scotsman's face before. He was disassembling the cylinder head on the M13/40 the last time I saw this doleful look. A good tank, the M13/40. Not strong enough, not well-enough gunned. But all right for its time. Mackeson reaches forward around Chowduri's shoulder with his good hand and pats me on the left shoulder. His touch is pain: yellow flows across my shoulders, green twists along my arm, my wrist, burns yellow bright with hurt. Chowduri's hand is on my wounded arm, a silver glint in his fingers. His arm and hand thrust forward. I smell vomit and blood. This is it, then. Spain again. The last numbered paragraph of the Spanish lesson.

The bluewhite light of the flares sputters and dies. I hear a rustle of falling leaves. Day is done.

I wake in darkness inside a canvas army tent. I am lying on a spindly army cot. My face is cold, but my body is wrapped in a warm brown army blanket. A rough hardness abrades my neck when I turn my head to look down at my left shoulder and arm encased in plaster. Each beat of my heart threads pain through bone and flesh. I pant and try not to cry out into the silence.

At least I still have life: through the open flap of the

tent in which I lie I see pale gray light sifting through the dark. My pain, and the new day dawning in the desert, revive dreams of guns firing near at hand and voices full of casual Australian idiom calling to one another through the reverberating concussions of the cannons' fire. I have a memory of bright flashes beyond the walls and roof of the tent. Muzzle blast? Flares? Twice, I recall, someone came out of the dark night into this tent, stood listening above me, touched me here and there. Probing for evidence I still lived? Checking bandages and dressings?

Somewhere outside in the faintest beginning of dawn someone coughs, calls out, knocks tin against metal. The clean sound rings in the silence. "Aw, shut the fuckin hell up there with yer fuckin tin and spoon, you sod," a groggy voice shouts. I smile. The movement of the muscles in my neck thrusts a sharp steel probe here and there among my wounds. Tin knocks again, twice, against metal, and a second voice answers the first: "Yer talkin to a noncommissioned officer, mate. So fuck off, why don't you?"

The army. The Australian army. I remember the insouciant colonel at the general's elbow. I also remember his calm confidence that he and his general would break through the wall of these hard men from far away and take Tobruk. And do so in a night. Clearly the general failed his brief last night. I wonder how many of his soldiers' corpses will lie out in the sun this day, the kites planing above them, the tilt of their wings marking the sources of putrefaction.

With care I turn my head from the open flap of the tent and look into the gloom beneath the canvas roof. Beside me, no more than two feet away, Mackeson sleeps on a cot identical to mine, under an identical brown blanket, his left hand swathed in a boxing glove of white gauze. I wonder how many fingers they have left him. It doesn't matter: even if he has been left with a smooth palm and nothing more he is lucky: he could have died inside the M13/40, pulped by the 88mm round that damaged him.

He could have been killed in his seat like Smythe, spattered and crushed like Mohammed.

Beyond Mackeson is Lister, and beyond him, sitting up on a cot and grinning at me like a veteran who has survived and knows the value of survival, is Allison. "Awake, Peter?" he asks. I nod. "Painful?" I nod again, and say, pain ripping across my shoulder and down my arm as I exercise the muscles in my jaw and neck, "Painful. Yes. You're all right?"

He raises his right arm. At the end of the arm a bundle of bandages gleams. Most of his hand seems to be gone, plucked from his wrist. "I'm sorry," I tell him.

"Don't be. I could be dead. This is better. I used to think this would be worse, but it's better."

"Pain?"

"I'm full of morphia. Very pleasant tingly feeling. *Much* more pleasant than the pain. Or feeling nothing at all."

"I'm sorry about the hand, though."

"It's all right. I wanted to study law anyway. I can turn pages with the left one well enough."

"Chowduri?"

"Not a scratch. Tied off your arm, tied off mine. Had us cleaned up and ready to go by the time our Australian allies came up."

" 'Allies.' Christ, they almost killed us."

"The sergeant told me, 'Natural kind of mistake, private. No need for you to worry.' " Allison holds up his bandaged stump. "I'm amazed. All the fingers and most of the thumb but not a scratch on the palm. Can't figure it out." His eyes glitter, the drug pushing him from one thought to the next. "The fire missed Mackeson and Lister lying in the back. When the Aussies came, Mackeson called them 'fuckin Arabs.' Lister shouted something in Australian. I couldn't understand it. A lot of phrases with 'fuckin this' and 'fuckin that' in them, though. I just screamed. Pain and anger, all that. Loss of the best part of a hand made me angry, I suppose. Their sergeant sounded like

my nanny: 'Don't make such a noise, there's a good lad.' "
Allison gives me a quick embarrassed smile.

"Don't worry about it," I tell him. "I'm lucky I was out. I would have screamed loudest."

Allison nods, considers this. The morphia pushes his thoughts another way. "When the Australian lieutenant apologized for shooting us up, Chowduri said, 'That's all right, Lieutenant. We're grateful your gunners are such bloody poor shots. With more practice they might have killed us all.' First lieutenant I've seen who had nothing to say for himself."

I glance out the tent flap. Dawn is coming. Easter Monday. April 14, 1941. Another desert day, clear and hot, with mild winds from the sea to the north. The movement of my head makes me grimace.

"Pain?" Allison asks. "Doctor ought to be here soon. He's been looking in all night."

"I thought I heard guns. During the night."

"We're a couple of hundred yards behind the gun line. The hospital's under canvas behind sand walls. They say they're going to move the medical people and the patients underground as soon as possible, though."

"I don't know why. It looks like only the Australians shoot at their own side's medical facilities."

"As the Australian sergeant said last night: a mistake. Just a mistake. After all," Allison says, "it's a war."

"I know."

"They say you'll be fine. Full use of the arm and the rest of the good news. I was to tell you if you woke and they weren't here. The fragments passed right through. Tore some muscles and tendons. I heard the doctors talking."

"I thought I saw my arm broken."

"You did. But they say they mended it. They were standing over you, complimenting one another on their work between salvos from the guns."

"You gave them the map?" I ask him.

"With my good hand."

"You learned something, then. The Spanish lesson."

"Spanish?"

"Nothing. You're a soldier now. You're out of it, but you learned something yesterday."

"I'm not sure what," Allison says.

"What it means. If it means anything."

"Learned that at my father's knee. He was in the Great War."

"A military family? You never said."

"Hardly. He was at the Somme, along with three hundred thousand others. Said everyone he knew was killed there in three hours. Every single one of them."

"I've read about it."

"We have it better these days," Allison says. "No over the top and at them. And better medical treatment, I expect." He holds up the bandaged stump of his right hand, nods at the plaster that encases my left shoulder and arm.

"The fighting's faster, though. And more mechanical. Everything's faster and faster."

"Yes. Too bad the war doesn't seem to get over any more quickly."

I hear more than one pair of boots marching across the sand toward our tent. A shadow falls on the triangle of gray desert I can see through the tent flap. Boots, shins and knees appear. An Australian sergeant in an Australian hat ducks through the opening. Like all sergeants, he begins with "Now, then . . ." but he sees Lister and Mackeson still sleeping and stops. He turns to hold the tent flap farther open for the major following behind to enter without having to duck down quite so far.

The major is Australian too. He also wears an Australian hat. He looks like a railroad conductor dressed up as an Australian soldier. He also looks like a railroad conductor nearing retirement, for he is somewhere in his late fifties. On the other hand, he wears the ribbons of the Military Medal and the Military Cross on his khaki shirt.

It seems the major has worked his way up to his present rank with hard work and hard fighting in Allison's father's Great War.

The major glances around, sees Mackeson and Lister lying asleep, and projects a strong whisper at Allison and me. "I'm Major Thomason," he says. "Acting commander of this regiment. Colonel Franklin was killed night before last. I've come over to apologize for a particular machinegun section's enthusiasm last night. They'll be disciplined at the proper moment, although I'll tell you for free that right now we need good machinegunners more than we need careful machinegunners. Nevertheless, I'm damned sorry you two were wounded, and damned mad they saw fit to fire on an ambulance. Had a few words with them about the law of war, etcetera, etcetera. They seemed properly impressed." The sergeant looks grim, as though he can't wait to get out of the tent and get his hands on them again. "In all events, you're alive. Corporal Chowduri has filled me in on the details of your journey, Sergeant," the major says, speaking to me. He fixes me with an officer's neutral look and says, "Most of them, anyway. I had the feeling he kept a few things back. I trust there's nothing of importance there that ought to be reported?"

"Nothing," I tell him. It is the truth. I can think of nothing to report. Not the knife in my hand and Colonel Steiger, blood sliding down his back, down on the ground screaming in terror and pain. Not the captain's slick pistol in my fist and the captain writhing on the ground, struggling the last bit of the way toward death. And certainly not the commander of the Panzer III shot dead last night by his proper German general: I will not call the general just, or help create his legend.

"I hope so. American, are you?"

"Enlisted in Canada, sir."

"So Corporal Chowduri said. Novel, having an American with us."

I wonder if he is trying to elicit some particular comment from me. I say nothing, for the major is correct: that I am here is unusual.

"I don't think we got anything with the guns last night," the major tells Allison. "I suspect they were off and away from there even before they fired flares for you. Jerry's not stupid. Knows better than to hang around in the desert." He gazes across the tent. "Would have liked to have gotten a Jerry general, though. Did he mention his name in passing? Corporal Chowduri had no idea."

"None of them gave names. A German general, that's all."

"Nothing you could identify him by?"

I remember the antique medal around the general's neck on its black and silver ribbon. The Kaiser's medal. The *Pour le Mérite*. There cannot be many German generals out here who wear it.

"Nothing," I tell the major. Allison gives me a look, nods, says nothing. "Just a general in a leather greatcoat with a strong sense of right and wrong."

"That's something to be said for the bastards. Not much, but this one seems to have shown he had some idea of decency. Pity it's not more of a general thing. Reconnaissance will send out an aircraft from the Delta, of course. To see if we got him. Doubt they'll find anything. No one likes to hang around out here. Particularly generals. Ours. Theirs. Generals like to keep on the move. Stop, and you'll end up like General O'Connor."

"Sir?" Allison says.

"General O'Connor was taken prisoner some days ago. Proper fuck up. One of the problems with retreats. Things get fucked up for fair when you're retreating." The major gives me a hard look. "It was pretty hard of you, Sergeant, noting the general's location. So you could tell our guns. Pretty hard, don't you think?"

"I think he expected it," I whisper. "He was pretty hard himself."

"Yes," the major says. "So Corporal Chowduri said.

Shot a tank commander out of hand." The major raises his eyebrows, as though he would like to know why I neglected to tell him about the general shooting the captain. "A captain, the corporal said. Yes. That's hard enough. Always difficult, shooting your own men." The major sounds as though he has had a broad experience of shooting his own troops. "Still, marking his location for our gunners on your map? That's harder. A *lot* harder."

"It seemed the right thing to do." It is one of the enlisted man's stock of standard answers to any officer's idiot questions.

"The right thing to do. Perhaps. Yes. I suppose so. The right thing." He looks around the tent. "Pity you're not fit, Sergeant," he tells me. "I could put you to use. Need a lot of people now. And the harder the better. And you, of course, private," he tells Allison. "After all, you gave us the information, didn't you? You must be as hard as the sergeant here. Am I right?"

"No, sir," Allison says.

"Pity about your hand. Didn't want to play the piano, did you?"

"No, sir. I'll study law, I think."

"Good for you. I'm a solicitor in Sydney when I'm not kitted out like this."

"Sir," Allison says.

"You'll like the law. On the other hand," the major says, gesturing at the space beneath the tent, at the triangular opening, at the desert outside and the war being fought there, "all this may make you wonder at times. Certainly made me wonder." He draws himself up as though to collect his thoughts. "Woolgathering. Philosophy. None of that out here. No time for it. No place, either. Out here, it's the guns that count. Isn't it, Sergeant?" He asks me this question as though I am the expert.

"Sir," I say. The major's sergeant gives me a mild admonishing frown: he thinks I should give the major an answer with more words in it.

"I'm glad you agree with me in such detail, Sergeant. I

233

mean, you *do* agree with me, don't you?"

"Yessir."

"Good. It's nice to have the sergeants agree with the majors."

"Yessir," I say.

"Anyhow, having listened—listened *agog,* I might add—to Corporal Chowduri's story, I can only say I hope that at some point we'll get more assistance from your country with this war. Met some of your people in the last one. Decent people. A lot to learn, but that's the way it is, isn't it?

"Now then, your immediate situation. The four of you, and Corporal Chowduri, are getting out of here today. By air. A transport aircraft, well-marked with red crosses. I trust our machinegunners will not shoot you down before you get to the Delta." He smiles. His sergeant looks as though he would like to see the machinegunners try it. "There you'll be dealt with as the powers that be decide. Chowduri will go back to his regiment, I suppose. To what's left of it, that is. And I can tell you there's not a hell of a lot of it left. For the four of you it's convalescent leave or discharge, depending on what the medical people say. I would think all of you will be discharged, although they might keep you on, Sergeant. Your wounds being the least serious, that is. Although our surgeon has made a couple of remarks about the scars on your legs. An accident, was it?"

"Spain," I tell him.

"Ah," the major says. His eyes flick at me, flick away. "Wounded, were you?"

"More of an accident," I tell him, remembering the T26B bursting into flame for no reason at all. "A technical problem with the fuel system in a Russian tank."

" 'Technical problem.' I like that. The scars and the arm may get you out, if you want out. For you to decide. You're an old soldier, you'll know what to do."

"Yes, sir." I hadn't thought about discharge. What will

I do without a war? I have not thought about *after*.

"Right then. The medics will be along in a while. It's almost seven. You'll be lifted out just after breakfast." The major, and the sergeant behind him, stiffen to attention and salute. Allison and I return their salutes as well as we can. When I move my right arm the pain almost makes me cry out.

"Best of luck," the major says. His sergeant nods and says, "Aye." The major ducks down and slips out of the tent, the sergeant right after him.

"Back to the Delta, then," Allison says.

"Yes. Lucky us."

"Know anyone there?" Allison asks. "I came through Suez and Alex. Never saw Cairo." I think of Susan. I wonder what she will think of the fresh scars clawed on my left shoulder and down my arm.

"A couple of people. We trained there for a while. You'll like it."

"No war."

"That and other things. But that most of all." I glance again at the entrance to the tent. The sun is up now and the sand I can see is copper. Soon it will be gold and by midday the sunlight will have pounded it into hard bright silver. Then the sun will descend through the afternoon toward the sudden orange sunset and at last the darkest blue will rise from the horizon before the stars come out in the black night sky. Another day.